FACELESS

Worn down by a job he hates and a stressful family life, middle-aged, middle-class Bradley picks up a teenage escort and commits an unspeakable crime. Now she's tied up in his warehouse, and he doesn't know what to do.

Max is homeless, eating from rubbish bins, sleeping rough and barely existing — known for cadging a cigarette from anyone passing, and occasionally even the footpath. Nobody really sees Max — but he has one friend, and she's gone missing.

In order to find her, Max is going to have to call on some people from his past, and reopen wounds that have remained unhealed for a very long time . . .

VANDA SYMON

FACELESS

Complete and Unabridged

AURORA
Leicester

First published in New Zealand in 2012
by Penguin Books (NZ)
This edition first published in Great Britain in 2022 by
Orenda Books

First Aurora Edition
published 2022
by arrangement with
Orenda Books

A catalogue record for this book is available
from the British Library.

ISBN 978-1-78782-923-7

Published by
Ulverscroft Limited
Anstey, Leicestershire

Printed and bound in Great Britain by
TJ Books Ltd., Padstow, Cornwall

This book is printed on acid-free paper

For Litiana Navai
My Bubu

Oh God, not the whip, Sweet Jesus, not the whip, please, not the whip, God, no, no, Jesus.

Billy

The arc of white spray paint mists the wall with abso-
lute precision, the microfine droplets highlight the
crest of the crashing wave with each graceful up-sweep
of her arm, and then contour the roiling fall into the
form of a triumphant stallion's head. She hums the
tune embedded in her head, the words '*something in
the water*' making her smile as she finishes the stroke
and stands back to gain perspective on her work.
Neptuna erupts from the ocean, radiating a deluge of
colour on a sea of concrete, her waterborne chariot
leaping out from the wall, but the edges leaching in so
the effect is of a vast splat of Botticellian beauty that
then seeps and evaporates back into the lifeless grey
of the building. Neptune's transformation is com-
plete. In the mythology of Billy's creation Neptune is
a woman, a woman with triumphant but warm brown
eyes, ringletted dark hair flying in thick tendrils in
the breeze, with the exception of the long strand that
snakes down her front and conceals the ripe curve
of her breasts. Victorious over the sea, with one hand
Billy's naked and muscular goddess holds her trident
aloft in jubilation, and with the other she extends an
olive branch — a Pasifika Britannia ruling the waves,
the volcanic form of Rangitoto Island behind her.

The tinniness of the ball bearing echoes inside
the empty spray can as Billy shakes the tool of her
trade. She looks down at the regiment of similarly
empty cans neatly lined up in front of her backpack,
next to the careful plan of her project, a miniature

masterpiece jumping out from a grid of graph paper. One more can of white should do it, white and a soft grey to dovetail the edges into the background colour of the wall. She smiles with satisfaction: this is her best work yet, the perfect fusion of classical art and mythology, and her Pasifika culture and dreams. She relishes the knowledge that she has created something to inject a vibrant pocket of life and beauty into the soulless canyons of concrete and polished granite that is her adopted city, Auckland. She cannot quite bring herself to call it home, but given time that might change, as she signs her moniker to more of her work, claiming ownership of the city one piece of art at a time. She can't sign this one quite yet; she never does until the work is complete — a small tradition, like christening a baby with holy water or launching a boat with champagne. It's a superstition, really, and an immensely rewarding one. She has to get more paint first, and to get paint she has to get money, and to get money she has to go to work, hit the streets. Max hates it when she turns tricks. She hates it, too, but it is a means to an end. She looks up at the image of her own exultant face, proudly looking out to a glorious future, an as-yet unknown future. Max will love it. She hasn't shown it to him yet; she's been saving it as a surprise when it's finished. She'll go to work tonight, she'll walk down to K Road and wait to be picked up by a stranger with a need, a need she can satisfy for a price. She'll do it for her art.

Bradley

'Fordyce?'

Bradley startled up from the sea of numbers on his computer screen; the burst of adrenaline shot like a bullet through the already dull ache in his temple. He tried to blink away the grittiness on his eyeballs and pull back his concentration, which was ebbing and flowing in vertiginous waves. He'd spent four flat-out days trying to sort out the mess that was the Colchester accounts, a company whose financial records officer he would like to have had arrested and shot at dawn. How could someone make such a hash out of something that should be straightforward? Their incompetence also impacted on his ability to complete the forecast and budget for next year, another part of the job that should have been finished last Friday; he'd been forced to come into the office over the weekend to play catch-ups on it. God knew he'd had enough grief about that from Ange. Her disapproval last night, like her tongue, had been venomous: 'Don't you even care about your family?' — Her parting words this morning, sanitised for the children but spat out, still rattled in his head. He could feel the cold sweat break out across his brow as he swung around on his chair to be confronted by the permanently scowled face of his boss, Crampton.

'Why haven't you finished Colchester yet?' The voice carried the tone of one for whom no answer would be satisfactory.

'I'm almost done, but honestly, I've been hamstrung

3

by the state of their financial records. Their software is hopelessly out of date, and I had to resort to trawling through hard copy to get an accurate picture. I've spent the whole weekend here working on the budgets and forecasts, so I'm just about to type up the final recommendations summary report and then it will be done.'

'You were supposed to have finished this on Friday.'

Bradley balled his clammy fists under the desk, out of Crampton's sight. He'd known full well there would be no acknowledgement from Crampton of the fact he'd spent the weekend slaving away on the job at the expense of his family, that there would be no thank-you for the overtime and hard work, but still he could feel the muscles in his legs tense further, taste the bitter bite of disappointment. No doubt Crampton would have spent yet another idyllic weekend away, sipping wine on the deck of his holiday bach overlooking the sea at Waiheke Island, a supposed holiday house that was more luxurious and had a larger square footage than Bradley's home. The staff and their families had been invited over there last year for a Christmas lunch — the ferry trip at their own cost of course. Most of them had gone back to their own humble dwellings vaguely depressed about what they could manage to afford. He'd wondered if it was a strategic move on Crampton's part to rub it in, assert his superiority. And of course Ange now saw that place as the gold standard of what to aspire to. When will we have something like that, honey? — it was a stab at his ability to provide for them as a family. Hell, even the gimp who kept such appalling records at Colchester had probably enjoyed a weekend of rest and relaxation in some palatial holiday house, while

4

he toiled away here thanklessly, tidying up the mess. Bradley counted to five in his head before replying, a strategy he'd had to use frequently with the girls to prevent himself from exploding at them. His Monday was going badly enough without having a run-in with the boss.

'As I said, their records were in such poor condition it took a lot longer than it should have. I will bill them for the extra time, and this week's red report is well advanced, so I'll catch up quickly.' Surely Crampton couldn't argue with any of that. It wouldn't cost their company anything extra in the long run, and money seemed to be paramount as far as the boss was concerned. The frown on Crampton's face slipped into what looked like smugness. Bradley felt the frown transfer onto his own forehead, and the kick as his heartbeat ratcheted up even faster.

'Well, I've just got off the phone from their managing director, Hickey. There's been a change in expectation. They have to shave another million off the budget for next year — a directive from the board — so you'll have to redo those figures; and they need them for tonight's meeting.'

Bradley's eyes flicked to the large clock in the middle of the wall, glaring down upon them like some battery-operated automated oppressor. It was ten o'clock now; shit, how many hours had it taken over the weekend? And a million bucks? Where the hell was he supposed to find realistic savings of a million? Not from the board wages, that was for sure. He felt the tug of pain bed itself in at his temple, intensifying with the tempo of his elevated heartbeat. 'I can't possibly get it done for tonight. And why the sudden change? They've had weeks to make an adjustment

5

like that.'

Crampton's voice dropped further into his smoker's growl, his bulldog eyes brooking no opposition. 'I've told them we'll have it through to them by four. You won't let me down. Everything else goes on hold until this is done. You understand me? Everything.'

* * *

A furtive glance around assured Bradley that no one was working nearby; this phone call didn't need to be overheard by flapping ears. He tapped the green symbol and waited, annoyed with the rising sensation of dread brought on with each ring.

'Hello.' Her voice held the bounciness she put on in case it was someone important.

'Hey, it's me.'

The bounciness dropped. 'Hi, Me.'

'Who's that?' he heard a little voice chirp in the background.

'It's Daddy.'

'Hi Daddy.'

And then another, even chirpier, 'Hi Daddy.' He felt a smile curl his lips despite the trepidation.

'The girls say hi.'

'I got that. Tell them hi from me.' He took a large breath. 'Look, I'm sorry, but something has come up at work, so I'm not going to be able to meet you guys for lunch today after all.'

There was a long pause, and he began to wonder if Ange had heard him. He was about to say hello, when her response came spitting down the line.

'You've got to be kidding me. You spend the whole weekend at that place and now you're not even going

6

to meet us for lunch? For God's sake, Bradley, we've hardly seen you — do we mean that little to you?'

He leaned back in his chair, hand against his forehead. She was an expert at firing barbs, always choosing the trajectory that would inflict the most pain. This conversation was never going to go well, but it wasn't like he had any choice. Couldn't she understand that?

'Look, I'm sorry, Ange, but they've thrown big changes at me for this report, all at the last minute, and I have to have it completed for tonight. Believe me, I'd be there if I could, but I'm snowed under, and Crampton has given me this deadline, so I have to get it done or it could jeopardise my job.'

He heard a sniff, and then another. 'Well, it's good to see where your priorities lie.' He closed his eyes, trying to shut out the disappointment in her voice. Then he heard a child's voice pipe up in the background.

'What's wrong, Mummy?'

There was a muffling noise, and he realised she'd put her hand over the mouthpiece of the phone. 'Daddy can't meet us for lunch anymore. He's breaking his promise to us, baby.' Bradley winced — the words were for his benefit, not Katie's, but she'd made sure he could still hear them loud and clear.

'But he promised. You're not allowed to break promises. He said.'

'I know, honey, but sometimes daddies can be really mean.'

His trepidation transformed into something else. He felt a tight ball of anger knot in his stomach.

'But why can't he come?'

'Because, to Daddy, work is more important than us.' There was another pause, and then the change

in volume indicated the voice was directed back at him. 'Well, you've upset the girls now, Bradley. You've upset all of us. I hope it's worth it.' There was a sharp click, followed by an accusatory *beep, beep, beep.*

<p style="text-align:center">★ ★ ★</p>

Bradley leaned his forehead on the steering wheel, the plastic providing a welcome stripe of cool across his brow. He banged it against the wheel a few times, before glancing up to see if there was any movement yet. Man, what an utter shit of a day. He sat in his car, stuck in the hell of rush-hour traffic. His stomach was a seething mass of snakes. Even his sweat carried a different kind of sharpness, the stale scent of the fearful and washed-up. Because that's what he felt like today, some limp rag that had spent hours being spun and pulled and twisted in the agitator and then yanked through the wringer. He'd got the bloody report done, but it was crap, and at the expense of everything else. He was too exhausted to face going to the gym, but he couldn't face going home yet. God, it would take a special kind of courage to do that — and he couldn't even opt for the Dutch variety, because she'd smell it on his breath and then there would be another lecture. What the fuck was he going to do? He couldn't stay here like this either, crawling along, metre by metre — the pressure building in his chest would explode. He wanted to scream and yell, to hit something, to feel pain, to break something, to fuck something. He needed some kind of release or he was going to have a bloody coronary, he was sure of it. And now here he was at a standstill on Victoria Street in the twilight of an overcast autumn evening

<p style="text-align:center">8</p>

that brought nothing but the depressing thought of a winter to come. The lights had gone through two whole cycles and he hadn't even moved. He could feel his breath coming quicker, the prickles of panic needling his skin. He lifted his eyes and looked up ahead, towards the massive shaft of the Sky Tower stabbing into the sky.

Got to get out of here. The car in front edged forward a metre; the space was all he needed. Bradley swung the steering wheel hard right, planted his foot on the gas and swung around in a tight U-turn. Thank Christ the traffic in the opposite direction was freer; but still there was a squeal of brakes and the sharp tirade of a car horn reprimanding him for the manoeuvre. He turned right into Queen Street. There, although progress was slow, at least it was moving. A light drizzle began to mist the windscreen, and as the wipers rhythmically squeegeed away the moisture he looked at the sea of humanity making its way home; he noted the uniform grimness on faces as they did the barn dance across the road in front of him, the tired, the disillusioned, all looking slightly surreal in the strange half-light on the cusp of twilight, the fluorescent underlighting of the verandahs and the higher streetlamps making their movements seem wooden. The drab masses fleeing the city like rats stepping off their treadmill and going home — to what? The same oppressive hell? How did he get so rutted in this job where he had no say, no respect, no appreciation? And the same could be said about his marriage. This morning's phone conversation replayed in his mind. He was turning into such a basket-case bore, such a fucking loser. The lights turned red as he approached the next intersection: Karangahape Road, with its

reputation for prostitutes and the darker side of the city — although it was all a lot more respectable-looking than it had once been. Could he? His heart leapt a little at even the thought of that kind of a risk. It would be outrageous. He indicated and sidled into the right-turning lane and waited. It wouldn't hurt to drive down and take a look. But would he have the guts to actually do it — or had he turned into such a fucking whipping boy he couldn't even make that kind of a decision for himself? With a sense of sickened excitement he turned onto K Road. He drove through one intersection, noting two women dressed in the uniform of the trade; they stood provocatively on the footpath, eyeballing potential business. He shied away, they were so overt, so in your face, the stereotype of what every Hollywood movie prostitute was portrayed to be. On the opposite corner he spied what surely must be a drag queen. She, or he, must have been over six foot tall even without the heels, and with the tasteless, garish wig and make-up was a giant parody of a woman. Who the hell would pick that up? Shit, this was not such a great idea after all. He shook his head and began to think that no, he didn't have what it took after all, didn't have the balls to just take control and pay for what he needed, didn't have the guts to treat it like some other business transaction.

'Loser, loser, loser,' he whispered to himself, and he put his foot on the gas to escape this road that was now just another reminder of his failings. Then a form caught his eye, fifty metres ahead on his left. She was wearing jeans, a hoodie, sneakers; a slight figure, perfectly normal-looking with none of the advertising, but parked out on the kerbside, trying to catch a ride, as it were. She had none of the over-the-top sexuality

10

the others screamed out; if anything, this one seemed almost shy. Shit, he could feel the thrum of his pulse hammering in his neck.

'You can do this.' He flicked on his indicator and pulled over to the kerb, and as she came over and her hand reached out to open the door he fought back the overwhelming urge to pull back out into the traffic and flee.

Don't be a fucking wuss, he told himself. *You can do this.* And before he could change his mind, the door pulled open, the hubbub and roar of K Road poured into the car, and there she was, sitting in the passenger seat.

'Drive,' she said.

Billy

'Sex or a blow job?'

His mouth forms an O of surprise. 'What? Oh God, right . . . um.'

He's a first-timer. God, she hates the first-timers, they talk too much; she prefers to get on with it and get it over and done with, businesslike, no polite chat, then she can get her money and go. She needs to do a few jobs tonight to get enough for the paint to finish her Neptuna, and to buy some food.

'Give yourself a moment to decide. Just turn left down here.' He indicates and turns the car into Gundry Street. It is an older car, an ordinary car, well looked-after, but not the car of a wealthy man. 'Yep, keep going, right to the end of this street, then left again, down that driveway.' She takes him to her usual place, behind some businesses that have shut up shop for the day. There are no people or cars around, it's as private as you can get outdoors in the middle of the city. It's also close enough to walk back to her spot on K Road. 'Park round there.' She points under the shelter of a carport. The car headlights swing around and illuminate a beatific Madonna holding her cherubic child, a halo of serenity and godliness surrounding them. Her brown, radiant face shines down upon that of the Pasifika Christ Child swathed in golden cloth patterned with tapa. This is one of her early works, and the fact it still remains when all the other graffiti and tagging has been conscientiously cleaned away or painted over makes her smile. She brings her johns

here because it reminds her of why she does this.

He kills the lights and turns off the engine.

'So, what would you like?'

He looks around wide-eyed, like an overwhelmed kid lost at the funfair. 'Ah, won't someone see us? Isn't there somewhere better we could go? I thought you'd take me to a hotel or something.' Like in the movies — why do they all think it will be like something out of Hollywood? God, he looks like a greying, friendly, middle-aged man who should be back at home with the wife and kids, not getting a cheap one in the front seat of the car. He is so timorous Billy feels a pang of pity for him. What is he doing here?

'There's no one around, we're quite safe here. I don't go to hotels.'

'Okay, well I guess, right, um . . . a blow job?' She smells the sharpness of his perspiration overwhelming the remnants of his cologne. 'So where do we do this, then?'

She gives it 80:20 that he'll change his mind and she's wasted her time — and she hopes he does; the anxious ones aren't worth it, even if it means it will take her longer and a few more jobs to get her paint.

'Here, in the car.' She makes her voice as soft and alluring as possible. 'Just relax.'

She angles her legs around so she can reach across to him, unfastens his seatbelt and then begins to unbuckle the belt on his trousers. She feels him tense up, push his heels against the floor and his back into his seat, and sees his hands grip the door handle and the handbrake so tight, they've turned white.

'I um . . . ah . . . Do you do this often?'

She ignores the lame question; she's heard it before and recognises it as the desperate attempt at

conversation of the nervous. She unbuttons his trousers and slowly slides down his zipper.

'Um, what? How? I . . . um.'

She carefully pulls down the elasticised top of his underpants to reveal a perfectly pink and perfectly flaccid dick. This one is going to take a lot of work.

'Ah, God, I'm sorry, I, um, haven't done this before and, you know, I . . . ' His voice is high-pitched, whiny. 'That doesn't usually happen, I . . . um.'

She leans back then and looks him in the eye for the first time. 'Look, just relax, you're doing fine.' And she gives him a reassuring smile as she reaches forward to take him in hand, harden him up a bit first. But a flicker of something passes across his face — something dangerous that jolts her senses — and she feels a split-second of alarm before she sees his right hand let go of the door handle and lash out, feels the crunch as his fist connects with her eye, gasps at the horrific sensation of her skin splitting and, as her head is thrown backwards, experiences an explosion of pain in the back of her skull as it hits the window, and then a flash of brilliant white light and then darkness.

Max

The cigarette butt was caked in what looked like vomit, but it was a long one, so he stuck it in his pocket anyway and moved on to the dumpster. He'd timed it well, the truck hadn't come yet, and he was early enough that no one else had beaten him to it. He'd spotted The Ferret on his way here and had ducked down the alleyway before he could be seen. This skip bin was on The Ferret's run, but if he was clever, he could get in quick, grab a few choice bits and still leave plenty of booty so he would never know. He knew his arse would get kicked good and proper if he was found out, so he wasted no time. He reached his hand down and felt something soft, plastic wrapped. He pulled it up. Pay dirt. A perfectly good ham bun. There was a touch of what looked like mould on the top, but that didn't matter. He could pull the ham out. Even he wasn't desperate enough to eat bad ham that he knew would give him the shits. Another grope down and he found an apple, slightly manky but reasonable. He tossed it back — that health food could kill you. One more dive down. All the while his eyes looked up the street, his legs poised to run. He felt something soft again, loose, rough surfaced, this time not wrapped. He pulled it up. A half-eaten lamington, a chocolate one. He brushed the dirt off it and shoved it into his mouth as he limped off down the street and around the corner.

It had been a cold night and his arthritis was giving him jip. He hated getting old. He hated feeling

cold. He hated being alone. He pulled the wrapper off the bun and tossed it on the ground, then carefully pulled out the piece of ham. He gave it a sniff. Nah, it was gone. He tossed it aside for one of the dogs that roamed around the place to discover. He didn't bother picking the mould off the bun. It made it taste earthy, like truffles. He giggled at the thought. Truffles. It was a long time since he'd tasted those things. Now he thought about it, it was utterly ridiculous to shell out huge dollars for what was effectively a bit of fungus. At the time it was the height of indulgence. He shook his head and pulled the cigarette butt from his pocket. This was his indulgence now, although it lacked the sophistication. He wiped the cigarette on his trouser leg, put it in his mouth and winced. It was vomit. But hey, beggars couldn't be choosers. He lit up, dragged in a deep breath and closed his eyes, waiting for the calm. He didn't have to wait long.

He was feeling melancholic this morning. Melancholic was a good word, descriptive, it rolled off your tongue well. It reminded him he was educated; it reminded him he was once able to afford truffles. It was better than thinking of people. People brought pain.

His mind was drifting towards pain, so instead he directed his thoughts to the girl. She hadn't come by last night. She always called by to make sure he was alright and to let him know where she'd be, if she wasn't dossing down there. And although she was nothing to him — well, other than company, and someone to talk to, share a fag with — he felt a proprietary pang of concern. But she could look after herself. He'd been on the street long enough to see people come and go; those that could make it, those

16

that couldn't. Those that drank themselves to death, or sniffed themselves stupid, and those who couldn't figure out the rules and got themselves dealt to by the likes of The Ferret. No, she was different. She had it all figured out, she played the game, but she had heart. He started to limp his way back to his digs, just in case. In case she came back. In case she needed something. He'd go back and wait.

Billy

Billy wakes with a start. Her body cringes back into the corner, and the plastic ties that bind her wrists to the cold metal pipe rake into her skin. She gasps, and with that sharp inhalation of air, whips her head around, listening. What has she heard? Is there someone coming? Is he coming back? She must have fallen asleep. How could she have fallen asleep? She is appalled that she's let down her guard. She won't make that mistake again. She holds her breath and strains to listen, but can't detect anything above the overwhelming noise of the rhythmic whoosh and buzz of her blood pulsing, the thud, thud, thud of her racing heart, which feels like it has migrated up to under her chin, and a high-pitched, almost electronic squealing that originates from within her head. The harder she listens, the louder it all gets. The silence is deafening. She knows she is in a room within a room; she recalls groggy impressions of a deserted street, of her concrete prison. She hears no one, and no one will hear her.

What little light there was before has vanished. Her eyes scan the blackness, darting, trying to land their gaze on something, searching for any change in tone, hint of grey, hint of anything to orientate herself. She turns her face to where she remembers the door is, squints even harder for a crack, a line of light, but there is none. There is only the blackness, blackness interrupted by the odd pinpoint flash of light from the puzzled firing of her retinal cells. The only source

18

of light is from within her.

She leans into the cold concrete wall, rests her head against its solid reassurance. Its rough texture is so real, so permanent, that she moves her head from side to side gently, scraping, scraping, until the action moves beyond discomfort and the pain makes her stop. She squeezes her eyes tight shut; the tears track their way down her face. She feels their warmth trickle past her nose, over the bow of her lip, tastes their saltiness on her tongue. That minute amount of moisture reminds her of how dry her mouth is. The thought triggers her swallow reflex, but the act feels thickened and difficult. She tries to swallow again, and discovers she can't. The swell of panic rises and she makes herself try again, breathing heavily twice and then chewing the insides of her cheeks to force some saliva into her mouth, moving the gobbet with her tongue to the back of her mouth and then with what feels like a gargantuan effort, swallows.

Her focus shifts to pain: the sharp sting of the fresh scrape on her forehead, the dull ache of the bands cutting into her wrists. The throb of her swollen eye. The dragging weight of her full bladder sitting like a stone in her abdomen. At this moment, in this pitch-black room, this is what she dreads. Not the man, not what he might do to her, not the dark, not the thought of vermin scuttling around, the rats, not thirst, nor hunger. It is this. What she has tried to ignore since she was brought here and what is now too urgent to avoid. She has to pee.

Her hands are tied. She can't pull down her jeans, can't pull down her undies. Of all the humiliations, this is the worst. But she can't hold on any longer. She has to let go.

Bradley

The pungent stench of stale urine made him recoil as he opened the door to last night's mistake. He should have thought of that, realised what would happen, but his mind was still coming to grips with the enormity of what he'd done. He shouldn't have panicked. He should have just paid her the money, taken her back to where he'd found her and driven away. Men used prostitutes all the time, and it was probably nothing new to her, but she had been amused at his inability to rise to the occasion. She may have thought she'd hidden it, but he saw the smirk curling the corner of her mouth, the derision in her eyes. And if he'd paid her then and there and driven away, all that would have been hurt was his pride. But he hadn't. He'd seen that look on her face and all he could think was, here was yet another woman belittling him, another woman he couldn't stand up to. A wave of anger and shame and guilt had overcome him, and before he'd even realised it, he'd struck out at her, hard, and then she was bleeding and shocked, and he had to fix it all somehow.

His eyes gradually adjusted to the dim light in the small inner room. He could make out the hunched form of the girl, slumped against the wall, her wrists secured to the pipe with cable ties. She was cringing against the sudden influx of light — or was she cringing at him? The sharp beam picked out the bruising around her eye, which stood out against her dark skin, the dried blood matted in her long, tightly curled

brown hair, the terrified expression on her face. Every ounce of her body seemed to scream out her terror. Jesus. He pulled his hands through his own thinning hair, dampened with a slick of anxious sweat. This was hardly what he'd call a fix, but last night it was all he could think of.

The old warehouse was part of his property portfolio, something he'd picked up for a song in an area no one wanted to know about. It was solid concrete. It had once been home to a mechanical-engineering firm, but times had been tough and, like many industrial businesses, this one could not compete against the influx of cheap product from China. Now the only hint of its original use was the network of pipes that snaked the walls, the gantries across the roof and the odd pile of scrap. The building was untenanted and isolated, in an area that was now pretty much abandoned — a white elephant sucking up money in the form of mortgage, insurance and rates, with not a hope in hell of anyone moving in anytime soon to relieve the burden. Not even the homeless bothered with this place. No one would look for her here.

She was staring at him; big, doleful eyes that made her look even younger — some fragile baby bird fallen from the nest. That had been what had drawn him to her in the first place, when he was cruising K Road last night. She hadn't been tarted up like the others, no crude neckline, no skirt up to her fanny, no extreme make-up or hooker hair. In her jeans and hoodie she had somehow looked like she needed him to rescue her. Now, with her knees drawn up to her chest, she looked like she was trying to push herself into the wall. Another wave of urine stench hit the back of his nose. He stared back at her, trying to think

21

of something to say — anything — but his mind was awash. He turned and slammed the door shut behind him, walked across the workshop space and kicked at a pile of car tyres thrown into the corner, kicked until the pain in his toes made him stop. 'Idiot, you fucking idiot. What the hell are you going to do now?' he shouted, then he picked up a metal bar and hurled it as hard as he could across the vast space; the clunk and clank of it hitting the concrete floor reverberated throughout the building. He heard her cry out and then she started to sob, the sound muffled by the concrete walls of her prison. No one else would hear her, not here, but it was enough to rip at his conscience, to make him begin to fathom the extent of what he'd done.

'Shut up,' he yelled at her.

The sobbing only got louder.

He paced up and down outside the door, his hands over his ears, chanting to himself, 'Oh fuck, oh fuck,' over and over. 'Oh fuck.'

Still she cried.

'Shut the fuck up,' he shouted at her. He searched the ground, found another metal bar and took it and started to hit at the door with it.

'Shut up. Shut up. Shut up.'

She began to scream then.

No, no, no, no.

'Stop it, for God's sake just stop it. Cut it out.' He whacked at the door again. He felt a surge of anger and frustration. What was wrong with her? Why wouldn't she just fucking be quiet? But no, instead the screaming was getting louder, hysterical, insistent. He was about to whack the door again when a moment of clarity came over him: he looked at the

bar and the dents in the door, and in his mind's eye looked through the door to what he imagined was a petrified and traumatised young girl, huddled on the floor, sitting in a pool of piss, bound to a wall, and it was all his doing. It was all his doing.

What the fuck was he going to do?

He dropped the bar, slapped his hands over his ears and ran for the exit.

Billy

Billy screams and screams as the cache of her fear detonates. She realises it is pointless, that she must stop, but at this very moment, this second, she suc-cumbs to her primal need to release her anguish, her fear. The sound of metal thrashing against wood only intensifies her terror, driving her to a hysteria of noise and blackness and pain and snot. Eventually the muted strains of her cries dry up, along with the saliva in her mouth. Their concrete echoes fade and are replaced by the rasp of her breathing, punctuated by fallow groans, as she sinks into an incoherent bun-dle of disbelief.

Bradley

Bradley Fordyce jumped in behind the wheel of his car, slammed the door shut and sat there for several minutes in the pine-air-freshener-smelling artificial sanctuary, cocooned from the terrors of the outside world, his fingers clawed around the steering wheel, trying to will away the swim of nausea in his stomach and the panic rising in his chest. His breathing came fast and tight, the sound grating at his ears, and he took to holding his breath for several seconds before exhaling in a burst of horror. He squeezed his eyes shut, as if by balling them up as tight as possible everything he'd just seen would disappear and his life wouldn't be completely fucked by the spectre of a beaten, bound girl. Her image remained etched in his mind.

As if in response to some primitive need, he turned the ignition, felt the vibration as the engine powered to life, thrust the car into gear and just drove. He had no destination in mind; he did not care. He had to get away, get as much distance as possible between himself and that apparition. The stereo was playing REM, and he cranked the volume up; unsatisfied, he cranked it up some more, to the very threshold of pain, to the point where the pounding of the bass overwhelmed the vibration of the engine. Still it could not drown out the turmoil in his mind, the constant questioning, the accusation, but it did transform it from a stream of dysrhythmic self-flagellation to the staccato stutter of *fuck, fuck, fuck, fuck* echoing around his head in 4/4 time.

Max

For the first time in more years than he cared to remember Max actually gave a damn about the time of day. He walked along the semi-deserted pavements of Karangahape Road, peering into the windows of shops and bars, trying to catch a glimpse of a clock. He didn't know what difference it would make to know the exact time, but it was a compulsion; and he felt so little compulsion nowadays, the strangeness of the feeling obliged him to follow it. It had been one of the small pleasures of his life on the streets, escaping the tyranny of the clock. When he thought about all of the pressures that had been brought to bear on him — work, home, life — the one item that he felt most acutely, and that had finally pushed him over the edge into his personal oblivion, was time. Where once the shrill electronic scream of the alarm clock used to haul him into consciousness to face the demands of the day, now his sleep cycles synched with his physical reality. If he slept at all, he woke with the sun or, more to the point, the cold.

He could hear the rising thrum of the motorway, the swell in noise as the roads filled up, the arteries of the city filling and clogging, each car another corpuscle fighting a way into its congested heart. His internal rhythm told him it must be around eight; the time on the dusty, off-white 1970s clock in the front of the tobacconist's window said ten past. He wasn't too far off. Leaning against the street-grimed wall was a series of wire-mesh frames holding the latest front

pages of the *Herald*, and the *Listener*, the *Dominion Post*. It had been a long time since he'd bothered to look at those, as well. He hadn't missed much. The *Listener* bleated on about the latest environmental scare-mongering; the *Herald*, the failures of the Super City; and the capital's newspaper headlined the latest MP spending scandal.

'Oi, you, move on. You can't stay here.'

They were pretty much the same headlines he remembered from when he'd last sat at a table with a plate of hot food on a placemat, cutlery, a mug of coffee on a coaster and company, even if he had chosen to read the paper rather than converse. How many months ago was that? Or was it years?

'Oi. Yes, you. Shove off.'

It took him a moment to realise someone was speaking to him. When he looked up, he saw a rotund, middle-aged Indian man in the doorway, a towel in his hand, flicking it towards him in a shooing movement.

'Bugger off, go on.'

Max felt a moment of confusion before his eyes were drawn to the reflection in the shop window. He tried to see around the gaunt vagrant in the way, before realising the derelict piece of humanity swerving his head around was him. He leaned in for a closer examination, his hand rising automatically to the matted beard on his chin, when he felt a sting on his leg. When he looked down there was nothing there, but then he caught movement out of the corner of his eye and saw the shopkeeper had flicked him, wet-tea-towel style, and was moving in for another shot. He dropped his eyes and moved off quickly, putting as much space as possible between him and the spectre he had glimpsed in the window, a wave of disgust and

27

humiliation breaking over him. His self-examination had been brief, but it had been enough. The reflected eyes had been sunken and haunted. The unkempt beard had gone some way to hide the dirt-ingrained skin, but it didn't cover it all. His hand drifted up to the crusted sore that festered near the corner of his eye. It felt crunchy and hard; a fleck of dried exu-date dislodged and the needle of pain it caused made him wince. He looked at his fingertips, struggling to focus on them, having to move them further away until he could make out the ridges and whorls con-trasted against the dirt. He slowly turned his hand over, examined the nails, yellow-stained, ripped and broken talons, with black impacted crud underneath. He ran his right index fingernail under the left thumb, flicking away the wedge of dirt and God knows what else. The person in the image had looked like the vic-tim of one of those disaster scenes from a famine or war zone, or from a concentration camp. The men-tal image he had of himself was still the strong, fit, though mentally desolate forty-five-year-old man who had walked away from his life. He shook his head and wandered off, all imperative lost in the fog of equating his remembered self with that thing in the reflection.

Bradley

Bradley stood outside the door, sweating fingers resting on the cool metal of the handle, poised to enter, but he couldn't, not quite yet. He closed his eyes and took several moments to breathe, trying to steady the reeling in his head. He had to steel himself, mentally prepare for what was on the other side of the door, but his mind was such a tangle of conflicting thoughts he didn't think he was going to be able to go through with it. Defeated by his indecision he dropped his hand and took a step back, but before he could turn and walk away the door was suddenly pulled open. A missile of blonde and pink hurled itself against his legs.

'Daddy, Daddy, you're home.'

The missile was soon joined by an older and more measured version. The sight of his girls wrenched at his heart, and for a moment he didn't know if he could breathe. A small, warm hand wriggled its way into his and started dragging him into the house. 'You should see what I made. I baked you stars, I knew you'd like stars.'

'*We* baked stars, not just you, Ellie. And I chose the stars. She wanted to make you angels, but I told her that daddies prefer stars to angels because angels are girls.'

'No, I chose the stars second, after the angels, not you, Katie. You chose the blue icing, and I chose the silver balls.' The words were spoken with the steadfast authority only a three-year-old could muster.

'No, I chose the stars, you picked blue and Mummy picked silver balls.' Even though she was only eighteen months older than her sister, Katie managed to get the 'I'm more informed' tone of condescension down just right. It was wasted on her sister, though.

Bradley didn't resist being dragged through to the kitchen; his legs moved automatically as he was manoeuvred in front of a tray of garish, blue-and-silver-decorated star biscuits that wouldn't have been out of place on a Christmas table. He had one girl tugging on each arm, and a constant wall of chatter drifted up towards him, but his mind couldn't absorb any of it. He stood there, his brain grappling to reconcile the absolute normality of this domestic scene, this vibrant moment of the reality of his life, with the unreal, the unfathomable image of that girl. *Daddies prefer stars to angels.*

'Daddy needs to go and get changed. They're great, girls, beautiful.' He heard his voice start to crackle. 'Just give me a minute, will you?' He didn't wait for their response; he had to get away, away from their relentless cheeriness, their innocence. He shook off the reluctant-to-let-go hands and beat a retreat down the hallway.

Shit, Ange was walking down the hall towards him, her expression a mix of 'pleased to see you' with a hint of accusatory 'what the hell are you doing here at this time of day?' He brushed past her, bumping her into the wall, mumbled some apology about dying to go to the loo. He heard a snatch of 'Watch out! Are you okay?' before he ran into the bathroom and slammed the door shut behind him. He leaned back against the door, eyes scrunched closed, breath coming in great gulps. He hadn't had to face her last night, she was

already in bed by the time he'd found himself home. Not that he'd slept. He'd lain there for what seemed like hours, trying to control the confusion of thoughts and emotions flying around in his head, before giving in and getting up to drown out the head noise with some crap on telly. He couldn't even recall what he'd watched. When morning finally dawned he'd had the convenient excuse of his usual 6.30 gym session to avoid any form of communication with Ange. Except he hadn't gone to the gym, had he? He'd gone back there, to see if last night had actually happened, hoping beyond desperate hope it had all been some bizarre but horrifically realistic nightmare.

'Bradley?' The familiar voice from the other side of the door was weighted with concern and a hint of caution. The mere sound of her, the one he had betrayed, that bloody stupid betrayal resulting in the biggest fuck-up of his life, triggered an enveloping wave of guilt that manifested itself in a very physical and urgent way, and he dove at the toilet, barely making it before his stomach gave an almighty lurch and he threw up misery, bitterness and bile.

Max

It was the gnaw of hunger that pulled Max out of the darkness into which he had retreated. He was familiar enough with the sensation to ignore it, but it had broken the spell, and clarity made its return. With that clarity came one thought: Billy. He looked around and noted he was in an alleyway off K Road, sitting in a carport behind the shops. He wasn't alarmed that he had no recollection of getting there — that was nothing new. When the darkness descended it was total, as if he somehow lost himself. Back at the beginning, when he'd first slid into his self-induced exile, he had tried to resist the darkness; but then, exhausted by the relentless attack of his memories, he had succumbed with gratitude to its pull. Billy had been the first person whose presence managed to halt that retreat. Other well-meaning people had tried — people from the City Mission and the Salvation Army — but they had swiftly given up once they saw the hopelessness of their endeavour. Even saints had limits. With her it had been different.

She'd appeared one evening, it must have been nearly a year ago. He remembered it well as it was a cold night, one of those nights when a grey pall of drizzle had blanketed the city, the kind of misty rain that smothered the streetlights and made them hum with an almost evil intent. The sound of car tyres swishing along the nearby road had been dulled by the deadened air. The cloying dampness had stuck to his clothes and then his skin, making him feel heavy

and wooden. He'd smelled like dirty, damp wool, wool from the dag end of the sheep. He'd settled into his usual spot under the overhang of a verandah at the back of the abandoned theatre, dragging flattened cardboard boxes from out of the nearby skip as protection from the weather. There had been a couple of the other usuals who had taken up their evening residence further down the way: Grizzly Adams, a bearded and long-haired mountain of a man — well, Max imagined he had once been a mountain, but the streets and the years hadn't been kind, and he now had the gauntness of someone a long time between meals, but not so long between bottles. Then there was Skeet. He looked wiry and mean and had about him a hint of rabid dog. He was a true loner: no one got too near to Skeet. Grizzly had long since shuffled off this mortal coil, but Skeet was still here, drinking himself into oblivion whenever he could.

On that gloomy night Max had watched the nervous steps of the newcomer. He'd initially thought it must be some teenage boy, the figure was so slight, hoodie pulled down tight against the rain. The kid kept to the shadows, moved with an air of indecision, wavered; it didn't take a rocket scientist to figure out he was scared. He'd looked up and down the alleyway then hunkered down in the recess of a doorway directly opposite where Max sat watching. The kid had wrapped his arms around himself and started rocking slowly, backward and forward. It looked less a movement to keep warm than a means of solace, the kind of self-soothing of someone at their wits' end. The rocking stopped dead, and the head turned slowly towards Max, as the boy became aware he was not alone. His eyes met Max's, and Max had realised with a shock

33

he'd been mistaken — it was no boy, the kid was a girl. A girl with huge eyes and a panic-stricken look on her face. In that locking of eyes it was as if something clicked within him; he felt a visceral turn in his guts. Was it recognition? It couldn't have been that: although the light was dim, he was sure he'd never seen her before. Her skin was dark, and her facial fea-tures were Polynesian rather than Maori, but that was irrelevant. What ripped at his heart the most was her abject look of terror. Some deep instinct called on him to reassure her, allay her fears. His face had curled up into a sort of a smile; it had been so long the sensation had been foreign, the muscles pulled in ways long for-gotten. But it must have appeared somehow sincere, as he was certain she looked a little less likely to flee. His next action surprised even him; he found himself rising to his feet. She immediately tensed, as if she was about to bolt out of the hole, but as he moved across the alley towards her, he extended the boxes, made it clear they were a gift, a token of something, of shelter, of safety. He didn't get too close, just held out the boxes and let them fall against the wall near to where she huddled. The boxes were huge compared to her, enhancing the aching sense he had of her vulnerability. He'd then backed away several steps before turning up towards the dumpster, where he burrowed down to extract a couple of dry replacements. Her eyes were on him the whole time, an itching between his shoulder blades. He saw her head track his passage as he walked back to his spot. He'd settled himself back into his corner, shaking off the rain and pulling the boxes in tight around him. There was a noise like a clearing of the throat, and when he glanced up he saw her watching him.

'Thank you,' she'd said. He thought he saw a tear tracking its way down her face, but it could have been the rain.

He'd made sure she had an undisturbed night, telling Grizzly to piss off when he'd come down to investigate the newcomer. But he'd slept fitfully, his radar on full alert, waking with every noise that could be a threat, someone or something coming their way.

The girl had left at first light. She'd stopped a few feet in front of him, given him a curt nod, before dropping the boxes into the skip on the way out to the main street. A tidy teenager. He hadn't expected ever to see her again, but come sundown the slim form had slunk back down the alleyway, picking up boxes on the way like she was an old hand at sleeping rough. Again there was the cautious acknowledgement of him, and with it an unspoken pact. He had known he would look out for her, and she knew someone had her back. There had been no question in his mind.

And there was no question in his mind now. She was in trouble. It was like some little mass of dread was weighing down his guts. There could be some perfectly innocent reason why she hadn't shown up last night, but in his heart of hearts he knew that wasn't the case. It wasn't pessimism or defeatism or even paranoia. It was the simple truth. He could feel it. But where did he start looking?

Bradley

'You're working yourself too hard.'

'I'm okay, really.'

'How many times have I told you you'll make your-self sick if you carry on at that pace?' Ange sat on the edge of the bed, looking at him as if she didn't believe a word of what he said — a look he had seen laid upon the girls with great effect. The cold facecloth on his forehead wasn't doing anything for him. She'd insisted on it, the cold facecloth being her treatment of choice for any bump or bruise for the children. Its clammy dampness wasn't about to cure his condition, but it made her feel better. Ange always needed to feel she was looking after everyone and everything, a mother hen clucking and fussing over her chicks, and anyone else who fell within her jurisdiction. Most of the time it wasn't worth putting up a defence; the force of her character ground away even at the most resistant.

The truth was he had been working himself too hard. Just look at the weekend gone and all the grief that had caused. He'd been putting in huge hours of overtime just trying to get through the bare minimum of his workload. He was barely treading water. He'd survived the last round of restructuring, but at what cost? They called it 'efficiencies'. Those at the coalface called it inhumane. He wasn't the only one feeling that way, but what could you do? Speak up? He knew what the result of that would be. There were plenty of others out there eager to take his job. Hell, there

were eight people who'd step in, the moment they could — the eight staff who had been shaved off in the restructure. The eight whose workloads had been spread out across the remaining ten. He was beginning to think they were the lucky ones. But when you had an enormous mortgage, several so-called investment properties not paying their way and a family to feed you didn't have the luxury of whinging about the conditions. But that was by the by. It sure as hell wasn't work that was making him feel sick.

'Maybe you should go see a doctor. You've been under a lot of stress lately; I'd feel better if you got checked out. Make sure there's nothing else causing this. You're not getting any younger, you know.' She smiled, and it held such warmth and affection his heart cringed at his duplicity. 'There are a myriad of things that can sneak up on people our age. You should probably get your cholesterol and blood pressure checked out, and your prostate.' She knew just how to tip it over the edge from concern to badgering. She'd been harping on about him getting that PSA blood test for years; it had only made him more determined not to go. And as for her bringing it up now, Jesus, the last thing he felt like was being prodded by a well-meaning doctor. There wasn't any health professional who could cure his affliction.

'Look, I'm just tired, that's all. I didn't sleep so well last night, and I probably overdid it at the gym.' Only half of that was a lie. 'I probably shouldn't have gone in the first place, to be honest, but it helps me deal with the stress.' After all these years he knew the right words to say to appease her, or at least fend off the haranguing.

'I'll ring Dr Morton's for you, see if I can get a time

37

today.'

He shook his head, making the facecloth drift down over his eyes. He pushed it up with the back of his hand and closed his eyes to avoid her gaze, those chameleon-like blue eyes that could change from charm to cold in a millisecond.

'No, I think you should go, you need to look after yourself.'

There she went, having to fix everything, like he wasn't capable of taking care of himself. Firing those unconscious little barbs, all pointing to the unspoken assertion that he was useless, that everything came back to her, that she would shoulder the burden. It was always delivered with that little sigh.

'No, there's no need to do that. It would be a waste of money. I'll just see how I go. If I'm still feeling crook tomorrow, then I'll get an appointment.'

She stood up from the bed. 'Well, I'll ring anyway and book for tomorrow. We can always cancel if you don't need it.'

It was an eternity before she finally left the room.

Max

Max wandered his way down K Road, trying to formulate his thoughts into some kind of order. What would cause her to not come home, or at least not let him know where she was? There was no shortage of ways a young woman on the streets could come to strife. He was pretty sure that for Billy, drugs wasn't one of them. From what he had seen of her she wasn't someone suffering the scourge of addiction. She didn't bear the hallmarks of crystal meth. Although she was thin she had an air of healthiness about her, and he knew from the times he had seen her smile that her teeth were strong. Dental hygiene had been one of the things she was fanatical about — she'd even kept him supplied in toothbrushes and toothpaste, and she checked that he used them. 'Have you brushed your teeth today, old man?' she'd say, with that sparkle of cheek in her eyes.

'You're not my mother, stop nagging.'

'It's not nagging, it's reminding.' She'd do that mock eye-rolling thing. 'Why did I waste good money buying you the stuff if you don't use it?'

'Told you I would have preferred fags.' He'd wave the brush. 'This thing is too hard to smoke.'

He ran his tongue over his teeth and felt a twinge of guilt at their furriness, reached into his pocket and extracted the splay-bristled toothbrush and popped it into his mouth. He had her to thank for the fact his teeth were still there — the only part of his body that could be described as minty fresh.

Her vices were few. They'd shared a smoke and the odd joint, but as far as he was aware that was the extent of it. He'd never seen her completely out of it; if anything, she was a bit of a control freak. He couldn't imagine she'd allow herself to get wasted to the point of insensibility. It was one of the many things he admired about her, that she had the strength of character to avoid that pitfall of life on the streets. But there was one element of street life she did participate in that he hated. He'd made his displeasure clear, but considering he'd benefited from the proceeds, he was in no position to lecture her on the pros and cons of street prostitution. She was old enough to make her own decisions on that front; she was not some poor, hapless twelve- or fourteen-year-old, the likes of which he'd seen too many of on the streets of Auckland. He knew she didn't do it regularly, and he knew she didn't have a pimp; he'd had to tag along as a watchdog for her a few times when some of the local boys had tried to pressurise her into their fold. She did it to eat; her dietary standards were a bit higher than his, and she even slipped food his way at times. It also kept her in spray paint. He smiled at the memory of her chastising him when he once made the careless mistake of calling her a tagger.

'I am not a tagger.' It was amazing how she could puff up her little frame, like some cat, when she was riled. 'Taggers are mindless vandals who piss all over their own neighbourhoods. They're worse than feral dogs. Don't ever call me a tagger. I'm an artist. I make things beautiful; I don't destroy things like those arseholes.' The lecture had been delivered emphatically and he hadn't made that mistake again. She was right, of course. He'd seen her work and had to admit it

was beautiful in its wild and colourful way. What she created was mythical, captivating, something that enlivened the blandness of the city, her spirit exploding into vivid relief on the grey walls of Auckland. Prostitution was one of the sacrifices she made for her art. What higher ideal was there than that? But that side of her life also posed the biggest risk, as far as he was concerned. Sure, there was the chance she'd been the victim of a random act of violence or something, but it was more likely a trick gone bad. There was a heaviness resting in his heart — the thought of her having come to harm was causing a tinge of something like panic. It was an alien sensation, and one that was driving him to action. He walked further down K Road, across the motorway bridge, his eyes instantly seeking out the spindle shape of the Sky Tower, lips curling into a smile at its reassuring presence on the skyline. It was too early for the regular streetworkers to be out; at this time of day men looking for a no-strings-attached thrill went to the establishments, and there was no shortage of brothels now that it was legal. No, in his work he'd seen plenty of pros who had suffered at the hands of their trick or their pimp — black eyes, broken teeth, bites and, for some unfortunates, they'd paid the ultimate price for their source of income. He'd have to wait for the cover of night before he could ask if any of the girls had seen her.

His mind flirted briefly with the idea of her family snatching her away in some form of intervention, but he dismissed that quickly. In the time he'd known her none of them had shown so much as a flicker of interest in their daughter, and she didn't like to talk about them either, passing on the basics but little more. He

Billy

She hums to herself, trying to break the otherworldly
silence of this place, as if the sound will repel the dark-
ness as a fire repels the creatures of the night; but she
soon realises her parched throat can't sustain sound,
and it dries up, fades into the concrete walls, and she
has to do something, anything to distract herself from
this place, from him, so she starts rocking backward
and forward, ignoring the twinge in her wrists as the
rhythm of the motion, the pull, relax and pull, tugs
her bonds against raw skin, and she finds the pain
oddly comforting; it reminds her that she is alive; for
now, she is alive.

Max

The picture demanded reverence, and Max stood in front of it in a state of humbled awe. He had to call it art, there was no other word to describe it, even though it was essentially vandalism, which he usually hated with a vengeance. But this image was different, it was a thing of pure beauty. His eyes took in the astonishing detail, the way it reflected classic art. It reminded him of Renaissance paintings he had seen in books and galleries long ago, when he had cared about such things. Its shape and form definitely gave a nod to Botticelli's Birth of Venus. Compared to the other hip-hop-styled crap some liked to call graffiti art, its mastery stood out. He loathed those big 3D words spray painted on the sides of buildings, fences, trains, under bridges; even if you tilted your head sideways they were so elaborate and stylised you couldn't figure out what the hell the words were, what message the writers were trying to inflict on an unappreciative public. And it did his head in when do-gooder city councillors actually commissioned murals of this style of rubbish, mainstreaming it, making it acceptable. The masterpiece in front of him was wasted, hidden here under the bridge. Why hadn't she painted it somewhere prominent, like all the other crap taggers did? He took in the shapes and the form, the mythical quality of it, as the goddess rose out of a caldera of fire — although there was nothing bird-like about this phoenix. Her arms were crossed over her breasts, fists clenched in a sign of strength.

The long, curled hair streamed out in a halo of gold and brown, surrounded by the licking flames; and the face, the beautiful chocolate-toned face with the defiant eyes, was Billy, it could only have been Billy. He walked up to the wall and traced his finger over the signature — Girlie, her street name, the type of nondescript name chosen by someone who wanted to stay under the radar. He needed to find those others. The collective she belonged to was called the BMX, short for Bullshit Mix, because she'd said they were from a multitude of cultures. Although he had no specific idea where they hung out, she had pointed out their work when they had been walking together, so he knew where it tended to occur. There were one or two places around the central city that were deemed legal or legitimate places to graffiti; although for the truly die-hard artists, putting up a piece somewhere illicit was part of the thrill. There was always the rail — for some reason rail wagons drew them like moths to the flame. They were as good a place as any to start.

Bradley

Thank God, silence had fallen upon the house. Ange had taken the girls to the park for half an hour and their absence finally allowed him to relax, as far as was possible given his predicament. He scanned the *Herald* and *Stuff* apps on his iPhone, needing to hold the device at arm's length occasionally to re-establish the network connection. If he had the money he'd buy a better wireless router, or at least a wi-fi extender, but that wasn't a priority; he'd never be able to justify it to Ange when as far as she was concerned they had a perfectly reasonable one now. The only way he might manage to sell the idea to her would be if he angled it towards making it easier for her to stream her Netflix shows anywhere in the house, not just the lounge. After a bit of arm waving he found the right spot and enough signal, and watched with satisfaction as the page downloaded. He relaxed a bit when he saw there was no mention of any missing girl in Auckland; no one had reported her gone. Maybe they never would. He knew there was that seedy side to the city, like in any big city in the world — an underground of illegals or homeless or runaways. Maybe she was a runaway, and her family had all but given up looking. That still didn't solve the question of what the hell he was going to do with her.

He couldn't concentrate on scrolling the internet, so turned his phone off and threw it on the duvet. His head turned to his bedside table, to the stack of books and magazines there. He laughed out loud when he

remembered the novel he was trying to read. How appropriate: a crime fiction thriller, *Captured*, about someone whose life spirals out of control in a real bad way. Shit, now he had started laughing, he couldn't stop, it was like the dam that was holding back his pent-up fear, guilt, shame and anger had burst and the giggles slipped the border between laughs and sobs. His life had turned into a fucking novel.

Max

After a few hours of wandering the back streets and parks of central Auckland, and with the bonus score of someone's half-eaten packet of hot chips, he finally came across a group of youths hanging out in the cemetery under the imposing arches of the Grafton bridge. They had the look: they were all young men, wore caps or hoodies, most carried backpacks, and there was a mix of ethnicity that suggested a common purpose had brought them together in the first place. Why else would you get Asians, Pasifika, someone who looked like an Arab and white boys comfortable in a group together, rather than facing off? They also had that shiftiness of the habitually persecuted. Their banter was the bluff and bravado of youth, punctuated by expletives, exaggerated accents and Americanised street slang, although the noise levels dropped markedly as he approached. He caught the tail end of a few rapid 'what the fuck' and 'check out the loser' comments that drifted on the air. Max came to a stop about three metres in front of them, and when he saw how big the Polynesian boys were it occurred to him that perhaps he should be nervous.

'What do you want, old man?' The speaker would have been mid-twenties, a ginger, and considering the youth of a few of them was most likely the oldest and the leader. The sight of his red hair threw the image of another redhead into his mind, and the thought made him reel slightly. The leader reached down and grabbed a backpack that had been on the ground

in front of him and slung it over his back, as if he expected Max to make a dive for it. The others moved in tight around him, a classic aggressive defensive move. Strength in numbers — as if he was any kind of threat. He could understand the posturing if he'd been some young skinhead, or carried the insignia of a gang, but it was a bit excessive for some sad geezer alone. He cast his gaze around him at the scattered, time-ravaged graves dotted across the tree-studded slopes and the significance of how isolated he was dawned. The cemetery may have been an oasis of calm and green in the city, but it was noisy, the inhabitants certainly did not rest in peace and quiet. The thrum of traffic on the nearby motorways a constant backdrop to the closer roar of buses and cars along Grafton Road and Symonds Street. He could yell for help here and no one would hear him. For the first time in a long while he felt the dance of butterflies in his stomach. He tried to think back to how he had handled groups like this in the past: direct, be direct but civil, he told himself.

'Do you know Girlie?' he asked.

'What?'

'Do you know Girlie?' He made a movement with his arm as if he was holding a can and spraying something and made a pshhhh noise.

They all fell silent.

'Billy,' Max said, 'her real name is Billy.'

'Why do you want to know?' He heard the note of suspicion, but, as well as an escalation of the storm in his stomach, the sound triggered a wash of relief. He'd found them.

'Do you know where she is?'

Again, the silence. They started to stand taller, their

49

shoulders-back, chest-out posture making them even bigger, readying for action. From the look of distaste and distrust on their faces they probably thought he was some paedophile or pervert who preyed on young women. After seeing the train wreck of an image of himself in the shop window this morning, he didn't blame them.

'She's missing,' he said. 'She didn't come home to her usual spot last night. She always tells me if she's going to be away, because she knows I worry, but she didn't come home last night. Do you know where she is?'

One of the Polynesian guys tapped the leader on the shoulder and whispered in his ear. Max watched as they nodded and whispered back and forth to each other, knowing full well everything hinged on this interchange. Then the Ginger faced Max and gave him that 'yeah bro' head flick. 'Eh, what's your name?'

Max hated the 'eh' and he hated the gesture. What did it matter to them? But he didn't want to annoy them more than they already were. He wasn't in a position to be picky about manners.

'Max.' The sound was reed thin, like its owner.

'Well, fuck me,' he heard another one say above the outbreak of murmuring, but they all appeared to relax.

'Shit, you're Max.' The Ginger looked astonished. 'Fuck, from the way she described you I thought you were a bodyguard or something, not . . . ' He let the words trail off; further explanation was unnecessary. Max saved them all the embarrassment by getting to the point.

'Do you know where she is?' The head-shaking, shrugged shoulders and confused looks on their faces

were answer enough.

'You reckon she's missing?' the leader asked. 'Are you sure she hasn't just crashed on someone's sofa or something?'

'She always told me if she wasn't going to be there for the night. We kept each other's back, you know? She didn't show up last night, and she didn't say anything about staying elsewhere.'

'Maybe she got a boyfriend, got shacked up with him.' A few of the younger ones sniggered. 'She'd be a sweet little catch,' another said. 'I'd fuck her.' 'Me too.' 'Me first.' 'We could share, eh bro, take turns.'

Max felt a twist of something hot rising in his chest, something ragged driven from somewhere deep, a sensation he hadn't felt in a long time. It exploded out with words, words delivered with rage-fuelled passion:

'She always talked about you lot like you were her brothers, her family. She told me that you all looked out for each other, that you cared. And I have to stand here and listen to this bullshit, listen to your crap pimply-arsed fantasies. Seems she was wrong.' He looked from face to face, eyeballing each and every one of them, the contempt he felt in his heart steeling in his gaze. 'You guys aren't worth it. You don't give a shit. Great lot of friends you turned out to be.' Two of the youths took umbrage at his words and stepped forward, chests out, attitude compressed into lanky bodies.

'Stand down,' the leader said in a tone that gave no room for debate. 'Stand down, he's right.' He turned to the bravado club. 'Shut it.' When he turned his attention back, Max noted the concerned look. 'You're seriously worried about her?'

Max nodded.

'How long's she been gone?'

'One night.' Even as Max said it, he knew it made him sound like a paranoid parent. The Ginger's eyebrows raised and gave him a look that had no doubt been delivered to his folks along with some attitude over the years. Was he being paranoid? No, that nagging disquiet wouldn't go away.

'Look, Girlie is cool, you know, and she's tough. She can look after herself, so I think if it's only been a night, you don't need to worry.' He was right, of course, but that didn't explain the hollow feeling in Max's gut, the certainty that something was wrong. 'Tell you what, we'll keep an eye out, and if we see her we'll tell her you're looking, okay?'

'And if she doesn't come back tonight?'

'If she doesn't come back, we'll get looking tomorrow.'

It was better than nothing, and he couldn't really ask for more than that. Max's eyes found a young man who had been standing at the back of the group, his hoodie pulled up around his face. He looked so young. His features threw a snapshot of someone else into Max's mind, and the thought triggered a buzz in his ears so loud that he had to walk off, he had to walk off now, away from the memory. With a curt nod to the leader, Max turned around and made his way down the nearest path to his right. He walked on in a haze, his feet on automatic, as his thoughts began to run through every conversation he could remember with Billy, to search for anything she had said in the last week that could possibly explain her disappearance. She'd mentioned a surprise for him, but wouldn't elaborate on that, just gave him her cheeky smile and

told him to be patient. He was certain she hadn't mentioned staying over anywhere else. She didn't know many people who could let her sofa surf — and if any, the motley group he'd just met were the most likely candidates. He felt disappointed in her friends and their lack of practical caring.

The drop in temperature under shade of the trees in the Grafton cemetery made him shudder more than the graves. He stopped for a moment, orientating himself now that he wasn't relying on autopilot. This area was usually a place of calm for him, a sanctuary in the manic bustle of this city; but today the gravestones only increased his sense of unease. Now he was aware of which way he'd come he set out again, upped his pace, heading up towards the concrete solidity of the street, away from the ethereal atmosphere of this place with its dilapidated reminders of mortality.

'Hey you.' He'd been walking along in such a reverie that until now he hadn't noticed the group of youths under the cluster of cabbage trees to his right. He put his head down and walked faster. 'Hey you, shitface, I'm talking to you.' He heard the light pad of feet running towards him and picked up his pace even quicker, but it was pointless, two bodies appeared before him, and he didn't need to look to know he was surrounded by several others. They were all Polynesian, and judging by the predominance of black bandanas, were gang boys. The one in front of him, who looked to be the leader, judging by the sneer, shoved him in the chest. 'What you running away from, old man?' The sneer shifted to a look of distaste, and then disgust. 'Fuck, you stink — you stink like piss and shit. Don't you wipe your arse properly, old man?' The words were followed by a chorus of

53

bass and tenor laughter and taunting from behind, along with another shove, one that threw him into the leader.

'What, you think you can touch me, are you trying to take me on? You wanna take me on?' Before he could react, Max felt the blow to his stomach. The explosion of pain felt like someone had shot him in the guts. He doubled over, and more by luck than design managed to deflect a second blow, but he was unprepared for the kidney punch from behind. It felled him like a ton of bricks. As he crashed to his knees, survival instinct kicked in and he curled up, foetus-like, and thrust his arms up to cover his head. Their voices sounded like they were filtering down through water, his vision matching the illusion.

'No, bro, don't kick him, specially not in the arse, that stink will stick to your shoe, and you'll never get rid of it.' The comment was met by laughter and the thump of hands slapping backs. 'Eh bro, you'd better wash your hands after touching him, eh? Those germs might kill you.'

He heard a big sniffing sound. 'Aw, my hand stinks now, argghhh, it's going to drop off.'

And another, 'Fuck, my hand stinks too, and I'm gonna wipe it on you.'

'Nah, get away, bro, ugh, that's gross.' Among the laughing and the jostling he only copped two kicks before the group, bored with their prey, moved on in a cackle of trouble to torment someone else.

Max stayed where he was, breathing deeply, for several minutes before he emerged like a turtle from his shell. He'd copped enough beatings in his time to know he'd got off lightly, that they'd only been playing with him; if they had meant it, he wouldn't be walking

54

away right now. He crawled over to a park bench to lie down and catch his breath. He still had work to do, he knew it, but his body ached, and the impetus had been kicked out of him. Maybe the BMX boys were right, maybe she had gone home with someone for the night and would turn up tomorrow, full of apologies for worrying him. She might even be there now, waiting for him, holding a peace offering of food or booze for causing him grief. The best thing he could do was go back to the haunt and wait — wait and see if she came back. Because he'd always be there for her, he'd promised that.

His body resisted his commands to move, but eventually spirit overcame flesh, and he pulled his aching self up off the park bench and started the walk up through the headstones and home.

Bradley

He lay in bed, staring up, watching the negative image
from the light shade flit across the ceiling with the
flicking movement of his eyes. For once he was glad
of the comforting glow of the children's night-light
in the hallway, because right now he couldn't face
being in the dark, like she would be. He didn't dare
close his eyes because when he did all he saw was
her, crouched low into the corner. The vision was so
intense he could smell the urine, feel the waves of fear
that came off of her. He had to make it right some-
how — but how? It wasn't the sort of thing he could
enlist Ange's help with. Hi, honey, you know how you
always fix things for everyone? I've got a pearler for
you: it might be quite a challenge, accidentally kid-
napped a girl — actually, she was a prostitute I picked
up — but can you make it go away? He let out a snort
of laughter, then held his breath as he heard Ange's
gentle snoring in the bed next to him falter, then set-
tle back into its quiet rhythm. His mind began to roll
down the well-trod path of self-abasement and abuse
for getting himself into this mess, but he hauled it
back, because that didn't do anyone any good. He
was employed to find answers for difficult problems
at work, and he did it bloody well. Admittedly they
revolved around the safe area of budget structure
and efficiencies, but surely the same principles could
be applied here? He would find a solution if only he
stayed calm, was logical about it. There were basics
that needed to be attended to. He didn't want to

accidentally kill the girl out of neglect, like that poor pet rat he'd had when he was ten. He'd stuck it out in the shed to clean out the cage because it was making his room too smelly, then had got distracted for a few hours, which had turned into days, which had turned into weeks, which turned into a dead rat. There was enough chewing on his conscience now without that. He rolled over onto his side, consciously relaxing the frown tightening his forehead. He had to keep calm, keep logical. He had to take control of the situation.

Billy

She dreams that the hulking, lurching shadow is edging ever closer to her, she looks over her shoulder and tries to see what it is, she squints, but its amorphous form shifts like winter mist and all she can feel is the dread, and she tries to run, to flee from the horror of it, but the harder she tries to run the more the ground beneath her shifts, it slips like sand, liquefying sand, and the more her legs pump and her muscles strain and the more she struggles the deeper she digs herself in, and still she can hear it coming, she can feel the darkness coming, she can hear it, hear its breathing coming in hot ragged gasps, and she is trapped, she can't escape and she knows it's right behind her and in her desperation and her all-encompassing panic she gives one more almighty kick out with her legs, and a flare of pain rips through her foot and she screams, she screams as she wakes up with the agony of her foot hitting the cold concrete wall, and as her lungs gulp for air and her heart drums in her chest, her face crumples as she realises her nightmare is her reality.

Max

The dawn sidled in under cover of cloud, with no fanfare or fuss. Max looked out over the top of the cardboard, across at the vacant space opposite. She hadn't come home. What had been a twist of concern had grown into a gnaw of anxiety with each hour of darkness, hours passed in vigil rather than in sleep. Tiredness weighed heavy on him now, his body ready to give over to the desire for sleep when his mind could not. He knew what he should do, he knew what he needed to do, but a painful inertia dampened his body and soul. Five more minutes, he'd wait five more minutes. His fingers groped about in his pocket for a lengthy stub of cigarette he'd found the day before, and his hands shook as he tried to light it. Food was probably a good idea too. He could do the round of the skips, hope for something reasonable, then maybe he could bring himself to do what was necessary. No, he couldn't think like this, for Billy's sake he couldn't. If the tables were turned, she would take action, she would make finding him her mission, he knew she would. He stood up abruptly, and the boxes that sheltered him fell to the ground. He started walking without looking back, left them where they fell, the scattered remains of a night's sanctuary. He had to go, he had to walk there before the desire left him.

Now that his destination was within reach, this course of action didn't seem like such a good idea after all. The whoosh of six lanes of traffic roaring past only added to his growing sense of unease and

disorientation. His pace slowed with each reluctant step forward, time stretching out between each stride like some slow-motion replay, so by the time he stood on the opposite side of the road, the Auckland Central Police Station loomed over him, the crest of an imminently crashing concrete wave.

I'm doing this for Billy, he reminded himself, and he impelled his shaking hand to reach out and press the large metal button at the pedestrian crossing. He flinched with the loud click, snatched back his hand from its cold, impersonal surface. The glowing red man on the opposite side swelled and receded with the ever-growing throb inside his head. He fixed his eyes across the road and up the street, on the front door of the building, the destination, a clear goal, focusing his willpower on that one small place. He could do this. It was as simple as walking through that door.

The angry red man turned to an assertive shade of green, the demand to cross reinforced by an insistent electronic clamour. Max's feet obediently propelled him over the threshold and onto the road; but by the time he got halfway across, his heart was hammering so hard and the whoosh in his head was roaring so loud, it was as if every primitive impulse to flee was screaming at him. With that blind instinct to protect himself against danger and pain, and before he was even conscious of doing it, he turned around and ran back to the sanctuary of the traffic island, a haven floating in the sea of traffic, with the shelter of its trees. Once within the protective confines of the triangle of safety, he leaned over, hands on his knees, and panted for breath. Rivulets of sweat ran down the sides of his face and the pounding pain in his head threatened to make it explode.

Jesus, what was wrong with him? What was so hard about walking in that door, reporting a missing person? What was so bloody hard about that? In his frustration he punched out at the air, trying to deliver a knock-out blow to his own failings. Had he turned into such a pathetic creature he couldn't even perform a basic civic duty? He could feel the black dog of darkness nipping at his heels, its seductive pull lulling him down, promising the comfort of oblivion.

Billy.

He said her name out loud

'Billy.'

He yelled it out this time, punching at the air again, catching a branch and flushing an eruption of startled birds out of the bush. The sting in his hand pulled his consciousness into the here and now. The blackness retreated enough that he was able to suck in deep breaths, steady himself, feel the percussion in his chest ease to *andante*. He forced himself to step through the protective barrier of the trees, walk forward to the seat, position himself so he could see the monster. And then he sat, sat and tried to stare it down.

Bradley

Avondale didn't exactly provide a high-street shopping experience, and that was precisely why he was there. The long night had not been wasted, and the seeds of a plan had emerged with the dawn. And with that plan had come the beginnings of a shaky confidence, so he'd managed to lie to Ange about going to work, and he had enjoyed a swell of victory when he had asked her to cancel that doctor's appointment she'd insisted on making. He'd had to dress the part to convince her, of course; and now he was here in Avondale he wondered about the appropriateness of his clothes. It was too late to worry about that. As he drove along the main street there appeared to be a disproportionate number of money-lending businesses in the shopping centre — that and takeaway food joints. He seldom passed this way, only on family expeditions, the odd Sunday drive to explore the sprawling city; the type of houses and the people who lived here were about as far removed as you could get from their substantial home in well-to-do Albany. He'd noted then the emporium-style shops — they were hard to miss, with garish displays of goods spilling onto the streets — in fact he had often scoffed about their tackiness. But until today he had never had cause to stop. Until today, he hadn't had a bloody huge cause — one that threatened to overwhelm him. Hell, it had overwhelmed him; he hadn't slept in days, he felt sick to the stomach and his heart didn't seem to have dropped below racing speed in all that time. He

tried to tell himself he was imagining the tight feeling in his chest, the snaking pains across his shoulder, the shortness of breath. He wasn't having a heart attack, it was just stress — stress at the stupid, fucking unbelievable mess he'd got himself into. He had a plan. It wasn't ideal, and it had the potential to come back and bite him, but it was a plan — his plan. He was doing something about it, taking action. Although the thought might not have calmed him, it did make him feel a little more in control of the situation.

Bradley looked down at the leather satchel on the floor on the passenger's side. He hoped it would be enough. It held the contents of his rainy-day account. He hadn't told Ange about that money, and why should he? He was the breadwinner, he was the one who toiled every waking hour in that toxic shithole of a job. He was the one who did the overtime, didn't get home until seven o'clock most nights, and was then expected to do dishes, or iron his own shirts, or mow the lawns, or look after the kids while she went out with the girls or to some art class or Pilates or whatever exercise fad she was following that month. What was her reason the other night? — 'It's been a hard day. I'm going out to catch up with Cathy. I need some time out from the girls' — when he'd just put in an eleven-hour day. She already had her bag and coat in hand, ready to leave, and he'd barely set foot in the door.

'But I'm going out. Tonight is my lodge night, you know that. Have you arranged a babysitter?'

'No, sorry, you'll just have to miss it this month. I'm strung out, I need to get out for a bit. You have no idea how hard it is to be constantly on call, constantly in demand from them. You get to walk out of

that door every day. I don't. There's no let-up.'

She thought he had it easy?

'Look, we've had dinner, so you'll have to fend for yourself tonight. And you'll need to give them a bath before bed. I'll see you later.' She gave him a quick kiss on the cheek and headed down the hall towards the garage, end of discussion.

'But I can't just not show up, they're expecting me,' he called after her.

'They'll get over it.'

The door through to the garage had barely clicked closed — he was still standing there, coat over his arm and briefcase in hand — when a wail erupted from the girls' bedroom.

'Muuuummm, Katie hit me.'

'I did not, you pulled my hair.'

And there went his time out, out the window. He was last in the pecking order in his own household.

He looked at the bag again. No, he'd earned it. He felt fully entitled to skim a bit off the family finances and put it away for a rainy day. And if this wasn't a rainy day, he didn't know what was. There had been a number of times recently, as their debt and lack of cashflow had threatened to trip them up, that he had been tempted to raid the account and ease their burden, but then he had thought bugger it, why should he be the one to make all of the sacrifices? Thank God he'd resisted, because now more than ever he needed that cash. He just hoped it would be enough. What was the price of silence?

He parked the car around the back of the shops, out of view of the main road. Not that anyone he knew would be out this way at this hour of the day, but it didn't hurt to be careful. Still, as he walked up the

street in his business suit he felt like he stood out like a beacon. He had a plan: if anyone asked he'd say he was picking up some spare clothes for a church camp for youth outdoor activities — or something like that. The first emporium he approached had stuff on every available surface; and where there wasn't shelving, it was hanging from hooks in the ceiling. It was wall-to-wall colourful crap. He'd never seen anywhere quite as crammed as this. It had a Pacific feel to it, with vibrant leis, hibiscus-patterned wraps, singlets and T-shirts with flowers or beach scenes. In contrast to that were the shirts with skulls and death-metal images. He sneezed — the smell of long-stored tat heavy in the air. Where the hell did he start? He moved further back towards the rear of the shop and found a stand of nylon trackpants. What size would she be? She was shorter than Ange, thinner, with less curves. He looked at the size labels on the racks — *14, 12 . . . 10.* Would that fit? He pulled a pair out and held them up. They looked tiny. He looked around to make sure no one was watching and held them against his waist, trying to gauge the size and length. Hell, they'd have to do. He could feel the beads of perspiration begin to roll down the sides of his face. Man, it was so hot in here, he had to hurry up. T-shirts. He grabbed a white one with a rainbow across the front. It was the sort of T-shirt Katie would love. The thought stopped him dead, the mental merging of his two distinct worlds jarring so hard he felt the knot in his stomach tighten even further and a taste of bile rise in his throat. He shoved the T-shirt back into the rack and grabbed a lime-green number instead. She would need something warm, if she hadn't frozen to death already. His hand was starting to shake as

65

he reached for a black hoodie with some unfamiliar brand name spread across the chest. The first one was so big it would have fit him. He tried to push it back in the rack, but it was so jammed full the bloody thing wouldn't go back in. In his frustration he dropped it on the floor, kicking it underneath out of sight. He turned his head around to see if anyone was watching and met the suspicious eyes of a young Polynesian woman, the shop assistant. The age was the same. The size was the same. The hair was the same. The eyes were the same. A wave of cold prickles washed over his face, bees buzzed in his head, swarming, getting louder by the second, and a grey maelstrom started to tunnel in the edges of his vision. His hands fell open and the bundle of clothes fell on the floor at his feet, the walls started to tip over and the floor shifted beneath him. With a Herculean effort of will he drove his leaden legs to propel him out of there before the walls collapsed in on him, before his world caved in completely. He had to get away, get far away from those eyes, those dark, accusing eyes.

Billy

She takes stock of her surroundings. Although the darkness is complete, she senses the dimensions of her prison. Her skin feels the chill, thick mass of cold concrete, the hairs on her arms erect, pulled to attention by the army of microscopic muscles supporting them. She shivers at the weight of those prison walls. In the death-like stillness of the room she detects the minute air movements reflecting off the smooth surfaces. They tell her the ceiling is not far overhead, the far wall is four metres away with a small table in front of it; the only other object occupying the space is her. It is as if the hair on her head is amplifying each echo, each echo of her breath, transmitting the tiny vibrations down each tightly spiralled strand, through her scalp and skull, to reverberate within her brain. Although her mind has memorised the space — a photographic image captured in that brief flood of light that came with him — it is what she senses that provides the realism. It is what she senses that she trusts. She feels the room.

Bradley

He turned off the street beyond the forlorn remainder of the landscaped verge, now more weeds and thistles than flax and toitoi, and drove down the narrow side ingress to the rear of his building, the vibration of tyres over loose gravel trembling its way up his spine. There were no observers around to note his arrival; the whole area was pretty much deserted, with the nearest scattering of parked cars at least a block away. They belonged to a small engineering firm that didn't need street appeal to catch potential clients. The low rent was probably the only reason they were still here and hadn't abandoned the area for newer industrial parks like everyone else. Mind you, with the recession he was sure a number of those businesses wished they hadn't been so hasty; if anything, he fervently hoped the economic climate would make sites like his — large and cheap — appealing to those struggling with their bottom line. The building had become a millstone around his neck in so many ways.

The only other business in the near vicinity, other than the engineers, was a long-term storage place. No one staffed it: high chainlink fences, razor wire, alarms and surveillance cameras were security enough. If you wanted human contact you had to ring the telephone number, painted in turquoise, six-foot-high numerals across the wall. There were no locals to see him and cars seldom drove past; but still, he wasn't about to take another risk.

The memory of his trip to Avondale made him

cringe. How could he have been so stupid? To panic like some skittish colt was unforgivable. A guilty-looking, suit-clad businessman running out of a store like that was far more likely to attract attention and etch him into someone's memory than if he'd just sucked it in, made his purchases and left. Dumb, dumb, dumb. And now here he was hiding in his car with a pile of cash, a failed plan and nothing else.

He leaned forward, head on the steering wheel, berating himself for his own stupidity. He knew he should go in, check how she was. Check if she was even there. She might have escaped for all he knew. Part of him wished she had. He fantasised for a moment that she'd got out of there, become disorientated and couldn't remember a thing about where she'd been imprisoned, and that she couldn't describe the dumb prick who had kidnapped her. The bile-flavoured churn of panic re-emerged at that thought. It was the one sure thing that wouldn't happen.

What the fuck was he going to do now? He couldn't leave her in the room, that was for certain. He owned the bloody building. If anyone discovered her there, he'd be the first person they'd come a-visiting. And if there was one thing he'd discovered in the last twenty-four hours it was that he couldn't cope with that kind of pressure: he wasn't cut out to be a criminal, and his conscience was eating him alive. The police would take one look at his guilty face and frog-march him down to the station, quick smart. He'd crumble under the tiniest bit of scrutiny.

He had to come up with a solution, and fast. The longer this stretched out, the less chance there was of anything ever getting back to normal, and at the moment, normality was the one thing he craved.

Never again would he moan about his lot. So what if his job was giving him high blood pressure and an ulcer? Who cared that his wife wore the pants and didn't appreciate his needs? Hell, he'd gratefully bend to her every whim and demand, if only this would all just go away. He was desperate to get back on his personal treadmill of tedium.

'Come on, Fordyce.' There had to be something he could do, something that would salvage the situation. He tossed a few ideas around in his head. He could stick the girl in the car, hidden in the boot, like he had when he brought her here, drive her out somewhere in the Waitakere Ranges, dump her in the bush to find her own way back. But what if she got lost, or fell and hurt herself? He didn't want to have any chance of being responsible for her death; his soul was wrestling enough now. That knowledge would surely tear him apart. He could gag her and dump her in a park under cover of darkness, somewhere where the early-morning dog walkers would be sure to find her, get her help. But then she would still remember him, describe him; they would make one of those identikit pictures, splash it all over the news and he would spend the rest of his life waiting for a knock on the door.

The bag of money on the floor of the car drew his eye. Buying silence still seemed the best solution, or at least the one with the best odds of working. Twenty grand was a hell of a lot of money for a teenager. It could buy a shitload of clothes or jewellery or smartphones, or whatever it was teenagers bought nowadays. His mind jumped to the reason he had picked her up in the first place, that fateful drive down K Road, and he felt a jolt of hope. Twenty grand could get her off the

70

streets. Somehow that thought made him feel a tiny bit better. It could change her life; she could escape from prostitution and set herself up with anything she wanted — study, travel, anything. Of course he could threaten her with all sorts of things he'd inflict on her if she ever dared to break his trust, but surely she wouldn't betray him with such an opportunity in her hands.

What about his own future? There was no reason he had to stay in Auckland. Ange's parents lived in Wellington — he was sure she'd jump at the chance to move closer if he played the proposal right. And surely he could get work down there — it was the country's capital, for heaven's sake. There were always public-servant jobs coming up. New start, new city, great opportunity for the grandparents to support Ange and the kids, better lifestyle. It could work.

A smile threatened to break out on his face for the first time in days. He could pull it off. But there was only one way to do this: he was going to have to harden up and get back out there, buy the clothes, get the girl cleaned up, give her the money, pay her way out of his life. It was the only way.

The growl of the engine as he turned the key in the ignition strengthened his resolve. Holding on to the chance of redemption, he pulled out of the parking lot and headed towards the city.

Billy

She feels the faint vibration travelling through the concrete floor and whispering up her legs, and when she turns her head, straining to listen, she can just make out the muffled sound of a car. It's him, he's coming back. She shrinks against the wall, her heart racing as she feels the swell of panic rising, hears the ever-louder ringing in her ears threatening to overwhelm her senses . . . No, she can't do this, she has to stay with it. She blows her breath through her lips, determines to clamp the terror down, to control it. She has to stay alert, she has to quell her fear, because losing herself to the horror serves no one, losing herself achieves nothing. Again she calls on the physical to draw herself into the moment. She rubs her head against the wall, and the sharp bite of pain pulls her mind into focus. She listens, she waits, in the darkness that envelops her, but doesn't swallow her.

Then a minute tremor moves up through the base of her spine, followed by the faint rumbling sound, and she realises he is leaving. Relief floods through her. Her tensed-up muscles relax their cramp-like grip, she flops against the wall. But relief is followed by alarm as her mind leaps through the possibilities. What if it wasn't him? What if it was someone else, someone who could have found her, freed her? The ache of thirst in her throat becomes all-encompassing; the fetid stench and cold, clammy discomfort of urine- and crap-soaked trousers becomes overwhelming, intolerable.

She calls out.

The sound is a hoarse crackle, accompanied by the iron tang of blood in her mouth. 'Don't leave me here. Come back.' Her eyes are too dry to shed the tears. 'Come back.'

Max

The last retreating strands of afternoon sunlight had disappeared between the concrete and glass valleys of downtown Auckland, replaced by the glow of the streetlamps and the brilliance of the Sky Tower bathed in its cloak of light. His joints ached, more from the seeping chill of evening than from his self-imposed stillness. He cursed himself inwardly for his cowardice, his inability to step across the six-lane boundary and enter that world, not even for her. In penance for his shortcomings he had not sought food, nor water, and now thirst and the growl of hunger fought for his attention. He knew he couldn't stay here. He'd failed. He'd failed her, he'd failed himself. The trouble was, failure was nothing new, so although it rankled, the guilt of it was still not enough to force him to act. Well, not here anyway. The first of the society ladies would be appearing for their nightly business on K Road, where she used to ply her trade when the occasion demanded. He'd go up there, ask a few questions, find out what they had seen, if anything. That he could handle, talking to creatures of the night, creatures not too unlike himself. Unlike the monstrosity before him. Today, dealing with that building and what lay within had proven too much. A frown rippled up his forehead as his eyes tracked the progress of the uniform crossing the road. He'd noticed the constable when he'd first come out of the station doors, but now, as he moved towards the traffic lights and waited to cross, instinct told Max the visit was for his benefit.

He rose to his feet, wincing at the sharp pain that ripped through his hip, and waited.

The constable was young, early twenties he would have guessed, but well muscled and clearly not apprehensive about the task at hand as he walked straight up to Max, not stopping until he was a metre or so away. Max felt himself being sized up; he noted the unconscious twitching of the young man's nose and the more conscious frown on the constable's face. He kept a respectable distance.

'You've been sitting there all day. Time you moved on, mate.'

He was in a small way gratified that someone had taken notice of him. Most of the time he felt invisible, just one of the faceless, nameless lost minions of this city that the everyday people automatically filtered out of their consciousness. But then you'd like to think the police would notice someone staring at their building for way too long.

'Yeah. Ah. Sorry.' He stood still, wrestling with indecision.

The constable's eyes narrowed, like he had been expecting some movement instead of, or as well as, a half-hearted apology.

'Is there going to be a problem?' His stance had subtly shifted to make it clear that if there was going to be any problem, it was going to belong to Max.

'I, ah . . .' He looked once more across at the forbidding building and tried to conjure up the image of Billy in his mind — small, vulnerable Billy, Billy who needed him to find her, Billy who needed him to just open his mouth and say the words.

'I need to report a missing person.'

There, he'd said it, and he felt a surge of lightness

at having taken that first step.

'A missing person?' Again he could feel the young man's appraisal. 'Who?'

'A girl, young woman.' He paused, piecing together in his mind how he would describe her.

'Is this young woman,' the constable slowed, finding the right word, 'an associate of yours?'

Max knew what he was asking, and he knew how seriously this case would be taken depended very much on what he now said.

'She has been living near me, but she has not returned to her home for two nights. She always returns home or, if she isn't going to, she informs me of where she will be. She is very reliable, so it's unusual for her not to come home, or to let someone know. I'm concerned about her.' He made sure his words were as clear and concise as possible, and he maintained eye contact with the young man throughout, which was a hell of a struggle — he hadn't done that with anyone in a very long time.

'What is her name?' He could see from the attentiveness of the constable that he was being properly listened to, and he was surprised to feel he could have cried with relief.

'Her name is Billy. She's Fijian, eighteen years old, although she looks younger than that — she looks more like a sixteen-year-old. Her English is excellent, although she speaks with a slight accent.' The constable had taken out a notebook and was jotting details down, so Max continued with a description. 'She is five foot two, or about 158 centimetres tall, would weigh about fifty-five kilograms. She has brown eyes, with a small crescent-shaped scar above her left eyebrow, dark-brown hair in long tight curls, usually

76

pulled back in a ponytail. And last time I saw her she was wearing blue jeans, an olive-green hoodie, and she had red-checked Skecher-style shoes on. She also wears a very distinctive greenstone necklace in the shape of a whale fluke with a white plaited cord and a bone fastener.'

The constable stopped writing and was looking at him with a curious and somewhat surprised expression. 'What is her full name?'

This is where it all fell short for him. She'd never told him her full name. People who came to live in alleyways often did this, because they wanted to remain anonymous. They came to live a different life, either out of choice or necessity, though more often the latter. If they didn't tell, you didn't ask. He'd sure as hell never told anyone his name other than Max.

'I'm sorry,' he said, his eyes dropping away. 'I don't know her full name. I only know her as Billy.'

'What is her address? Have her parents or family been concerned she is missing?'

What the hell did he tell him now? He had to tread very carefully.

'She didn't live with her family. They were estranged, so she didn't talk about them much, so I'm afraid I can't tell you their names.' He hesitated before giving their address. 'She lives in Lorne Street.'

'What number?'

'No number.'

The constable looked at him again, and he knew that look — it was the 'you had me hopeful for a minute there, but . . .' look. There was always going to be a but.

'Look, people who live rough often disappear for a few days. They pop up somewhere else. I know you

said this young woman was reliable, but maybe she's gone off to visit someone and forgot to tell you.' He flipped his notebook closed and slid the pen's clip over the end. 'There's nothing here we can go on. You've given a very thorough description, but without her full name we don't have a place to start checking.'

'You could check the hospitals, or,' his throat caught at the thought, 'the morgue.'

The constable's eyes softened. 'Look, I can see you're concerned, and thank you for reporting this, but there's nothing we can do right now. Half the people reported missing turn up within two days, and almost everyone does within a couple of weeks. You can report someone straight away, but with so little information we're not really going to be able to do anything, especially with someone who is homeless.'

'So you won't do anything?' That feeling of helplessness had returned; the hunger gnawing at his stomach was replaced by a cold, hard fear.

'I can check the hospitals . . . ' Thankfully he didn't add the second part to that train of thought. 'But after such a short period of time and without a name or any other details we can't do much.' He pulled the notebook out again. 'What's your name?' he asked, pen poised.

Max felt paralysed. He should have expected that, with his years of experience on the other side of life, he should have known he'd be asked that very simple question, but his overriding concern for Billy had blotted out his memory of all the formalities needed in these circumstances. He wavered, unsure of whether he wanted to give that information, unsure of whether he was capable of it, as the sickliness of anxiety rose like a wave in his throat.

'It's not important,' he said, dropping his eyes and walking off fast in the direction of home.

Bradley

This time, when he pulled up outside the deserted industrial building, his heart fluttered with an anticipation, a quickening. It was part nerves — he knew that, because he had to admit to himself it could still go wrong — but mostly it was the surge of adrenaline that went with knowing you were about to finish something, something big. This time he'd gone to the Big Red Shed at Sylvia Park to do his shopping, and this time it was mission accomplished. There had been no sudden attack of paranoid guilt, no looking over his shoulder in case someone recognised him. He was one of the faceless masses slavering over cheap goods in a huge store, so no one took any notice of him. He didn't have to deal with some bored-looking checkout assistant avoiding eye contact as he'd used the self-service aisle. Normally he liked the human connection, even if it looked long-suffering, but today anonymity suited him just fine. In the car on the way over he'd listened to the news on the radio, stomach gripping in anticipation of a report of a missing young woman, but none came. The same weight of dread had overcome him this morning when he'd read through the Herald. His eyes had manically scanned the headlines, but there had been no mention of her. Would there ever be? Did she have family or friends who would report her missing? You'd think there would be someone who would realise something was amiss, but then maybe she was a street kid and he'd struck it lucky — no one would ever report her. Playing

odds wasn't his style, though, so he wasn't about to take any chances. He grabbed up the bulging grey reusable bag, made a mental inventory of its contents. Black nylon trackpants with a stripe down the leg and a bit of red trim. They were elastic-waisted, in case he'd guessed her size wrong. When choosing a shirt he'd selected a plain, navy, long-sleeved T — she didn't strike him as a pink kind of a girl. Pink was a colour he was all too familiar with. He hated that Ange insisted on dressing the girls in pink. It wasn't like they could ever be mistaken for boys, they were as girly girl as you could get, with long hair and ponytails, and the prettiest of pretty faces. It wasn't as if anyone needed clarification there. To him it lacked imagination and smacked of Barbie. Boys blue, girls pink. What was wrong with the rainbow of colours out there? Even purple would have been an improvement on the layer upon layer of pink inflicted on the girls. God help them if she made them wear it into their teenage years; everyone would assume they were ditzy and thick, like wearing the colour automatically wiped twenty points off your IQ. In some ways he hoped they'd go gothic on Ange — it would be the ultimate revenge. In protest he'd bought a green hoodie for the girl, with some nondescript music-themed graphic on the front. He had been going to get red, then he remembered some high-profile gangs wore red and black, and the last thing he wanted to do was get her into trouble on that front. It was better to be safe than sorry. He'd bought underpants and socks, but hadn't bothered with a bra, that would have been a bit too attention-grabbing. What he was most pleased with himself about was he'd thought to buy wet wipes so she could clean herself up properly, and rubber

gloves, because the way she smelt, it wasn't going to be a pleasant job. He'd thought of everything, without the unwanted prompts from his wife, or a secretary, to procure the right things. Food and water had also been on his shopping list: chocolate bars, muesli bars, some potato crisps. It wasn't what you'd call nutritious, but it was something to get her strength up so she could get moving and get the hell out of his life. He noticed with a lurch he'd need plastic bags to chuck her soiled clothes in, and then he'd have to get rid of them somewhere. So he hadn't thought of everything after all, but then, it would have looked a little too suspicious in his mind if he'd chucked in some bin liners. There was a supply of reusable bags in the boot — he'd just have to sacrifice one of them. It was a testament to his heightened nervous state that it hadn't occurred to him before.

Everything sounded loud to him — the clank of the metal door closing behind him, the echo of his footsteps across the cavernous workshop floor as he approached the room, the rustle and thunk from the shopping bags as he lowered them to the ground. He stood outside for a few moments, rehearsing what he was going to say, how he'd pitch it, and then he slid the key into the lock and opened the door.

The stench was, of course, worse. Even though he'd anticipated it, he felt sickened and even disgusted by it, by her. She cringed into the corner, trying to hide her face from the sudden influx of daylight. Light. Damn, that was another thing he had forgotten. The power was off in the building — why pay for a connection no one was using? It did mean he couldn't close the door behind him, to prevent her from bolting. It meant a slight rethink, and of course, it all depended

82

on her. Always her. There was no point prolonging the agony, for either of them.

'I have a proposition for you,' he said. His voice was amplified by the small room and its hard surfaces, the tremor in his words made more apparent by the reverberation. It smacked of weakness, and he worked hard to continue on without the quiver. 'This is a fucked-up situation I never meant to happen.' He just about uttered those socially conditioned words, 'I'm sorry', but somehow held them back, the ghosts of many TV lawyers past echoing the words 'never apologise' in his head. 'I have no intention of hurting you, and I have a way we can both walk away from this.' He watched as her head began to turn towards him, as her eyes tracked up towards his. It took an age, and when they finally made contact the intensity of the fear and exhaustion in them created a hollow in the pit of his stomach.

He waited for her to say something, but she remained silent. The huge orbs of her dark eyes staring began to disconcert him, and he looked away, felt his hands start to shake more. The bags with the clothes and food in it were on the floor, so he bent over and grabbed them, swinging them slightly to hide the trembling, then walked properly into the room and placed them on the small table that had for some reason been left behind in the room. 'I have clean clothes for you, and stuff to clean you up.' Then he swung the bag on his back around and held it up for her to see — the bag with the money. When she didn't react, he opened it, pulled out a wad of notes and fanned them with his thumb. 'Here's the deal. I have twenty grand in cash, right here in the bag. For the twenty grand you go away, you do whatever you want with it, I don't care.

You can blow it on booze or drugs, I don't give a shit. But you don't go to the police, and you never tell anyone about all this, about me.'

He caught a glimmer of something on her face — was it hope? Was this going to work after all? 'Like I said, I don't want to do you any harm, I just want this whole awful episode to go away. Jesus, I want you to go away, and I'll pay you to do it. But believe me, if you ever betray me, if you ever go to the police or turn up again in my life one day demanding more, I will kill you. Pure and simple. You do not want to fuck me about, because I will do it, I swear, because I am this close to the edge. Do I make myself clear?'

She nodded her head, and the cascade of relief that flooded through his body nearly made him stagger forward. But he had to make sure.

'Do we have a deal?'

She nodded again, but he wanted more, he needed to hear her say it.

'Do we have a deal?' he yelled, the sound detonating like an explosion in the tiny room.

She flinched, and he could see her throat bob up and down as she tried to say the word.

'Yes.' It was small and hoarse, but it was enough.

Billy

She sees his hands are shaking and his voice, his voice, so loud in the confined space of her prison, it quakes, and she sees he is as scared as she is, and as his words filter through the dehydrated murk of her brain, her heart leaps in a glimmer of hope.

'Like I said, I don't want to do you any harm, I want this whole awful episode to go away. Jesus, I want you to go away, and I'll pay you to do it. But believe me, if you ever betray me, if you ever go to the police, or turn up again in my life demanding more, I will kill you. Pure and simple. You do not want to fuck me about, because I will do it. I swear. Do I make myself clear?'

He doesn't want to harm me. She feels a burst of elation. The money is a mind-blowing figure for her, but it's not about the money, the money is incidental, it's about getting out alive, and she realises, *He wants to survive this as much as I do.* The thought repeats a mantra in her head. She hears his threat, delivered with a quivering voice, and she knows it is purely that, it's hollow, a facade of strong words because he is scared, he is shit-scared. But he doesn't need to worry, doesn't need to worry at all because she will take his money, she will take his money and she will run and she will get the hell away from this place, from Auckland, from her life, from this hell, and he doesn't need to worry about her coming back and demanding more because, above all else, he is the last person on earth she wants to ever see again.

85

'Do we have a deal?'

She nods her head, her eyes unwavering from his, she wants out, she wants out as fast as she can, she doesn't give a damn about anything else, as long as she can feel the sun on her skin, breathe in the sharp, salt sea air, just get the hell away.

'Do we have a deal?' His shout makes her flinch, and she knows he needs to hear her, because his fear is as livid as hers, but her throat is so dry, so very dry and she tries to force out the words, to scavenge up a trace of moisture to lubricate her vocal chords, help her find her voice, but it won't come and all she manages is a crackled 'es', but it is enough, she can see from his face, it is enough. She can see from the way his shoulders slump forward and he nearly stumbles, it is enough.

'I'm going to trust you now,' he says, 'I'm going to cut your hands free so you can clean yourself up, but if you do anything stupid, anything at all, the deal's off, and I'll tie you back up and leave you here to rot in hell. Do you understand?'

She nods.

He moves towards her then, warily, like she is a ticking time bomb of indeterminate fuse, and he fumbles slightly with the multi-tool he draws from his pocket before he selects a fine blade. He is next to her now, and she sees in his screwed-up face his revulsion as he is assaulted by the full strength of her stench. She can't watch as he slips the blade between her skin and the plastic of the left tie. She cringes at the stab of pain from the dragging pressure as he pulls the blade up; feels the physical and mental relief as the tie cedes to steel and the cut band drops free to the floor. He steps away from her then, towards the door, and she

understands with an ache of shame that it is to breathe fresher air — she is that putrid, that repugnant.

'Let me get you some water now.'

She feels a swell of gratitude that again threatens to overwhelm her, feels her body lurch with the arid gasps that would be sobs. She tries to rub at the insulted skin of her freed left hand with her still bound right one, but only succeeds in stinging, not soothing. He passes her the water bottle and steps back, and it is the most beautiful thing she has ever seen, the light from the outside glinting off the curves of the plastic. He's left the plastic cap on and she tries to flick it off with her left thumb, but it won't budge, so she brings it across to her right hand, but the cap is stuck tight and she groans with the frustration. Without warning the bottle is snatched away and, as her head whips around to follow its path, she sees him pull off the cap with ease, she sees him pull up the sealed sipper and even as his hand moves it back towards her, she is up on her knees, reaching out for it, like the devout at prayer appealing to God, all inhibition gone for the sake of that blessed liquid, and she grabs it and lifts it to her lips and she slumps back onto her heels with relief as wetness bursts into her craving mouth, the spring of cool water gushing down her throat, its reassuring weight hits her stomach and she groans with the absolute pleasure of it, then sucks deeply on the bottle again, and again. But something is wrong, her eyes open wide with shock as she feels the intense spasm grip her stomach, instantly rues her greed and, as her stomach clenches in violent protest, she is horror-stricken and hopeless to resist as her body rejects and ejects a stream of liquid, hot and hurried, up out of her throat, out of her nose and all over his suit-clad legs.

Max

He was right, the first wave of ladies were out on the streets, plying their trade. Max walked further down the road until he reached the spot Billy favoured when she was on that game. He recognised the two women whose territory was closest. One of them was older — well, she looked to be in her forties with a face like a weathered hag and dyed black hair that just made her look all the more severe. Her body was lean, junkie lean, and she emphasised what few curves she did have with a satin-look bustier, a black mini that was borderline obscene and standard-issue fishnets and stilettos. There was nothing subtle about her approach, either. Max couldn't help wonder what magic she could perform to keep a steady stream of dedicated clients. The girl — and she was a girl — was dyed blonde, again with the standard mini and tights, but this one was a little more adventurous with colour. As he got closer he corrected himself: the girl wasn't dyed blonde, she was wearing a wig, and she was Asian. He liked to think she looked younger than she was, but it was an unfortunate fact that there were many underage girls in the trade. He walked up, near to where the hag was stubbing out a cigarette with her shoe and waited until she noticed him. She glanced at him, and then returned to her task.

'No way, fuck off mate, I don't do the likes of you,' she said, her voice gravelled by years of smoking. 'Even I've got standards.'

The young one stood there chewing her gum like a

cow on the cud and gave him a look of abject disgust.

'I'm not buying,' he said.

'Then fuck off, because you're bad for business.' She looked up the street over his shoulder and gave a little incline of her head. He turned his head to follow her gaze and saw movement in the shadow of a doorway, a large movement. Shit, he knew what that meant, he had to be quick.

'Look, I'm just wondering if you've seen Billy at all — you know, the short Fijian girl, the tomboy one? She's gone missing. Have you seen her in the last few days?'

A massive hand whumped down onto his shoulder, he felt his neck crick under the sudden weight, and a voice charged with menace and wafting the scent of stale fish sounded in his ear.

'You're not troubling the ladies, are you?' The voice belonged to an Island guy — he was a good half-foot taller than Max and three times his size at least. This was what he'd been worried about. The pimps didn't tend towards mercy when it came to anyone interfering with trade. The only reason Billy had gotten away with it for so long was that she flitted on the fringe of their territory and was infrequent enough that they didn't bother. They had tried their methods of persuasion to get her into their stable, as it were, on a number of occasions, but to her credit, she had fended them off.

'No, look, I'm not bothering them, I just wanted to ask them a question about someone.' The hand squeezed even harder on his shoulder, and Max waited in horrified anticipation for the crack of bone giving in to pressure.

'Fuck, you stink, get the hell out of here.' He shoved

Max down the footpath, away from the women, away from his chance for some information. The force of the shove knocked him to his hands and knees, and he felt the sting of skin abrading against footpath. The chorus of aches in his body complained as he scrambled back to his feet. He rubbed his hands against his trousers to wipe off the grit embedded in his skin, and then tested his shoulder, relieved it was still intact. It was so tempting to walk away, but he couldn't give up that easy. Billy had been gone two nights. Time was the enemy at this stage — any snippet could be vital, and the ladies might have seen something. He turned back around to have one more try at the questions.

'Hey, look,' he said, bloodied palms up in supplication, 'I just want to know if anyone's seen Billy, you know, the little—' He didn't get to finish the sentence as a fist barrelled into his stomach. The force lifted him off the ground and threw him to the pavement. His head smacked back and the crack of it hitting the concrete launched a flash of pyrotechnic stars. Through the burst of pain, self-preservation kicked in and he flipped over and started crawling away, trying to put distance between him and the punishment, but he wasn't fast enough, and the excruciating pain of a boot up his arse ripped like a rocket up his spine. Still he crawled, waiting for the next blow, but it didn't come: objectivity lesson of the day had been dished out; as far as they were concerned the threat had been dealt with. He crawled onwards and around the sanctuary of a corner to the accompaniment of deep rumbling laughter and a witchy cackle cutting through the air.

Bradley

Fuck. He had just about told her to slow down, to take it easy after so many days without water, but the immense guilt of knowing he was the cause of her desperate thirst had made him hold his tongue. But now, as the feeling of dampness soaked through his trousers and touched his skin, the guilt was replaced by a surge of anger and revulsion and, without conscious thought, his hand had drawn back and then slapped her across the face, hard. The sharp echo of the slap that resonated around the room, the screech of the dropped bottle as it scraped across the floor and the look of wide-eyed shock on her face sent him reeling back a step. A burst of confused feelings coursed through his body, and he backed out of the room, slammed the door behind him and then spun around, leaning his back against its solidity, his eyes closed, heart racing, breath gasping. He had lashed out again in anger, and it was precisely that destructive explosion of anger that had got him into this shit in the first place. He couldn't believe he'd done it again. How could he be so bloody stupid, so impulsive? He was never like that with anyone else. He'd never hit a woman before this in his life, never even come close. So why was it different with her? God knows, Ange had riled him enough in their time together, but he'd always bitten back the anger, swallowed it down and forced himself to stay calm. What was it about this girl that seemed to bring out the worst in him? Shit, he'd hit her not once, but twice now. What shook his

91

mind and his heart more was that this time it had been different. He flexed the fingers of his right hand, which still stung with the shock of the slap. It was that difference that scared him the most. He screwed his eyes up, chanted to himself, 'no, no, no, no,' all in a pointless effort to distract his mind from what it was trying to tell him, and what he didn't want to admit. But he couldn't, he had to face the truth: this time it had felt good. It had felt so very good.

He leaned against the door, and willed himself to walk away, willed himself to walk back to his car, to get in, to drive away, to just drive away and leave it all behind. With what felt like an immense act of will he stood up straight and took one step forward towards the exit, towards escape, and then another. Then he stopped. He stood still, dropped his head back, his chin up, to look at the ceiling, the words 'Jesus, Jesus, Jesus', falling out of his mouth. Then he slowly turned, he turned and looked back at that door and the knowledge of what was behind it, with feelings of fear, and disgust and self-loathing, and with the undeniable stirrings of excitement. He breathed out long and slow, and then reached out for the handle.

Billy

The darkness engulfs her, as consuming as the spasms that still grip her body. How can she have been so stupid? She knows she should have sipped, that her stomach wouldn't cope with so much at once, but once she had the water in her grasp, it was as if the insatiable demand of her body had taken over, and it was impossible to stop. Despite the cramps, and the hot sting of the handprint on her cheek, she gropes around, fingertips searching, trying to find the bottle. She pauses, and to her horror registers the sound she can hear is the quiet glugging of the water spurting out onto the floor. The sipper was open. She imagines the entire bottleful emptying away. In her desperation she reaches out with her feet, ignoring the pain in her one tied wrist, stretching as far as she can reach, carefully probing with her toes to ensure she doesn't inadvertently kick it yet further away. But it remains out of reach, tantalising, teasing, glugging.

Her attention is broken by the *skreek* of the door handle turning, and the graduated influx of light as it swings open. He is silhouetted in the doorway, and immediately she senses a change. She pulls her body back into itself, kneels, huddled, close to the wall, waiting, the twist of uncertainty charging in her heart. He stands there looking at her, his weight transferring from his toes to his heels, as if he's teetering on the edge of something.

And then he moves. He walks over, with purpose, not with the uncertainty of earlier. He stands over

her; she can hear his breathing and it is ragged, the heavy sound of someone who is feeling — what? Is it excitement? Her eyes rise to meet his. All she sees is blackness, then the sudden blur of movement as his hand swings back followed by the shock of pain across her cheek as he slaps her.

Moments pass, time expands as they stare at each other. Then he hits her again.

Max

It was late: the streetlights pushed back the encroaching night; the usually manic road traffic had quietened to a steady thrum. The sear of pain up through his tailbone had compelled him to lie on his side in the alleyway where he had retreated to lick his wounds, where he had tried to descend into the oblivion of his personal darkness and its comforting nothingness; but he found, with an unmistakable sense of irony, that when wished for, it remained elusive. Instead his thoughts were a whirling miasma of Billy. Their first encounter, the slow journey to trust, late-afternoon walks in the parks, quiet conversations. At times her image morphed into that of another girl of similar age, the composite a play of laughter and light and hope, but which evolved into a shifting montage of fear and despair, the impact of which lurched him back from the abyss of his mind into the hard reality of asphalt, of pain and an underlying ache of anxiety. Billy. He had to get up. He knew his conscience would never rest unless he got himself up and did something about it. His mind had run through the potential courses of action he could take. Some were simple; others required some serious choices. All were about the timing. And at this late hour, there was only one prospective avenue available.

His eyes opened, took in the tagged brick wall opposite. The sight of the mindless yellow spray-painted moniker before him made his teeth grit with irritation. First things first: he had to continue with his line

95

of inquiry.

It was as if every muscle in his body yelled out in protest as he first got himself up onto his side, waited through the inevitable head spins and then lumbered to his feet. He stood there a few moments, bent over, hands leaning on his knees, eyes screwed shut, trying to block out the thud in his head as he worked up the fortitude to get on with it.

'Oh, for fuck's sake. What have you turned into?' He hit his balled hands against his thighs several times and then stood up straight. With as much presence as his aching body could muster, he walked around the corner and back out onto K Road. There was no sign of witchy-woman or her younger hag-in-the-making; they would be servicing the needs of the night-crawlers. But it wasn't them he was after. He caught movement further up the street to his left and, before his courage deserted him and his body quit out, strode as confidently as he could towards it.

'Are you fuckin' stupid or something? I thought I told you to get lost.' The man mountain looked less than delighted to see him and stepped forward, right in his face, his aggression plain for even the least intuitive to see. 'Or did you like the feeling of my boot up your arse?'

Max stood his ground, hoping his exterior looked staunch, even while his innards turned to hot liquid.

'I don't want to cause you any trouble,' he said, raising his hands, a peace offering between them. 'A friend is missing, that's all. I'm just trying to find her. Trying to get some information that will help.'

'Is she your bitch?' It was a typical question from someone to whom everything was a business transaction, although this one was delivered in the mocking

tone of one who knew it was an impossibility. Max ignored the slight and continued.

'No, like I said, she's just a friend I look out for. Billy. You might have seen her around here. Small Fijian girl, bit of a tomboy.'

A glint of recognition showed in the pimp's face. 'You mean that pretty one, the one who comes and turns tricks around here sometimes. She pisses me off, I've had to have words a few times. Why would I care if she's missing? She steals my business. Better off without her around.' He moved back a step. 'Fuck, you stink.'

A flush of embarrassment crawled up his face. It surprised him. Since when had he started caring about what people thought? Especially scum like that.

'She's been gone two nights. I'm concerned, okay? She's got no one else who looks out for her except me. I know you look after the ladies around here. Do you photograph their rides?'

His eyes narrowed. 'What's it to you? You a cop or something?'

'No.' He felt a pang at the question. 'Look, I'm not interested in your business. Like I said, I don't want any trouble. I just thought you might have caught the girl on your camera, in the background or something. It's a long shot, I know, but I just want to find her.'

The man looked at him for a while, and Max noted with relief of sorts that he was no longer in imminent danger of getting his butt kicked back to the alley. Although the expression the Polynesian was wearing still made him feel far from comfortable. It was too calculating for his liking.

'What's in it for me?'

'What do you mean?'

'You know how it works. Nothing's for free. If I help you find the girl, what's it worth?' He should have expected this. He realised with despair, he had nothing of currency worth trading. No money, no possessions, no cigarettes. He couldn't even trade his arse, because no one in their right mind was going to take him in this condition.

'I have nothing,' he said with utter honesty, and turned to leave. It was pointless, and the sense of failure he felt weighed his shoulders down.

'You have something I want,' Man Mountain said, with a combination of amusement and malice that was chilling.

Max felt the frown wrinkle his brow. 'What do you mean?' The one-sided sneer brought with it a dawning premonition of what was coming.

'Her. I help you, you find her, she's mine.'

Oh God, not that. But what price was he prepared to negotiate without her permission or even knowledge? She used her body occasionally as a means to an end, but she held the power over that. It was her choice. This kind of bastard would use her relentlessly for his own profit — she would be trapped and helpless, used until spent, like that hag. She would never forgive him.

Max shook his head and began the tired walk of failure again.

'You ain't got much choice,' Man Mountain called out after him. 'And I'm pretty sure I've got something that might help.'

Max stopped dead. Fuck. Win her back but sell her soul? Still, the pimp was right, what other option was there? He'd do what he had to do. He turned back.

'You can help me find her, then? You've got something?'

A half-smile curled one corner of the man-mountain's lips. 'Where will you be in an hour?'

'I'll wait around the corner, behind the café.'

The pimp gave him the head flick that went as a greeting, or a seal of agreement. 'And don't you fuck me over, or you will pay in ways you never imagined possible.'

Max nodded, and limped away. His imagination was pretty good. But still, one thing was for sure: find her or not, he had absolutely no intention of living up to that deal.

Bradley

He was having trouble reconciling the exquisite sense of guilt he felt with the unbearable euphoria that surged in his heart. The warring of such potent emotions left him vertiginous, confused, yet somehow energised. A giggle burst from his mouth. He took a hand off the steering wheel and slapped it over his mouth, but too late, another escaped, and yet another, and he wondered if this was what happened when the thread of your sanity let go. It took all his strength and concentration to steer the car through the throng of traffic, the occupants of other cars blank with the tedium of the Auckland shuffle, or in conversation with passengers, or singing noiselessly, looking happily moronic. Seeing them, hermetically encapsulated beings, oblivious to the secret he carried, made him laugh all the louder. He noticed a little girl in the car next door looking at him like he was crazy. She would have been the same age as his Katie. On the spur of the moment he poked his tongue out at her. She looked surprised, then smiled back broadly, dimples punctuating her cheeks. The similarity to his daughter pulled him back towards the here and now, and the laughter faded on his lips. In fifteen minutes he'd be home. In fifteen minutes he would have to walk in that door and somehow find the mettle to carry on as if nothing was wrong, as if nothing had changed, as if he was his normal, hard-working, middle-class, conservative self. But he was nowhere near normal. He knew he had crossed a line, stepped over a forbidden border to

a foreign land that made him something he had never conceived himself to be. His Catholic schoolboy guilt told him he had become the worst kind of a monster. That thought terrified him, but it also excited him. And that was what scared him the most.

Max

From the perspective of someone for whom time was just another element to be weathered, an hour was nothing. Max shook himself back to attention when he heard the approaching slap of heavy footsteps in jandal flip flops, and pushed himself up from the wall he had been leaning against. He noted the exaggerated waddle of someone whose thighs were so fat he had to walk with his feet shoulder-width apart, and he couldn't help but feel disgust at the thought that this man's corpulence had been fuelled by the proceeds of many exploited women. He had a fleeting compulsion to find a way to rid the world of this pestilence, but it fled with the realisation of his impotence. The man mountain stopped two feet in front of him, his face twitching his revulsion.

'You remember our deal?'

Max nodded.

'Don't fuck me about.' Before he could react, the ham-sized fist once again barrelled into his stomach, and his body folded in half and dropped to the ground. He knelt there clutching his stomach, waiting for the next blow, but it didn't come. Instead an A4 piece of paper drifted onto the ground in front of him, and the jandal-clad feet waddled away.

Fighting the urge to vomit, Max reached out and flipped the paper over. The image was a little pixelated, but it was unmistakable. It was Billy, and she was getting into a car.

Billy

She sits in her pitch-black prison. She sits still, cross-legged, spine straight, as if meditating but with her captured hand up and her other out, a meditating ballerina at an unlikely barre. Her face still buzzes with the stings of his attack. She breathes slow and even, and in her mind she is reaching for something, some anchor, something to keep her earthed, grounded, present. For she knows the game has changed with his return, his conscious determination, it has changed for good and she senses she has become his outlet, his toy. The fleeting opportunity for redemption has passed, destroyed by the greed of her thirst. Her physical being cries out in shock and pain and need. For the moment she ignores it, and in her mind she searches, searches for something to sustain her. She thinks of her art, the piece she is yet to finish and the new project that had been flirting in her mind, Medusa reaching out from the wall, the terrible beauty of her Polynesian face surrounded by a writhing mass of hibiscus flowers, snaking tendrils of green ending in a floral eruption of red, replacing the serpents of myth and lore. But now, instead, she thinks of Persephone, kidnapped by Hades, Lord of the Underworld, and dragged into the bowels of hell, and she shudders, because it is too close to home, she is Persephone, this is his hell, and she shudders because she knows he will come back.

Max

The first rays of thin, autumnal light greeted him from a fitful sleep, a sleep that had been haunted by dreams of melting faces — like waxen candles, grotesquely consumed by their own flames. There had been the image of Billy, whose ethereal form kept slipping from his grasp, his hand raking through the misty trail of her passing, vortexes and eddies forming from between his spread fingers. And there was her, another girl — younger, blonde, whom he couldn't bring himself to put a name to, and whose presence made him ache in such a visceral way it had woken him, disorientated, confused, relieved.

He pulled himself out from beneath the makeshift shelter of boxes, his battered body responding to the chill southerly wind with a shiver that did not stop. On any normal day the weather would have been enough to send him back into the refuge of the doorway, but not today. He hunched his shoulders forward, put his face to the wind and started walking. But before he'd even gone seven paces he paused, turned back around and looked over to Billy's spot, felt his feet drawn there. He squatted down on his haunches, ran his fingers across the asphalt, flicked away a few loose pieces of gravel. Then, with as much ceremony as he could muster, Max pulled the squished tube of toothpaste and toothbrush Billy insisted he use out of the scraggy depths of his pocket and slowly, deliberately brushed his teeth. The action brought a sudden expanding hollowness into his chest and a visceral

ache to his heart, and he marvelled at the sensations. It was as if Billy's disappearance had uncovered the well that had been his suppressed emotional self, and although these sensations were coming back sporadically, each one cut like a knife and threatened to take his breath away. He feared being crippled by his inability to deal with each attack — because that was what they felt like: repeated assaults on his soul. And at this point he didn't know if they were strengthening or weaking him.

Homage given, he set out for the only place where he knew he could get proper help, where the precious slip of paper he carried might be examined, potential evidence extracted, a trail formed. Well, he hoped it could. At the moment it was all he had, all she had. Max practised in his head the words he would use, hoped they would be enough to get through to the person he needed. This time he took a circuitous route so that he approached the Central Police Station from Vincent Street, ensuring he couldn't use the six-lane road in front as an excuse for inaction. Head forward and heart racing, he drove his legs towards the target, barely paused for the automatic doors to open, and walked straight up to the front counter. He could feel the sweat breaking out on his brow, each pore responding to the sudden change in temperature and screaming out in distress. His empty stomach squirmed like a seething mass of worms that threatened to escape.

The constable behind the enquiries desk was joking with someone behind him, but when he saw Max and looked him up and down, his countenance dropped mid-expression. There was no cheery greeting; his body language said it all, the slight lean back, the

scrunch of the nose, the judgemental eyes. Max had hoped it would be the young officer who had come out to the park to challenge him yesterday — then there would have been less explaining to do, and less chance for him to obey his body's urge to bail and run back out those doors. No such luck.

'How can I help?' The politeness was forced, but it was there, and Max was grateful for good training. This constable was of a similar age to yesterday's but was rangy and tall, without the solid look of someone who worked out a lot.

He cleared his throat. 'I am here to report a missing person who I believe has disappeared in suspicious circumstances. I am wanting to talk with Detective Meredith Peters, please.'

'Is she expecting you?'

Max almost smiled. He would be the last person she was expecting to see. 'No.'

The young man's eyes narrowed, and Max knew he'd been instantly classified and filed as a nuisance, nutter and bum. 'If you want to make a report about a missing person, I can get a constable to take a statement from you. If you wait a moment I'll grab someone.' He turned to move towards the back, dismissing the specific request off hand. But Max couldn't let him go, couldn't give in so easily.

'Excuse me, I really would prefer to talk to Detective Peters, please.'

He paused and turned back around, irritation clear on his face. 'Detective Peters isn't available. I will get a constable to take your statement.'

'I would like to talk to Detective Peters. Can you call and see if she is there?' He was trying to keep his tone as neutral as possible, but Max could hear the

hint of annoyance and desperation in his own voice.

'Look, mate.' The constable had come back to the counter by now and had raised his voice a couple of notches. 'Let me make this clear: you will not be talking to Detective Peters. If you would like to continue with a missing-person report it will be with a constable, no one else.'

Max could feel his resolve beginning to crumble. He had thought it would be hard to get to Meredith, but he hadn't planned on such immediate opposition. His shoulders felt heavy and the ache in his butt and stomach from yesterday's impacts intensified. He must have been mad to think anyone would listen to a man like him. Maybe a constable would do, at least it would be something, get things moving; but then he thought, God, no, he couldn't be such a pushover. After everything he'd been through in the last few days, he had to see this through. Out of desperation he called up the image of Billy, and with it came a spark of something harder within him, of resolve.

'Look, young man.' Jesus, that made him sound like his father; the moment the words came out of his mouth he regretted them. 'I have dealt with Detective Peters before, she knows me and I am making a simple request to see her because I have useful information. Are you going to get her for me, or do I have to go to your superior?'

The constable looked at him then as if he was some lick of dogshit stuck on his shoe. 'Look, old man,' he emphasised the 'old'. 'There is no way in hell you will be seeing Detective Peters; get that into your thick head. At the rate you're going the only person you are going to see is the constable who drags your arse down to the cells. So shut up and give a statement, or

107

clear off.'

The raised voices had attracted attention, and a few moments later the constable was no longer alone behind the counter.

'What's going on?' the sergeant asked. He too was younger than Max but carried a bit more rank than his colleague. It gave Max another welcome shot at voicing his concerns, another shot at Meredith, although again, judging by the look he got from the new arrival, that chance would be slim.

'I am merely . . .' He barely got his mouth open before he was interrupted by the flush-faced constable, who had appeared to have taken it as a personal crusade to shut Max up.

'This vagrant wants to make a statement about a missing person but has become demanding and uncooperative.'

'I have not been uncooperative,' he said. A surge of — what was that, anger? — coursed through his veins. 'I have asked repeatedly to see Detective Meredith Peters as I have some information for her, but the constable here is not listening and won't follow my request.'

'Why is he wanting Peters?' the sergeant asked the young man, completely ignoring Max.

'God knows, he's just some bum causing trouble.'

'Time he left the premises?'

'God yes — as you've probably noticed, he stinks.'

The anger that had started in Max's heart flared out and stung across his skin like chickenpox.

'I am not just some bum causing trouble,' Max said, no pretension of kowtowing in his voice. 'And I am neither deaf nor stupid. I have just as much right to be listened to as the next man. In fact I have been

more than cooperative with the constable, but I'm getting tired of being ignored. I would like to see Detective Peters, and I would like to see her right fucking now.'

'Hey, that's it, mate, you're out of here.' The young constable headed out the back, and it didn't take a mastermind to know he'd be appearing around the side door sometime very soon. Max knew he was going to get kicked out, and he couldn't let that happen, because he had to speak to Meredith, he had to get her to listen to him, to see that something bad had happened to Billy, that she needed to be found. The sergeant had followed the young man, and sure enough there was a click, and the two of them appeared at the side door into the atrium.

'Right, you, leg it, get out of here,' the sergeant said, shooing him like he was some fly intent on the family picnic.

But Max didn't, wouldn't, couldn't. He stood his ground. 'I want to see Meredith,' he said. 'I'm not leaving until I do.' He tried to will himself heavier, more solid, to make himself leaden.

'Either you leave of your own accord, or we will arrest you for obstruction and public nuisance. Now move it.'

But Max wouldn't move. Where, before, every instinct had been to flee the building, now every impulse was to stay. 'Meredith,' he started yelling. 'Meredith.'

Firm hands grasped him on his shoulders and he twisted in them, trying to throw them off, but his emaciated form was no match for fit, driven men, and before he knew it his face was up hard against the cold wall, his hands were being wrenched behind his back

109

Bradley

Bradley had been awake for hours, but the first threads of light were only just beginning to sneak under the curtains. He'd fallen asleep last night with the sheer exhaustion of someone who had been wrestling their conscience to the ground, then had woken up early to continue the self-assault. The trouble was, the more he thought about what he had done, what he was doing, the closer the single voice inside his head came to being a chorus. The underlying bass of self-recrimination had been joined by the tenor of *I didn't ask for this to happen*, as well as the soprano of *What the fuck?* It was the alto that was perplexing, the rich middle voice that hinted at the promise of something more. When he focused in on this voice, it offered seductive emotions such as control and power, even dominance; and the more he thought about these, the stronger its siren call beckoned. He became aware of the woman beside him in the bed, aware of her tangible presence, the way the depression she made in the mattress pitched him towards her, her smell — a blend of something lightly floral combined with a muskiness — his skin felt the heat radiating from her body.

Ange was a woman with a strong sexual appetite. Even having children had not diminished her need and enjoyment of it. The fact they only made love once a week or so had been down to him, to his drive or lack of, his needs. When they'd been younger they'd been at each other whenever they got the chance, with

111

that first flame of lust and romance that intertwined and consumed them into a bonfire of heady pleasure. Public parks, parents' houses, even a graveyard — you name it, they'd done it there.

They were days he frankly missed, days of youthful indulgence before the pressure of kids and mortgage and the grind of work quelled the fire for him; and thinking about those days gave him that all-too-familiar pang of guilt, because he knew damn well Ange would jump at the chance to revisit them. He thought about how strong he'd felt in those days, god-like, invincible; and he realised he'd experienced a hint of that this afternoon, in that moment when he'd turned and gone back into the room, when, whether right or wrong, it had been entirely his decision to do so, his choice, his alone — and although terrifying, it had also been exhilarating. With the memory of that exhilaration came a physical manifestation of the excitement the moment had carried: he felt goosebumps tremble across his skin, his heartrate climb, felt the pull of his erection, and felt most of all need, overwhelming need, and he had to sate it, sate it now. He reached out for his wife.

Billy

You need some are to look after you... he'd said
one day when they sat in the rotunda at "Bert Park",
sheltering from a scramble Auckland summer's day,
watching humanity surge by. The memory of that
warmth enveloping her body brings her

The cold she feels is that seeping, fingering cold that
wraps its exploring, exposing tendrils around muscle,
sinew, bone, and leaves in its path an intransient ache.
Sleep comes easily now, too easily, which scares her.
Where once she willed herself to sleep, now she cajoles
herself to stay awake. Without the cue of daylight she
doesn't know the time, but senses it is morning. She
recognises that drop in temperature that comes with
the dawn, when, if it's cold enough, the frost crystal-
lises over the land, rebelling against sunlight, and she
recollects the days she would have huddled further
under her shelter on the street. Will the cold kill her
before he does? She hopes the mental drift into hypo-
thermia will be kinder than her reality.

Has anyone missed her? Will anyone come for her?
When she thinks of her parents, all she feels is pain.
She imagines them warm in their Otahuhu bungalow,
surrounded by her younger brothers and sisters, being
all love and light, grace before dinner, prayers before
bed, yet hiding their hypocrisy. There's Frankie, but
he's only fifteen, and although he's sought her out
occasionally, pressed cash into her hand, hugged her,
said he misses her, his visits are sporadic and he is
careful not to provoke the wrath of their father. No, it
is too much to expect of Frankie.

Max, her mind settles onto Max. He will know
she's gone. He cares, he will be worried about her,
she knows it. He will realise she is in trouble, he will
do something, he will find her. They made a pact.

'You need someone to look after you,' he'd said one day when they sat in the rotunda at Albert Park, sheltering from a scorching Auckland summer's day, watching humanity walk by. The memory of that warmth enveloping her body buoys her.

'Speak for yourself, old man,' she'd flipped back. 'If anyone needs looking after it's you. Have you looked at yourself lately? Arnold Schwarzenegger you ain't.'

He'd struck a ridiculous bodybuilding pose that left them both chuckling. 'Yeah, but unlike the Terminator, I will always be back.'

'That's what you say. No offence, but you're not exactly my idea of a hero.'

'This is just my clever disguise. You'd be surprised what I can turn into when provoked.' The line had been delivered with an odd intensity, like he was trying to tell her something, but on that particular day, and in that place, she wasn't in the right frame of mind to pursue the invitation.

'Well, looking at you, it won't be the Hulk.'

'True, not that,' he'd said waving the loose folds of fabric of his trousers. 'But seriously, I'll always look out for you, you know that?'

'Yeah, I know.' The conversation had lost its levity. 'And I'll do the same for you too, deal? Two-way street.'

'Deal.'

But will it be enough? She has seen the rapid decline in him in recent weeks and fears for his wellbeing. Where once he seemed wiry but robust, now he looks skeletal and sickly; where once he at least tried to keep clean, now he stinks. They made a pledge, but will it be enough to move him, to pull him from his self-imposed exile from reality? Will it be enough to

114

drag him back up from his downward spiral? It has to. She hopes. She can only hope. He is all she has left. Her mouth opens, and instead of sound, only thought comes out.

Max.

Max

The police cell was not designed with comfort in mind, but was still a vast improvement on the places he loosely called home. It was warm and dry for a start, which was always a bonus. The built-in bench was appealing, even without any padding, and his aching body longed to lie down; but now was not the time, there were more important things on his mind. He folded his hands back around the bars and rested his forehead against one.

'Meredith,' he bellowed, with what little of his voice he had left. He had been yelling it for the last half-hour, and he knew he had right royally pissed off the duty staff. He could imagine the colourful words being muttered about him from the watch house, but he didn't care, in fact he didn't give a damn: what they thought was the least of his concerns, and if pissing them off got him some attention, then so be it; if it got *her* attention, perfect.

'Meredith, I want to see Meredith. Bring me Meredith.'

A sharp voice shot down the corridor.

'You'll see the business end of the firehose if you don't shut the fuck up.'

His ploy was working. The young ones didn't get it, there was nothing they could threaten him with to make him stop calling, because you couldn't intimidate the desperate. When someone had nothing, you couldn't take anything from them. As far as he was concerned his existence was as low as it could go.

116

Even a jail term would be an improvement, because at least then he'd get three meals a day, a shower, fresh clothes, a warm and comfortable bed. But he couldn't let it come to that, because he had a job to do. And from what he could see, there was only one path out from here.

'Meredith.' He wished he had something metal to bang on the bars to add to the irritation. He'd thought of the toothbrush, but after a few test dings had decided it didn't make enough noise.

He heard a commotion from down the hallway, and for a brief moment wondered if he'd pushed it too far, and the constable was unrolling the firehose ready for a drenching. Then he heard voices approaching and, as one became clearer, he felt a jolt of recognition. They were still down the hall, so he closed his eyes in an attempt to filter out all distraction and listen in on the conversation.

'What the fuck's going on?'

'Look, sorry, ma'am. Some bum has being kicking up a stink, demanding to see you. We've chucked him in the cells, but he won't shut up.'

'Well, what does he want?'

'Claims he wants to make a missing-person report, but insisted he would only give the info to you.'

There was a pause. 'Why me?'

'Said he'd dealt with you before. Got real upset when I told him he couldn't see you and would have to give his statement to a constable. That's when we chucked him in the cells.'

'So, who is he?'

'What do you mean?'

'What's his name?'

There was another pause then, a long one. Max

could feel the embarrassment.

'Please tell me you actually asked him his name?'

Max's face couldn't help but curl up into a smile. He knew the kind of look the constable and sergeant would be withering under at that moment. He didn't envy them one little bit.

'Which part of the "identify the person you're throwing in the cells" protocol did you clowns find hard to comprehend?' She was still as subtle as he recalled.

'It all happened so fast, we didn't get the time.'

'And he's been down here how long?'

The reply was mumbled.

'Half an hour? Well, why don't you get the fuck down there right now and ask him. It's kind of useful to know who you've got locked up. Jesus, imagine if his lawyer got hold of this.'

The clomp of reluctant footsteps echoed off the concrete walls as they approached. Max still had his hands grasped around the bars. He raised his head enough to look into the reddened face of the young constable who had first met him at the reception desk. He resisted the temptation to look smug and instead just stared back, waiting.

The constable took a big breath, then asked quietly, 'What's your name?'

'Max Grimes.' He couldn't recall the last time he had told anyone his full name. Even Billy only knew him as Max. It sounded alien, like something from a long forgotten time. 'My name is Max Grimes.' He said it again for good measure.

The constable nodded at him then headed back down the hall. Max closed his eyes again. The twang of anxiety pulled at his chest. This is where it was

make or break. He couldn't predict how she'd react, what kind of a reception he'd get. When he started to feel giddy he realised he had been holding his breath, trying to hear Meredith's response.

'And?'

'Max Grimes, he said his name was Max Grimes.'

He could hear her sharp inhalation of breath from down here. 'Shit,' exploded from her lips, then there were footsteps, the sharp clack of heels striding along the hard floor. They walked straight past, further down the cellblock. She had glanced at him on her way past but kept walking, not recognising him.

'Meredith.' He spoke her name, quiet, hallowed. The long, trouser-clad legs stopped, the whole body rigid, and then she slowly turned around. Her face looked incredulous as she came to stand before him, arms akimbo.

'Jesus fucking Christ, Max, is that you?'

'Good to see you too, Meredith.' She was just as striking as ever: statuesque, deep auburn hair pulled back into an easy ponytail, high cheekbones, intense green eyes. Not classically beautiful; with her sprinkling of freckles and too full mouth, she was better described as fascinating, with a presence that turned heads. The few extra years had only made her more appealing.

He saw her face battle as she took him in, her nose twitch, the look of disgust that started to form despite her attempts to hide it. He looked away.

'Jesus Christ, what the hell happened to you? Oh, and God, you stink, do you realise that? Fuck, that's just awful.' Her hand came up to cover her nose, and for the first time in an age Max felt truly ashamed of what he'd become. He stepped back from the bars

and retreated to the bench, leaned back against the wall and sighed, looking up at the ceiling. His peripheral vision caught her positioning herself as far away as possible, but still in sight.

'Why are you here?' she asked. She was never one for small talk.

'He called you ma'am. Have you had a promotion?'

'Detective sergeant, but mostly they call me that because they're scared of me, and I like to keep it that way. You didn't answer my question. We haven't seen you for — what? Over two years? Suddenly you're here, hollering and making a ruckus like a school kid. What do you want?'

He found her eyes then. 'I need your help.'

'You look like you need a lot more than my help.' Again, he winced at the harsh judgement. 'You been living rough all this time?'

'Pretty much.'

'Why?'

Such a simple question, but one that sent a cascade of images tumbling through his head, images that provoked emotions that made him reel, and he had to grasp on to the edge of the bench to prevent himself falling. She'd seen it, too; she always was one of the sharpest observers he knew. He heard her sigh, sensed the change in her demeanour. When she spoke again, her voice was cautious, softer.

'Jesus, you're in a bad way. Helena said you'd walked away from everything, said you had fallen, but I had no idea it was this bad for you.'

He hadn't expected her sympathy, and he certainly hadn't expected to hear she'd been talking to his wife. His ex-wife, he reminded himself. Again he felt the choking in his throat, and vertiginous spin of mem-

ory and emotion playing centrifuge in his head. If this kept up he would unravel completely, and then he'd be no good to anyone, least of all Billy. He focused his mind on her.

'I need help to find a friend who is missing.'

'They said you kept harping on about some missing girl. You know front desk could have helped you with that.' Like they would take him seriously. At least the young constable in the park had tried, but in reality Max had no credibility, and he knew it.

'Yeah, but I thought you'd listen to me.' The only place the front desk had helped him to was the cells.

'What can you tell me, then, that you couldn't tell them.' Her voice had gone back to the businesslike version, with a hint of the old antagonism.

'She's a street kid. Her name's Billy. She's been missing three nights. I don't know that much about her personal details, only that it is completely uncharacteristic of her to disappear. We kind of looked out for each other.'

'Were you fucking her?' Direct as always.

'No.' He paused, then added, 'She's only eighteen.' He chanced a look Meredith's way, and saw the look of pity and comprehension in her eyes. And that was why he knew she was the only one to help, that he needed her. 'What can I tell you? She is Fijian, family somewhere in Auckland but didn't have anything to do with her, turned the odd trick for cash.'

'Drugs?'

'Bit of weed, otherwise clean.'

'Family wouldn't have staged an intervention?'

'Not likely, and if by some chance they had picked her up she'd have left a note or something. No, she's just gone, and she's in trouble.' He knew it, with

absolute certainty. Every instinct in his body screamed it so.

'That's not a hell of a lot to go on.'

'I've got this.' He reached his hand into his coat pocket and pulled out the folded piece of A4 paper. He stood up to give it to her, but she waved it away.

'What is it? Tell me, I'm not touching it.' She knew how to twist the knife.

'K Road pimp caught her on camera as she was catching a john. It's dark and the picture's grainy, but you can make out a couple of numbers from the plate.'

She was staring at him again, and he recognised the look. He shifted position and tried to sit up straighter, like the teacher was looking. She was calculating something. What exactly? He hoped it was in his favour, in Billy's favour.

'Max, I'm going to be upfront with you.' A twinge of fear and apprehension relayed around his stomach. 'You're a mess. You stink — fuck, you stink — and you're a bum.' Each word pained like repeated punches to the kidneys. 'I think I know you well enough to be dead sure you wouldn't have come here unless you absolutely believed this girl was in danger, so I'll give you the benefit of the doubt there. But,' the look she gave him settled like a cold brick in his guts, 'I'm not doing anything for you until you do something for yourself.'

'What do you mean?'

'You go, clean yourself up, shower, for God's sake, then come back here and we'll talk.'

'But the clock's ticking — she's been gone three days. You know what the score is, you know time is everything. Can't you at least take this,' he held out the page, 'at least start looking into it.'

'Not until you clean up.'

'But it will take too long.' His voice sounded pleading, feeble.

'Then you'd better hurry.' Hers was concrete.

'Well how the hell am I supposed to do that? Don't you think I would have by now if it was that simple?'

'We all make our own choices, Max.'

'You think I had a choice?'

'You always have a choice. Personal responsibility. You elected to opt out of life, that was your decision. And before you protest,' she held her hand up, physically and verbally halting his riposte, 'I know you had the worst burden to bear, and I would never want to go through what you all went through; but still, it was your choice.'

She wasn't going to budge. He knew it, and he knew the only way he was going to get any help for Billy was to do as she said. Fuck, she could be a heartless bitch.

'How the hell am I supposed to clean up? This is all I have.' He stood there, a picture of decrepitude.

'Go find an op shop, get some new clothes, for Christ's sake bin those ones, go shower, shave, then you can come back.'

'Easier said than done. I haven't got any money, and where the hell can I go for a shower? Are you offering your place?'

'Hah,' she said with a snort. 'Get real. Use your imagination.' Imagination could only get you so far. Who was going to admit him anywhere, looking and smelling like this?

'I'll need money.'

She sighed, and then reached into her jacket pocket, pulled out a billfold. 'If I find out you've spent this on booze or fags, it's over. I'll make sure no one listens to

123

your concerns about this girl — at any station around town, not just here, you understand? And that's a promise. It's all up to you.' She handed over a twenty-dollar note.

'I'll need more than that,' Max said. Even his mathematical ability and dated grasp of economics knew twenty bucks would get him nowhere.

'Too bad, it's all the cash I've got, and I'm sure as hell not giving you my credit card. I'm not some charitable trust. Make do.'

Max looked at the note, folded it and then stashed it in his pocket.

'A thank-you would be nice.'

Max mumbled a 'thanks', but couldn't look her in the eye.

'Hey, McDonald,' she yelled down the corridor. The young constable hurriedly walked down towards them. Max wondered how much he'd listened in on their conversation.

'Ma'am?'

'Let the former detective here out of the cells and see him on his way. If he turns up at the station again looking like this, don't let him in. If he's cleaned up, give me a call.' She turned her attention back to Max, a grim look on her face. 'Take care, Max,' she said. 'You know the score. It's all up to you now.' With that she turned and walked away.

Meredith

She hadn't even made it out of the watchhouse from sorting out the mess made by those clowns this morning before she was accosted by people asking scurrilous questions. And here was yet another one walking down the corridor towards her, probably on the way down to the cells to have a look for himself and have a poke at the prisoner so he could make his pathetic excuse for an ego feel a bit better. The look on his face alone gave her a premonition of the coming conversation. The echoey click of her heels slowed as he blocked the way, forcing her to stop and pay him attention.

'Peters.'

'Johnson.' As far as she was concerned he lived up to his name.

'Have you seen him? Is he as big a bum as they say?' His voice sounded eager, conspiratorial, as if willing her to buy into the latest tabloid sensation.

'And are you as big a gossip as they say?'

The detective shrugged the insult off, intent on other things. He'd clearly missed the warning tone in her voice.

'Seriously, they were saying Grimes reeked of piss and shit, looked like a skeleton who hadn't had a bath for a year. Is he really that pathetic?'

Meredith's face twitched at his throwaway choice of word, and she felt the itch under her skin intensify, the acerbic knot in her stomach tighten.

'How the mighty fall, eh? Who would have thought

that — '

'Shut it, Johnson.' She didn't give him the opportunity to finish his sentence. She pulled herself up to her full height, poised slightly on her toes, so that she looked down on the smarmy, smug face before her. 'And what is it to you? That is none of your fucking business. And if I find out you have been down there to stare or jeer at him I will have you hauled before the disciplinary panel faster than you can blink. Jesus Christ, the poor bugger's had enough to cope with without having the likes of you rubbernecking. I thought you were supposed to have been his fucking friend.'

She pushed her way past the now-gawping detective, bumping him off balance, and strode away — strode away before she lost it completely and did something she'd regret. Arseholes like that were the very reason she played her cards close to her chest when it came to anything even remotely personal. The rubberneckers were no better than the paparazzi and their fascination with the scandalous and scurrilous. It was unprofessional, and it was contemptible. Her fist banged against the wall with the rhythm of her strides, and the clack of her heels echoed up the stairwell; the hollow sound seemed to emphasise how repellent company would be right now, so she veered off towards the women's bathroom. A quick check of the cubicles confirmed it could provide the solitude she needed. She moved over to the basin and placed her hands on either side of the smooth porcelain, feeling the refreshing shock of its cold on her palms, and she rocked backward and forward on the balls of her feet, trying to calm the emotion that bubbled up within her. When she looked up at herself in the mirror she

126

wasn't surprised to see the redness in her eyes and tears welling. She blew the breath out from between pursed lips and tried to steady the cramp of nausea in her stomach.

How could he have sunk so low? She had known she would bump into him again someday; New Zealand was too small a country, Auckland too small a city not to eventually rub shoulders with the past — but nothing could have prepared her for this. It was difficult to comprehend, and a part of her wondered if she'd got it wrong, if it wasn't actually Max Grimes down there, but some miscreant who'd stolen his identity and was trying to con them into thinking he was a broken-down version of Max, for his own gain.

But as was often the case in life, the truth was harsh. Max had fallen and he'd fallen hard. Part of her could understand why, but a larger part of her was both livid and saddened, and also felt a smear of guilt. No, she wouldn't allow herself to feel that. He'd made his own choices, and she wasn't going to carry the burden of his poor decisions any more than she'd already had to. He did that to himself.

She stood upright, wiped under her eyes, taking care not to smudge her eyeliner and mascara, blew her nose on a paper towel, and checked to ensure all signs of emotion had gone. One thing she knew for certain: it must have taken immense courage for him to come back here, to face her. It would have been the step of absolute last resort. He must have been consumed by fear for the girl's safety to crawl back to this place.

Would he do as she said — would he clean himself up and come back? Or had that been too much to ask? Regardless, she would make a few phone calls,

Billy

I've got to get that water, what is left of her dehydrated logic keeps chanting: *Get the water, get the water*. It has stopped leaking, so she knows there is at least half the bottle left where it is lying on its side, out of reach. She also knows approximately where it is, the direction from where that heartbreaking dripping, glugging sound came is emblazoned in her brain. Her mind works through the possibilities. Her right hand is secured to the pipe. She gives it a small tug and winces as the plastic band digs into abraded skin. She has a flash of an idea, and then chides herself for not thinking of it earlier. She reaches forward with her left hand and undoes the shoelace on her left sneaker. She slips it off and places it alongside the wall. She undoes the right and places it next to its mate. She leaves her socks on, a token barrier against the cold. The uncoordinated fingers of her left hand fumble against the button on her jeans; with a twist it comes free and she pulls down the zipper. This is where she pauses, steeling herself for what is to come, because the wet, reeking fabric of her jeans is sodden with her own urine, her own shit, and her skin has been marinating in this festering sludge of excrement. She gets to her feet as best she can, riding with the spin of her head, breathing deeply to push away the need to fall back down, then slowly reaches across her body and begins the side-to-side wriggle of fabric over her hips. The fresh wave of released stench hits her, and she screws up her face and persists, grimaces with the sting of

damp denim scraping across the macerated flesh of her inner thighs, and feels relief when the jeans drop the rest of the way to the ground. She shuffles her feet out of them, and then, dry-retching at the smell, she holds them by the hems and gently casts them out, a reeking denim net arcing through the blackness in search of life-giving water. She is rewarded with the scrape of plastic over concrete, the victory swelling in her heart as she pulls them in and the scraping sound nears. She casts out again, and again, each time hearing that bottle inching closer and closer, until she reaches out with her hand and her fingers nudge plastic, they grasp for it and, with a mewling noise like an excited kitten, she pulls it in to her chest. But she remembers what happened the last time she clutched the bottle and she won't let such greed and stupidity happen again. She raises the bottle to her lips, cringes at the slight whiff and trace of taste transferred from the jeans, and takes the tiniest of sips. With a groan of ecstasy she rolls the moisture slowly around her mouth before she dares to swallow.

Max

A complex mix of emotions engulfed him as he walked out the front door of the police station. Elation: he'd done it, he'd pushed himself past that immense mental barrier and made himself heard, made Billy's plight heard. There was relief that Meredith had deigned to speak to him; and with it he felt shame, a gnawing cavernous shame that transformed into a gut-wrenching guilt, grasping and clawing up from the deepest reaches of his soul. Now wasn't the time to examine the reasons for the guilt — that would be a Pandora's box of epic proportions. Now he had the more immediate physical issues to contend with. He had to get cleaned up, and fast. Meredith was not one for idle threats, and if she said she would black-mark him, she would. She hadn't earned her reputation as being a bitch in heels by backing down over anything.

The question was, how to go about it? Twenty bucks wasn't going to get him far. The charity-run op shop for clothes, that was the easiest option; but where the hell was he going to get a shower? There were public swimming pools, but where was the closest one to here? He'd have to walk all the way to the Point Erin Pool, or Parnell Baths, or Newmarket. The problem was he'd have to pay to get in — that's if they'd even let him in. Chances were the staff would get all worried about the creepy homeless man around all those good people, all those mothers with children. They'd decide that because he looked like nothing on earth, he must be a paedophile. All their white, middle-class

stereotypes and discriminations would come into play against him, whereas in reality they should have been more worried about the nice, tidy-looking man with the friendly smile. As far as he was concerned his money was as good as anyone else's, but that was the problem, the money. It would probably cost him, what, eight bucks or so nowadays to get in? And that was too big a chunk out of his precious little cash. He wondered if a backpackers or the YMCA would let him use a shower. Fat chance. When he recalled the apparition he'd seen reflected in the shop window, hell, he knew he wouldn't let someone looking like that anywhere near his premises if the shoe was on the other foot. The City Mission? Maybe. There was no point standing there in a freeze of indecision. First step would be an op shop, to at least get clothes fit to change into. There was a Red Cross shop in K Road. He'd start there.

Billy

She leans back against the wall, relishing the restorative effects of the water, amazed at how much her clarity has improved with even that little taste. She shakes the bottle in her left hand. About quarter is left. The sound releases an overwhelming urge to lift it to her lips and chug down the remainder, but she resists — she won't, she can't. She places it on the ground near where her right hand is tied to the pipe, and then takes several deep breaths before she starts on the next task she has to undertake. Her heart thuds in anticipation of the pain it will bring, but she knows if she is going to have any hope of surviving this, she has to look out for herself in the small ways. Getting her jeans off has only emphasised the point. She can't stay wet and cold. She won't die of hypothermia, she won't. She reaches out and feels along the wall to where she's managed to hang the jeans. Will they dry before she freezes? She doesn't know, but she has to try. She has to do something affirmative, something for herself. She starts edging down each side of her soiled underpants, inhales sharply at the sting of shit pulling away from her inflamed skin. She stops, holding her breath, waiting for the pain to ease before again working them down. Finally they fall to the ground with a sodden plop, and she leans her head against the cold wall, panting, working herself up to the next step. She closes her eyes, then reaches down for the disgusting things, carefully moving her fingers along until she finds fabric that is wet but not shit-covered.

And then, gritting her teeth in preparation, she begins to wipe her arse.

Bradley

He walked into the supermarket with a spring in his step that had been a long time absent. The corners of his mouth curled up in a smile at the thought. How did the saying go? — What a difference a day makes. Sure, there was what felt like a permanent stream of underlying panic flowing through him; but somehow, this morning he felt stronger, self-assured. It had been a good night, a bloody good night. There had been no problem rising to the occasion this time. He had forgotten just how incredible Ange could be, so responsive and adventurous — her body wouldn't have been out of place strutting it on a lingerie catwalk. Motherhood had been kind to her, and she worked hard at it, he knew; but how could he have gotten himself into such a funk that he'd forgotten she was hot? And she was all his. After last night's efforts, he was sure the feeling was mutual. He paused in front of the fruit stands. What did you feed someone who had been fasting a few days? There were muesli bars in the bags he'd dropped in the room, but that wouldn't be the right thing to get the girl starting to eat again, they'd be okay later . . . And he'd need to get more water, too. His mind drifted back to the shock and the intense guilty pleasure he'd felt when he'd struck her, and his initial feelings of remorse. Then he thought of Ange, and last night, and how he had taken the lead and rocked her world. Bananas would be good . . . perhaps something hot? Soup? She'd be chilled after another night. He'd get her cleaned up,

warm, fed. He needed her now. He needed her alive. He had plans.

Max

Max felt the heads turn as he shuffled through the doorway, felt the eyes follow him as he walked deeper into the crammed and dim interior of the K Road Red Cross shop. He looked down at the floor and walked hurriedly through the rows of racks until he found the men's trouser section. The shop carried that unavoidable musty fug of secondhand clothes, although the staff tried their best to disguise it with some pine-like scent — and he was also acutely aware he wasn't adding anything good to the already thick aroma. The array of colours and sizes of trousers on the rack overwhelmed him. What the hell size was he now? Once upon a lifetime ago, he'd been a fit-and-healthy size large. Now he was an unhealthy-and-emaciated size skeletal. The trousers he wore only defied gravity because of the length of twine pulled tight through the belt loops. He ran his fingers over the fabric of a grey pair of work pants; they slid over the shiny surface and he shivered at the alien sensation. He danced his fingers along the coathangers on the top of the rack until he came to some jeans. Somehow the coarse denim felt more solid, more real.

He looked around the shop and noticed the other three customers had gone, and the two staff were gathered over at the counter in conversation, glancing towards him then quickly away. He knew that look, and he knew what would soon be coming. Which one of them would draw the short straw? Which one would get to deal with the bum? He had his answer a

137

few moments later when the young brunette woman approached him. She had that modern hippy look about her, with a long, patterned skirt over trousers with Doc Martens boots poking out the bottom, a long cardigan and what looked like a crocheted tea cosy on her head. He wasn't surprised to see the nose stud as she got closer. She looked about eighteen. God, why did they all have to look that age? A lump formed in his throat.

'Can I help you with something?' she asked. He could detect the apprehension in her voice, although she was trying to hide it. He looked at the rack of trousers, and then back to her, but couldn't find any words.

'You know, unless you are buying something, you can't stay here, and I'll have to ask you to leave.' Her voice held a hint of steel, but he could sense softness behind it.

'I need to start over,' he heard himself say. He saw her frown, and again felt that hint of compassion. The words didn't seem his own, but they stumbled out, regardless. 'I have to clean up, I need,' he paused, eyes roving the store, trying to find the right word to express his situation, 'everything.'

She looked him in the eye, her nose twitching like a rabbit's, struggling with the smell. He could see her weighing him up: crackpot or genuine?

'Can you help me?' he said in almost a whisper.

'Do you have any money?' she asked.

He thrust his hand into his jacket pocket and felt around for the precious note and showed it to her. 'This is all I have.'

'And you need everything?'

'Yes.'

She nodded to herself and looked around the shop, then looked him up and down. In recent times that kind of appraisal always came with harsh judgement and condemnation, but this was different, she was different; he could see the sincerity in her eyes.

'You go and wait outside, not right out front though, around the corner a bit. I'll call you when we're ready.'

He nodded, 'Thank you,' and left.

Ten minutes later the young woman came and found him where he was crouched down, leaning against a wall watching the ebb and flow of traffic stopping for people traversing the rainbow crossing. She carried two grocery bags full of clothes, and he could even make out the shape of a pair of shoes in the bottom of one of them. He got to his feet, his body reminding him of how it had been mistreated over the last few days. He calculated how much that lot would be worth, even at op-shop prices. Please let there be some change left over. He reached into his pocket, pulled out the precious twenty-dollar note and held it out to her. She shook her head and waved it away.

'We don't need that, you keep it,' she said, and he felt the sudden prickle of tears in his eyes. 'Look, you don't smell very good, you need a shower if you're going to clean up. My boyfriend has a boxing gym — it's two blocks down and then take the street on the left. They've got showers, and there will hardly be anyone there at this time of day. His name's Matt. Tell him Jess sent you, okay, he'll help you out.'

A bolt of lightning shot down his spine. 'Jess, your name is Jess?' he gasped.

'Yes,' she smiled and placed the bags down by his feet. 'You take care, okay.' With that she turned and walked back towards the store.

Bradley

There was no hesitation this time as he reached for the handle — he welcomed its smooth, cold solidity. He swung open the door with a sense of drama and walked into the room, holding the lantern above his head. The stench was stronger than before and almost drove him back, but no worry, that would be dealt with soon enough.

The girl was huddled against the wall: the sight of her ground him to a halt and made him gasp. She was semi-naked — there was nothing on her bottom half — and he caught her trying to shift position to a kneel, pulling her sweatshirt down at the front to maintain her modesty. His eyes flicked to the jeans hanging from a hook on the wall, and a few moments later they found the underwear thrown into the far corner. His heart started to pound in his chest. He had expected a quaking, terrified figure, not this. It shocked him that she had taken matters into her own hands rather than being the timorous captive he had left behind. His eyes glanced to her wrist and he relaxed when he saw that the plastic tie still held her firmly to the pipe. There weren't going to be any more surprises.

Mind you, the figure hunched into itself on the floor didn't exude confidence of any kind; if anything she looked resigned. His pulse started to return to normal: she hadn't transformed into some kind of cornered cat woman, ready to take him on; and even if she did, surely she'd be pretty weak by now. No, all

141

was well, he could carry on with his plan.

He placed the lantern on the table, and then went back out to bring in the other bags. All the while he felt the large, dark eyes on him. In a weird kind of a way he liked that, too.

'Here's the deal,' he said as he started to pull items out of the bag. 'It's obvious I can't let you go anywhere now, but I'm not a complete arsehole, so I'm going to give you the chance to clean yourself up a bit.' He paused then, and looked at her. 'I see you've kind of started to do that already.' She did not look at him; instead she looked straight ahead, at the door. He went over and shut it, then locked it with the key. The click of the lock gave a most satisfying sound.

'I've got clean clothes for you, and some wet wipes so you can give yourself a wash. If you behave yourself, then this won't be too bad, you understand. I'm going to have to trust you and untie that hand so you can change. But just so you know what will happen if you try anything . . . ' He reached over to the table and picked up the short leather whip he had laid there. It had been something his mates had given him as a bloke-joke present on his stag night, but it had seen some delicious active service in the early days of his marriage. That had changed when the girls were born, and it had sat at the back of the shelf in his wardrobe ever since. He felt the firm coolness of the leather grip in his hand, shook it a little to feel the flex, then, before he could change his mind, walked the few steps over to her and lashed it, hard, down against her bare legs. Her scream split the room and reverberated like a gunshot in the small space. The sound at once froze and bolstered his heart. He was sure the lesson had been learned. The girl was

142

whimpering now, rubbing her leg with her free hand. Even in the low light he could see the streak of red across her dark skin, and he felt bad for it, but he had to make sure she played the game.

'That won't happen again if you cooperate. It's up to you.'

He placed the bags of clothes on the ground in front of her, then the wet wipes and a bin liner. 'I'm going to cut you loose now. You've got ten minutes to get yourself cleaned up, and stick all your dirty clothes in the bag. If you do it in time, I've got a reward. He held up the takeaway hot chocolate he'd bought on the way over. 'Right, let's get to it.' Holding the whip in his left hand, with his right he picked up the scissors. He felt her flinch as he slid the icy metal between her skin and the plastic. The tink of the plastic giving way was replaced by the sound of his own footsteps quickly stepping back as he swapped the whip into his right hand in case she rounded on him. By way of disincentive he cracked the whip against the tabletop. The sound made her jump and she reached out to grab at the clothes.

The anticipated resistance never came: for once, someone was doing exactly what he asked of them. How long since that had happened? Certainly not with the girls — they knew exactly how to work around him in their charming and playful way, smiling with mischief as they said no to his requests. It may have been cute, but it was still disobedience. And Ange didn't help the situation: she never backed up his authority, giving a united front; if he was honest it sometimes felt like she actively undermined it. Ange preferred to give orders rather than take them. Then there was work, where nobody appeared to respect him, let

alone listen to his opinion. His so-called autonomy was frequently overridden by the boss. To see the girl scrambling to fulfil his demands was liberating; and her unquestioning compliance threw some ideas into his head that he knew he shouldn't contemplate, but that held an illicit fascination. He watched the girl as she tried to clean herself up, back turned to him for privacy. Bradley finally allowed himself the satisfaction of a smile. It could all work out, after all.

Billy

He is gone. She sits there in the dark and chides herself for not trying to escape, for not at least having a go. What is wrong with her? She thought she was tough, had fight, but she did nothing. Nothing. Why? She sits there, feeling warm for the first time in days, feeling the soft caress of dry clothes on dry skin, the weight of the blanket around her shoulders, the sugary sickliness of the hot chocolate on her lips, the warm weight of the cup in her left hand, the uncertain sensation of how what she has drunk sits in her belly. Her right hand is bound once more, but this time it isn't flush up against the pipe; he's given her length, a chain, long enough so she can reach the lidded bucket he's put in the corner, so she can reach the water and food he's left beside her, reach the lantern and spare batteries. But she sits in the dark and berates herself.

Max

The boxing gym was right where the young woman described it. It was a nondescript affair with only a small sign to indicate its purpose. He'd walked right past it the first time, even though he was looking for it. He was surprised he hadn't noticed it before on his wanderings, as he had thought he knew all of inner-city Auckland and he'd been down this street many times before. The door swung open easily with his push and he walked into a small entranceway that led into a vast open space. He imagined it must have been an old workshop or warehouse building originally, the way the high ceiling was pitched and the windows were arranged, angled so they took full advantage of the light. The centre of the room was dominated by a boxing ring, and in many ways it looked like something straight from a movie set: spot lighting was suspended above the raised ring; three rows of rope pulled taut between padded corner posts. To the left was a large weights area, where two well-built guys were working out. Further down the wall were boxing bags and balls suspended from a lowered ceiling, exercycles and treadmills. It may have looked industrial and slightly grimy, but it was certainly well equipped, and the atmosphere was perfect. He felt himself relax, even though he still had a hard ask ahead.

To his right were some offices, a wall of lockers and the entrance to what he guessed were the changing rooms and showers. It was from one of these offices that a young man emerged: Matt, he guessed. He had

the build of a heavyweight, more of the David Tua mould than the Holyfield. He could sense the man's wariness as he approached.

'Can I help you with something, mate?'

'Are you Matt?'

'Yeah?' There was a definite wariness to his voice now. 'Why?'

Max looked over his head at the clock. Just about eleven, Jesus, had he wasted that much time already. For Billy's sake he had to get a grip and get to business.

'Jess sent me.' Saying her name had a profound effect on them both: the tears welled up again in Max's eyes, and Matt rolled his. Max wondered how many basket cases she sent his way. He held up the bags of clothes. 'I have to get myself cleaned up. I've got the clothes, but I need a place to shower.' He thought some extra ammunition might help his cause. 'I've got to clean myself up so I can help a friend.'

Matt looked him up and down.

'I can pay, I've got some money.'

'And Jess sent you, from the shop?' Again the name, again the stab.

'Yes, from the Red Cross. She's a nice girl.'

'Jesus, she's a bleeding heart.' Matt ran his fingers through his hair and looked over at the two men, busy pumping iron. 'Come on, then. She might look like a pushover, but you don't want to get on the wrong side of her. She'd never let me forget it if I didn't help you.' He walked off and Max followed him to the door he'd correctly guessed was the changing rooms. 'Have you got a towel?' Max shook his head. 'Soap?' He asked it like the rhetorical question it was. 'Hang on then, I'll get you some,' and he walked off, resigned. For

the first time in many years Max put up a prayer of thanks to God for angels.

* * *

He was bending over, tying up his shoelace when Matt came back in. The girl had made a good guess on the size of the clothes. He'd had to hitch the trousers in tight with the belt, and everything hung off him to an extent, but that was okay. He'd forgotten how truly exquisite it felt to be freshly scrubbed and clean.

Matt stood there looking at him, and he felt uncomfortable under the gaze. 'Better,' Matt said, 'but you still look like a bum. You just look like a clean bum.'

'Thanks.' Max was surprised at the note of sarcasm in his voice. He must have been feeling better. Matt's face broke into a smile.

'You got to help someone out, you said?'

He didn't even know where to start explaining on that front, so he kept it simple. 'Yes. And it's pretty serious.'

'You're going to need to shave then. And trim your hair. No one's going to take you seriously, looking like that.'

He didn't need telling. 'Do you know anywhere close that will do it cheap? I've only got twenty bucks.'

Matt shook his head. 'Tell you what. I've got spare shaving gear you can use in my bag. And we've got hair clippers in the office. I'll get them — but first you've got to put all your old stuff in the rubbish, it stinks. Pack it up in those bags, there's a dumpster out the back door. Get rid of it, then you can finish tidying yourself up.'

Now he was clean, Max appreciated with disgust and horror how low he'd let himself get. The only thing he kept from his old gear was the twenty-dollar note, the precious picture of Billy from the pimp, and the toothbrush and paste. It had been a relief to hurl the reeking, filthy mass into the bin. And now he stood at the sink, staring at the hollow reflection in the mirrors. He took in the wet, lank hair hanging down past his shoulders; the scraggly, unkempt beard; and suddenly he didn't want it, he didn't want any of it any more, he hated it, it made his skin crawl. He wanted it off, now — and he was tempted to tear it out. Instead, he took the clippers in his hand, flicked the switch and felt the powerful vibration thrum through his fingers and up his arm. He grabbed a fistful of hair, and then he reached up with the shears and set to work.

Max

The young constable looked up from the enquiries counter, not a flicker of recognition on his face. Max couldn't help the smile that crept across his chilled face.

'Can I help you?'

'I'd like to see Detective Meredith Peters, please.'

'Is she expecting you? Who can I say is here?'

Max cocked his head to the side and raised his eyebrows.

'Max Grimes.'

'If you'll wait a moment, please.'

The constable turned to head out the back and was partway to the doorway before he paused, and then turned around, a look of confusion on his face.

'You were the one here earlier?' he asked slowly, as if trying to avoid looking like a tosser if he was wrong.

'Yes.'

Max heard the murmured 'wow' as the constable went back to page Meredith. Now he was here, the all-too-familiar nerves started to plague him. He felt the pull of the wide-open spaces beyond the automatic doors; and he felt the deep squirm of uncertainty at how she might react. Maybe she'd thought he would wimp out and she'd never see him again. Maybe that was what she was counting on.

He didn't have long to wait before he heard the click of the side security door opening, the rap of heels across the hard floor, and saw the striking form of Meredith stride through. When her eyes found him

she pulled up so short her ponytail slapped around the side of her head. Astonishment splashed across her face before she pulled it back to her usual mask of brusqueness. There were four beats of silence as she finished her assessment.

'Good, we can talk now,' she said. She turned her back on him and headed to the security door, swiped her card and walked through. Max waited for further comment about his transformation, but none came. He scampered after to get through the door before it swung closed, and then followed her silently up to the second floor and along to an interview room.

It had been a long time since he'd been in this room, and it hadn't changed a bit — well, apart from being a more faded and stained version of its former self. If he was honest, the same could be said for him.

Meredith sat on one side of the table and indicated for him to sit opposite. He sat down, pulling the chair forward so he sat with schoolboy good posture. When he raised his eyes, he found her studying him intently in that exhaustive way that intimidated the good and the bad alike. He couldn't bear the scrutiny and had to look away.

'Right, you'd better tell me all about it, then.' No preliminaries, no 'How are you?' Straight down to business, with a tone in her voice that made him realise, with a stab, that she still blamed him. He fought back the flood of emotion that barraged him again. The last few days had been like an awakening. The intensity with which he felt every barb, every ache, every tinge of guilt was like the sharpness and relief of your ears popping as you come down from altitude, making you realise that everything until now had been muffled.

'Her name is Billy.' He spoke fast, and direct. It was not the time to gloss over what was real, and of all people, he knew Meredith appreciated candour. 'She's a street kid, occasionally worked it if she needed money for something specific. Mostly clean, only a bit of marijuana, nothing serious. She's a good kid.'

'How long has she been missing?'

'Three nights. And it is completely out of character for her. We kept an eye out for each other, so she would have told me if she was going to be away for long.'

'How old?'

'Eighteen.' His voice sounded very small as the number left his lips.

Meredith picked up the difference and looked at him closely. He saw the change come across her face again, that slight softening.

'The same age that—?'

'Yes,' he replied, before she could say the name and finish the sentence.

She nodded and he felt an immense sense of relief in that small acknowledgement of understanding.

'Her full name?'

'I don't know. It's just one of those things on the street, we only know each other by our first names — if even those are real. I'm pretty sure hers is short for Vilimena — is that the Fijian version of Wilhelmina? — which isn't that common, so it should help.'

'Better than if she'd been called Ella, I suppose — isn't that the current favourite?' It was a small attempt at humour, and he appreciated the effort. 'So she was definitely Fijian?'

'Is, is Fijian.'

152

She leaned forward, elbows on the table between them. 'Look, Max, let's be honest here. You know how this sounds. Young woman streetworker missing. You know the stats as well as I do. It's highly likely to be foul play, and you have to face the possibility she may already be dead.'

'Don't say that.' He spoke with more passion than he had in — what? — years. 'I refuse to believe that. She is alive. She's in trouble, but she's alive, I know it.' How could he explain that he could feel it, feel her? That she haunted his dreams; that he felt some long, thin line of connection with her. But he wasn't about to give Meredith more opportunity to think he was a washed-up kook.

She looked startled by the outburst, but pushed on regardless. 'Well, she must have family here. What did she tell you about them? You don't think they would have come and collected her?'

He shook his head, the question refocusing his energy. 'No. She didn't talk of them much. Basically they had disowned her. Came over from Fiji three or four years ago. They are very involved with one of the churches here; her father may even be a preacher of some kind. But they had a big falling-out and she was kicked out of the house.'

'The prodigal daughter?'

'She certainly wouldn't return home, if that's what you mean. She was very strong about that. Couldn't handle the hypocrisy. I think it had to do with a boy, and, well, as I said, they are a very religious family.'

'You don't happen to know her birthday, do you?'

God, did he? He thought back to some enormous muffins she'd bought one day, big iced decorated things you'd get for kids. Time had held such little

153

importance for him that even a vague date was a struggle. 'It was summer, light until late, so maybe December, January?' What else had happened on that day? Was there anything else that made it differ from the nothingness of every other day? Something was niggling at the back of his mind. There was something else, he was sure of it, but what? He wished he'd paid more attention — to many things, as it turned out. He thought back, tried to visualise that day — and suddenly it came. 'There was a bus crash that day, up on K Road, hit a pedestrian . . . the old lady died. You'll be able to look that up, that will give you the date.' The surge of hope he felt at such a small thing again threatened his equilibrium. With so little information, it was the small things that were going to count. He watched Meredith writing down the details.

'So where's this photo?'

He put his hand into his pocket, felt the dry tickle of the paper under his fingertips and pulled it out. He unfolded it and flipped it around so it was the right way up for her before passing it over. 'It's grainy as hell, taken from a pimp's cellphone on Monday night. K Road. Unfortunately you can't make out any detail of Billy, she's got her hoodie up.'

'And you're sure that is her?'

'Certain. The pimp was, too. She wasn't his, but he'd been trying to get her in his stable — probably why he was photographing her rides as well as his girls, trying to find a way to extort her in. Full credit to her, she'd held him off so far.' He didn't mention the unsavoury bargain he'd made on Billy's behalf to obtain the image.

Max tapped his fingers on the photo. 'You can't see the badge for the make and model of the car, but

154

it's definitely a dark colour — not black, maybe charcoal or navy blue — and you can make out two of the numbers of the plate.'

Meredith bent over the photo. 'A five and a nine,' she read aloud. He recognised the signs of her struggling to say something, or not say something. 'Look, Max, I know you think this is going to be significant, but this is Auckland, it's full of dark-coloured cars, there will be hundreds of vehicles that share those numbers. The simple fact is we have got precious little information about your girl to go on, and we don't even know that she is missing. She may have just gone away for a break or something.'

He started to protest, but she held up a hand to stop him. 'And before you say you're sure something is wrong, yes, I am going to give you the benefit of the doubt on that one, because for you to come back like this, after how you turned up this morning, you must be pretty damned certain.'

'Thanks.'

'Yeah, we'll see how charitable I am about all this later. If it's a wild-goose chase I'm going to be pretty pissed off.'

'It's not a wild-goose chase, Meredith.' He reached into his pocket again and pulled out the twenty. 'Here — here's the money I owe you.' He pushed it across the table.

'You didn't spend it on booze or fags?'

'Nope.'

'How did you get the threads?'

'It's a long story.'

She pushed it back towards him. 'When was the last time you ate something, Max?'

God, when had it been? He'd been so intent on Billy

155

Bradley

He couldn't go back home — as far as Ange was concerned, he was at work. He could have gone to the gym, but his mind was such a jumble of fragmented and warped thoughts he felt the need to escape, so he'd spent the afternoon in a café-bar in Mission Bay, looking out over the water, watching the pram-pushers and dog-walkers go about their daily business, listening to the inane prattle of a group of women at the relaxed end of a power lunch while he nursed a beer, and then a second. Beyond the trees the peak of Rangitoto drew his eye; the extinct volcanic island still held an air of threat and mystery. The chill effect of the beer buffered his turbulent thoughts, his way-too-fast pulse and the slightly sickened weight in his stomach. The third one helped to soften his inhibitions, and he allowed himself to acknowledge that he was beginning to enjoy this; that in analysing the risks to benefits ratio, the benefits — or potential benefits — were becoming more appealing. He had a captive; he had a captive audience, and a compliant audience. He didn't want to hurt her, he honestly didn't, but his drifting mind kept filling with ideas, ideas that could sate his needs yet not flagellate his conscience. 'Jesus,' he whispered to himself. How the hell did it come to this? His mother would be rolling in her grave if she knew her beloved boy held such dark desires. His parents had never been overly religious — he remembered going to church only at Easter and Christmas — but they believed in good

values and hard work. 'Do unto others as you would have them do unto you.' They were solid, salt-of-the-earth people, and he and his sisters had enjoyed the carefree childhood of most people of his age. His mother took care of all their needs, and his father supported the family, much like he did. His father worked hard, long days, like him, but he had been a mechanic, a man who worked with his hands; his was the end-of-day tiredness of physical labour, rather than mental exhaustion. He recalled the image of his dad slipping into his armchair with a beer at the end of the day, tired and happy. He didn't get that luxury. When he got home exhausted from another thankless day at work, Ange saw it as her time to clock off. She'd had a tiring day with the children, she'd say; it was his turn to be the parent, to do the bathing and bed-time routines, clean up after dinner, do the laundry, because she had a full-time job being a mother and he had to play his part, equal partnership. Trouble was, there was nothing equal about it. He didn't see why he should have to do half the housework when she spent all day at home. He spent ridiculous hours in that hellhole of a workplace to earn all the household income, and she spent it. Then he had to justify pur-chasing what he wanted. Shit, the grief he got about buying a decent stereo system, one that linked in with their smartphone apps and computers, and had the depth of sound he liked — you'd have thought he'd gone out and bought a bloody Harley-Davidson, the way she'd gone on. He felt the bitter tang of resent-ment and swallowed it back. Yet she always turned up with new shoes or clothes, and he didn't want to think how much money she spent on her hair.

He half-smiled at the irony of it, as he looked at the

view through the amber remains in his glass. The first thing that had attracted him to Ange was her hair, her beautiful, glossy, lustrous hair. The night he'd met her at a friend's birthday party he'd been bewitched by the drop-dead gorgeous, vivacious young woman with the mane of golden hair. He'd fantasised about running his fingers through that hair, smelling it, burying his face in it. It had taken four months of active campaigning before he had got the chance, and it had been a hard sell; but persistence had paid off, and the reality had lived up to the fantasy. As far as he was concerned, he'd scored his dream girl.

Reality was now far removed from those carefree days. Now his job was grinding him into the ground, and the woman he adored paid more attention to their children than to him. Not that he could blame her — he lived for those two little girls. But the undeniable fact was that now he felt less and less in command of his life. It was like the power was slipping through his fingers; like he was stuck on a treadmill that was getting faster and faster, propelling him forward with relentless motion. And over the past few months he had felt it was accelerating at a pace he had no hope of keeping up with, and that at any moment he was going to be spat off the back, wasted and torn, a mangled mess.

That had changed now. Everything had changed. Despite the fact it scared and horrified him, despite the fact it went against everything he believed himself to be, he had learned something today, in that room, with the girl. He had control, he finally had control over something, and it felt so damn good. He couldn't give that up now.

Meredith

She finally let out the breath it felt as if she'd been holding for the last hour. Yes, the transformation had been remarkable, but to her it only accentuated the true depth of his fall. The once handsome face was now gaunt, his skin pockmarked by the scars of infected sores past and the unhealed remains of those present. With his head shaved he looked like some prison-camp survivor; the thin lines of white skin showing through the stubble more signs of how tough life on the streets had been. The hardships were reflected in the haunted look in his eyes. He had been painful to look at, and she feared she'd been too abrupt, too harsh with him; but it had to be done, for both their sakes. She had to think about the girl, take her mind off the history that had just walked out the door.

When she had told Max the results of her hospital and morgue search she'd expected him to be relieved. He'd been unwavering in his belief the girl was still alive, in his grail-like quest to find her. Still, chances were she was a body in a ditch somewhere just waiting to be found. No one matching her description had turned up at the Sallies or the City Mission — although the lady at the mission thought she knew who they were talking about, only she hadn't seen that particular girl for a couple of weeks. It was reassuring news as it meant they were chasing a real person, not some phantom Max's mind had dreamed up in an effort to get attention. For now there were two avenues of

inquiry: her family and the partial numberplate.

She looked at the ghostly hooded form in the photograph.

Eighteen. Shit, this had become personal.

Bradley

The door loomed large in front of him, and he stood there, acutely aware that he was about to cross a line, consciously cross a line. This wasn't about lashing out in anger, this wasn't about acting on impulse: this was a deliberate act. Was he certain he wanted to go through with it? The undeniable rise of excitement in his chest, the surge of adrenaline in his veins, the dizzying apprehension of what he was about to do was intoxicating.

Because the simple answer was yes.

'Fuck, I can do this, I can do this, I am going to do this, I am going to do this.' Before he could back out, he reached forward and unlocked the door. He pushed it open and stood on the threshold, watched with a sense of satisfaction the look of fear that crossed the face of the girl, the way she shrank back before him; he felt a swell of pleasure at the sight, wanted more of it, wanted to wallow in it. It fuelled him. He strode into the room, put his bag of supplies on the table, let his fingers reach out to the leather object lying along the back of it.

'We have some business to attend to,' he said, his voice clear and strong as he walked over and stood above her. 'If you cooperate, you'll be fine, if not . . .' He lashed out and struck the whip against the wall, a mere foot from her head. Her eyes jerked up to his, her full understanding of the threat clear.

'Sit on the chair and hold out your hands.' He kicked the chair her way so she could do as he asked

within the constraint of her chain. He didn't trust her. He couldn't afford to trust her, even though he knew if she tried anything he could crush her resistance in an instant, because he had the advantage of size and strength. He didn't want it to get to that. In truth he still felt uneasy about hurting her: he wasn't a complete monster. So what he planned today wasn't hurting her. If she sat still, it wouldn't hurt at all. Which is why he needed her hands.

But she hadn't moved.

'Fuck off.' Her words were quiet, but defiant.

He felt a tug of apprehension. 'Sit down on the chair right now.'

'No.' She spoke louder, and pulled herself back into the corner as far as her chain would allow.

He lashed out at the wall again, and the crack echoed around the room. She cringed at the sound, but still didn't move.

'Move it,' he shouted.

'No, I won't,' she yelled. He felt his jaw clench and his mouth curl up into a snarl, and he strode forward, pulling his arm back and bringing the riding crop in an arc across her arms, which she was holding up to protect herself. She screamed, the sound ripping the quiet of the room.

'Do you want me to do that again?'

'No, please, no.'

'Well sit the fuck down and hold out your hands.'

After a pause, and much to his relief, she slowly sat down and held out her hands. The resistance had been brief and feeble, but still, the fact she had stood up to him at all had jolted the sense of complacency he had developed. He wouldn't make that mistake again.

'Closer, put your hands closer, wrist to wrist.'

Quietly sobbing, she complied.

He pulled a cable tie out of the bag containing today's necessities. He placed the whip on the table, grip end closest, so he could grab it quickly if she flared up again, but he didn't think she would. She looked defeated, utterly defeated, and it made his heart soar. After he'd tied her hands together he stood back, hands on hips, and looked at her. It was a bit of overkill. One of her hands was already tied by the chain to the wall, so it wasn't as if she could escape; but it would stop any further resistance.

Time to get to work. He glanced into her eyes and saw the fear and the tiredness. He wondered what she thought of him. Did she think he was going to rape her? Did she think he was that kind of a mongrel animal? He wasn't that kind of a sick bastard, a man who could debase a woman like that. But there were plenty of other things he'd been thinking about. Things he'd been fantasising about from the small hours of the morning, since he'd reached out to his wife again, and had run his fingers through her long, blonde hair. He'd always wanted Ange to try one of those really short cuts, like Charlize Theron, bobbed and sexy, daring. But she would never do that for him, never in a million years. She saw her hair as a trademark, part of her identity. It was a pity — she would look even sexier cropped.

He pulled the other instrument he'd brought out of the bag, and heard the little inhalation of breath from behind him as the girl saw what was in his hand. With her anxious sound he felt the increasing excitement of his own, the enticing prickle of goosebumps across his skin. He walked slowly around behind her, stood

at her back and slid the elastic tie out of her hair, and then he slowly ran his fingers through her long, ring-letted tresses, wiggling them free when they snagged on knots.

'No,' she whimpered, and she raised her bound hands up, trying to bat him away, but he grabbed a handful of that beautiful dark hair and yanked it back hard, pulling her head back with the force.

'Sit bloody still or you know what will happen,' he growled in her ear. Her hands dropped back to her lap, but he could see her shoulders were shaking. He smiled, happy in the knowledge. He ran his fingers through her hair again, drew a section up from her forehead with his left hand, then reached across with the right and snipped the scissors through it, hearing the *schlick* as metal slid across metal, and watched with deep satisfaction as the dark, curly locks fell to the floor.

Meredith

'You've got to be kidding me? You expect me to launch an investigation, an expensive and time-consuming investigation into a supposed disappearance based on the testimony of that bum?'

She closed her eyes and steadied the fire that was building within her, before reopening them and fixing the detective inspector with a look that she hoped spoke of sincerity and determination, and not what she actually felt, which at the very minimum would get her stood down for insubordination.

DI Williamson was an imposing man, physically and in demeanour. Her superior officer was also one of the very few men in the world who made her feel small, in every respect. He didn't take any crap, that was for sure, but he was generally fair, and she knew full well it wouldn't advance anyone's cause to lose her temper.

He got another salvo in before she could mount her counterprotest: 'And you above all people should have more sense than to believe anything that man says. Look what happened the last time you trusted him. That was the fuck-up of the century. I'd have thought you'd been burned enough not to believe a single word that came out of his mouth. And Jesus, you saw the state he was in. Max Grimes is a train wreck, a no good, washed-out, pathetic shell of a man. I'm not going to waste police time and resources on chasing a ghost dredged up from the mind of a nutter.'

Each word gouged another track of anger, shame and grief through fresh wounds. Meredith could feel the tide of heat that tracked up her face. She fought back the urge to scream at him. She dug her finger-nails into the palms of her hands and felt the sharp stabs of pain steady her, pull her focus back to the immediate.

'But surely the fact that he came here, that for the first time in two years he set foot in this building and asked for me, tells you that he is seriously concerned for this girl's welfare.' Her voice sounded high to her ears, thin and pleading. She moderated it before she continued; DI Williamson had never been one to be swayed by displays of weakness. There was only one shot at this.

'Max has stayed below the radar for all of this time, so it would take something extraordinary for him to resurface and bring attention back on himself. I believe he is genuinely concerned about the safety of this girl, and that we should be, too.'

'But where's his proof? A street girl? Prostitute? Does she even exist? He can't even tell us her name, for God's sake. How can I justify launching an investigation based on crumbs?'

There had been plenty of investigations launched on less, and Meredith couldn't help but think they wouldn't be having this conversation if it had been some rich white girl from Remuera who had gone AWOL. She could feel the corner of her left eye beginning to tic and tried unsuccessfully to blink it away.

'Isn't it our job to find the proof?' she said. This time the anger showed in her voice. 'That's what we are supposed to do. I've already had confirmation of a girl fitting that description having been into the City

Mission in the recent past. She isn't some ghost — this is a real person.'

Williamson's arms crossed over his chest. 'So, you've already started an investigation behind my back, have you?' The anger in his voice reflected her own, and Meredith could see the muscles tightening in his jaw. She cursed herself for the slip.

'No, I just made a few preliminary phone calls before I came to you, to make sure I wasn't wasting your time.' She knew how to suck up as well as the next person. The scowl that crossed his face said he recognised back-pedalling when he heard it. This was never going to be an easy sell, but it was going worse than expected.

'So, you don't trust him either?' It was a statement more than a question.

Jesus, it was far more complicated than a matter of trusting him, but for the sake of simplicity she shook her head.

'Good, and so you shouldn't, because at the moment I can't see how you could possibly be objective about anything to do with Max Grimes. You were far too close to him before, and made some extremely bad decisions that too many people paid the price for. We're still cleaning up the bloody fallout. No, your judgement is clouded.'

Again the pulse of blood at her temple began to thrum harder. Was she always going to carry the stain of that awful day? She wasn't the only one to blame. The circumstances had been extreme — beyond extreme — and how many bloody years had she worked her arse off to try and atone for that one decision? To prove that she was as good as any of her male counterparts; hell, that she was better, the best — and

168

here she was being fobbed off, still in the shadow of her past. After a shit of a day, it tipped her over the edge of her self-control. When she next spoke, her voice quaked with her shock, rage and hurt. Her hand drifted up, her finger beating accusation towards him with her words.

'No, I'm not going to wear that. For God's sake. I thought you would give me far more credit than to think I'd be swayed by past events. I'm a professional, this is my job. And you're forgetting one big, almighty great thing. This isn't about Max or me or the shit that happened in the past; this is about the girl. There is a young woman missing out there,' her arm swung around in a big arc, 'and it is our duty, our sworn duty, to find her. Don't you forget it.'

'You watch your tone, Detective Sergeant Peters.' His voice was low and dangerously calm. 'You do not talk to me in that manner, ever. And don't you dare remind me what my duty is or isn't. I have been in this game a lot longer than you have and I know far better than you do exactly what my duty is. Your behaviour just confirms my suspicions: you are not being objective, and your feelings towards Max Grimes have overshadowed any modicum of judgement you may have had. So *you* listen, and you listen very carefully. We are not going to launch an investigation into the disappearance of some prostitute street kid who may not even exist, based on the word of Max Grimes. Period. If someone else happens to report her missing, then sure, it will be corroboration, but until that moment we are not wasting police time and resources on it, understood?'

Oh yes, she understood alright, but she wasn't about to give up that easily. Meredith would almost

169

guarantee that the girl had had a life full of people giving up on her and letting her down, and she wasn't about to become one of them. She wouldn't give up on the girl, and she wouldn't give up on Max, not this time.

She turned and stormed towards the door, before coming to a halt and swinging back around to face her boss with what she hoped was perfect theatrical timing.

Then Meredith pulled out the trump card. It was manipulative, but fuck it, there was no other way. Public perception was everything, and her superior understood full well the politics of appearance. 'And what if he's right? What if Max Grimes is right and something sinister has happened to this young Pasifika woman? Imagine the field day the media will have if this girl turns up dead in a ditch somewhere and it gets out that the police chose to ignore a chance to find her alive because the victim was only a brown, prostitute street kid and the information had come from a bum?'

Meredith saw the flicker of hesitation furrow DI Williamson's brow and felt a stab of bittersweet victory as her barb struck home. She had him. She'd get her investigation.

Max

The park bench felt hard and cold against his bony arse. Max picked at the date scone he'd bought to eat, and gazed across at the station. Despite promising himself he wouldn't, he became fixated by each person exiting the building, hoping it would be her. The wind was a relentless sou'wester that bit through his new clothing. He had fond thoughts about his old coat, probably on its way to the landfill by now. 'No regrets,' he said to himself. To kill time earlier, he'd walked back down to the K Road Red Cross shop. On this occasion, when he'd entered the store there hadn't been a mass exodus of other customers; there were none of the conspiratorial whispers of staff members. He'd enjoyed the look on the young woman's face when he'd said thank you, and it finally dawned on her who he was. Then he'd felt moved once more when she'd looked at his shorn head and said, 'Well, you'll be needing one of these then,' and had handed him a beanie. His hand ran up to his head, fingering the fine knit, and the bumpiness of the embroidered logo for some kind of sheep dip. He whispered her name, 'Jess,' testing himself to see if he had the strength to shape the word with his lips, to form the sound, to picture the face. Pain shattered his heart and he begged for the darkness to descend.

★ ★ ★

'Max.' He started, as if awaking from sleep, felt the shift from the ethereal to the grounded, of reality to the vertical. He resented it. 'Max, are you alright?'

After the intensity of his earlier vigil, he'd completely missed her exit from the police station, her passage across the road, and then her approach across the funny little island marooned in the lanes of traffic.

'Yeah, I'm fine, must have dozed off.' It was far easier to lie.

Meredith stood before him, her green eyes holding both concern and a guardedness. He had to hold his hand up to shade his eyes from the brightness. The late-afternoon sun shone from behind her, creating an auburn halo through her flyaway hair, turning her into a ginger angel. The thought nearly made him giggle, and that kind of inappropriate response towards her, of all people, made him question his sanity. This emotional yo-yoing was exhausting. He had to look down at her feet to avoid losing it altogether.

'Do you have any news?' he asked.

'We do, but none of it is especially helpful.' She was always direct, which he found a good thing, although he knew many didn't appreciate her candour. She came around and sat on the bench, but as far removed from him as was possible. He didn't blame her. He didn't stink anymore, but even cleaned up he wasn't the most respectable-looking creature out there. Then there was that whole other thing. She didn't trust him, pure and simple. She probably didn't like him, either.

'What can you tell me?'

'Basically your girl doesn't exist. There's no immigration record that would fit with what you've described of her and her possible first name. From that we'd have to surmise her entire family are here

172

illegally, which will make them harder to trace. Did she ever mention going to school? If she did we will canvas the high schools next to see if she was enrolled anywhere.'

'Sorry, I can't help with that. She never mentioned school at all.' Max thought about some of the complex discussions they'd had. A number had been rather philosophical — although she could twist his brain in ways that gave him a headache at times. He'd enjoyed those discussions immensely. He'd never talked with such depth and had such a diverse range of conversation with anyone, not his parents, not even . . . well . . . those who had been close, the people whose memory he'd managed to bury in the recesses of his mind for such a long time. The bilious swirl of anxiety sloshed around his stomach. He steered his thoughts away from that minefield and steered his attention back to Billy. 'She's a bright girl. She was often reading books.' He felt a small jolt of realisation at what he'd said. 'And I'm pretty sure they were library books, so she must have a library card, and they require proof of address and contact details, so that could be an avenue to follow up.'

'Yep, we'll do that.'

Max took note of the reference to 'we', and the fact there had been no acknowledgement that it was a good idea. It was a them-and-us situation. It felt strange and sad to know he was now classed as one of 'them', when he had once been 'us'. The divide felt immense.

Meredith hadn't looked at him in this time. They both stared out at the cityscape, and he was glad that it negated the need for eye contact — especially hers, which felt so accusatory.

'From what you described, her family are very religious, so we'll visit some of the local churches. We'll start with the Pasifika churches first before spreading out further. A lot of Fijians are Methodists, from memory.'

A number of those discussions he'd had with Billy had been about religion, and he was no believer in God; he'd seen too much crap meted out by man to man to ever believe there was anything God-like involved: animal, yes; God, no. Billy was firmly in the God camp, even if she sprinkled the conversation with words like hypocrisy, materialism and unforgiveness. She'd often called him to examine his belief systems, and in some ways she'd made him feel ashamed that he didn't truly have any, other than a moral sense of what was right and what was wrong, and the mantra drilled into his head by his mother: 'Do unto others as you would have them do unto you.' He thought that was a perfectly good set of values to get by on. It had served him well enough. He pulled his thoughts back to the car, and the man in that car, and what he'd do to him if he found him.

'What about the plate?'

'We ran the numbers we have through the motor-vehicle database. As you can appreciate there are hundreds of vehicles that could potentially carry those numbers. When we narrowed the parameters to Auckland district, there were eighty-seven. When we filtered it by colour to darker-coloured vehicles, eliminating white, silver, yellow and gold, that left fifty-six vehicles. We didn't filter it by sex of the owner — that would be one assumption too many.'

'And someone will be calling on all those owners?'

'Yes, that will start tomorrow.' Too long, it was far

too long.

'Why wait till tomorrow? Can't they start tonight? You know as well as I do that every hour, every minute counts.' He could hear his voice rising and tried to pull it back, but his anxiety couldn't be contained.

'Look, Max, I know how much this means to you.' She glanced at him then, and her look said she was aware exactly how much this counted. 'But we're chasing a ghost. We're chasing someone who isn't on our records, who is homeless, who could be anywhere. Let's be honest here: we only have your word that something is amiss, and although I believe you are genuinely concerned, there are many others in the station who won't; I'm sure you wouldn't be surprised I've had to be very careful who I mention your name to. You know the politics involved in these kinds of cases. I have to justify every investigation, every expense. So it has to wait for tomorrow. That's just the way it is.'

Max flopped forward, his elbows on his knees, head in hands, trying to rub away some of the fear, some of the frustration from his temples.

'Is there anything I can do to help?'

She actually scoffed, laughed out loud, and Max cursed himself for uttering that thought. Again it was a case of wrong person, wrong question. She didn't bother answering, and he didn't bother repeating the query. It left an awkwardness in the air between them, which marked the time for him to leave. He sat back and was about to get up and go when she dropped a few words that stopped him dead.

'I ran into Helena the other day.' The words were said quietly enough, but the effect they had on Max was anything but. He felt the sweat break out across

his face, while a chill sensation swept along his back. The way his heart thudded in his chest, he wondered if he was going to have a coronary.

'She asked after you, if anyone had seen you, knew where you were. I had to tell her no. Maybe you should get in touch.'

Max's breath came in short gasps. He could feel the griping in his stomach and the lumps of date scone threatening to come back up.

'Jesus, I gotta go.'

He hauled himself to his feet and without looking her way stumbled off and across the turning lane, the blast of a car horn punishing him for his inattention.

'Max,' she called out after him. 'Max, you have to face up to this sometime.' He placed his hands over his ears, but he could still hear her words slip through his fingers, felt them chase him, stab into his back. 'You can't run forever. It's never going to go away.'

Bradley

He stood in his garage, in front of the workbench, and pulled the coarse, coiled tendril between his fingers, stretched it till it was straight, then relaxed his hands so the curl sprang back to its natural length. He did it several more times, and with each stretch and spring the smile that curled the corners of his mouth climbed higher, until he started to laugh out loud. He couldn't believe he'd done it. Couldn't believe he'd followed through with his plan, that he'd managed to work up the guts. He hadn't wimped out: he'd ridden out her protests, and actually gone through with it. And best of all, he didn't feel that bad about it — after all, he hadn't actually harmed her. But he'd done something he'd set out to do, he had been in command of the situation and he'd finished the job. And, fuck, it felt good. He felt elated, and strong, and horny, so fucking horny. The kids were in bed, and Ange was in the house, probably tidying up everything, getting the house picture-perfect as it had to be, nothing out of place, everything how she liked it, her way, and all he wanted to do was grab her, rip her clothes off and strip her naked and then to feel the softness of her hair running through his fingers while he fucked her. She was his, all his. He stretched the curl out one more time before raising it to his lips, and then placing it carefully in the bottom drawer of his tool chest. Then he turned back to the house and with an unbearable anticipation went to hunt out his wife.

Bradley

He lay spooned against her back, his body exquisitely aware of her skin touching his; he felt as if every pore was charged with electricity. He nuzzled his face into her hair, breathing in the scent of her shampoo.

'Bradley?' Her voice was quiet, uncertain.

'Hmmmm?' he murmured dreamily.

'Are you having an affair?'

He felt like he'd been slapped. His body tensed with her words — and hers responded in kind. What had she noticed? He'd dropped those stained trousers into the drycleaners, thank God that suit came with a spare pair, and he'd disposed of all her soiled clothes. Had she smelt something on him? Surely not — he'd showered. Then he asked himself her question, an affair? Was he having an affair? Technically, did it count? And he decided, with a sense of relief, of course he wasn't, there was no love involved, not even lust — well, not towards the girl, anyway. It was something entirely different — it was something . . . something indescribable but it wasn't an affair. He breathed out and let his body relax again.

'No, of course not. Why would you think that?'

There was silence for a while. He could imagine her trying to find the right words. She must have been worried, because words had always been her primary weapon and she generally fired them without pause. Finding the right words had always been his weakness.

'You wouldn't lie to me?' She sounded so vulnerable.

179

He pulled himself up onto his elbow and gently rolled her over so he could make out the outline of her face in the dark, the whites of her eyes softly reflecting the little light there was. 'You know I couldn't lie to you. I'm not having an affair. Why would you think I am?'

'Because you've been doing so much overtime at work. Because of this — because you're suddenly showing me some attention after years of not being very . . .' she paused, again hunting for the right word ' . . . giving. It's a classic sign, you know, a change of habits, suddenly wanting sex. You've been different these last few days.'

He felt different. Whereas before he'd felt withered by her dictatorial and perfectionist ways, now he felt empowered, that he was the one in the driving seat. He gently twirled a lock of her hair around his finger. 'I know I've been a bit different, but in a good way. Believe me, I'm not having an affair.' He paused, deciding how to spin this. 'I guess I just had a sort of epiphany. Work has been like a treadmill, and I guess I'd let that slowly wear away at me till I was always too tired, or distracted, and I felt so much pressure to be the best, to give them more and more. The workload and expectation has been ridiculous since the restructure, you know it has. And when I was at the gym the other day, and I looked at all the other sad, middle-aged bastards who looked as hounded and as tired as I felt, I thought, why am I doing this? Why am I letting it get to me like this? If I keep on at this rate I'll be dead in a decade, another bloody corporate heart attack, and you know, I want to live to see our little girls grow up, and I want to be around to grow old with you. And you know what's funny? I was

always worried you'd be the one to run off and have an affair, get tired of how much I'd neglected you and go find some better, more attentive man. I want you to stay with me and I've finally come to appreciate how much I've put my job first and how much that hurt everyone. I decided to change that.'

He heard her sniff; she was crying. Ange never cried, she was from the 'don't show your true feelings' school of life, and this sudden display of softness stirred something deep within him.

'I've decided to make every day count. I'm sure that I'll slip up occasionally and lapse back into my old ways, and when I do, you can slap me around a bit and tell me to snap out of it. But I've made that conscious decision. I love you, and I want to be here for you and the kids.'

'It's been so long since you said that.' She cupped his face with her hand.

'Said what?'

'That you love me.'

'Well, I do,' he said, and he realised he actually meant it.

Max

Max stood at the entrance to the alleyway, his alleyway. Somehow, in the course of this single day, its significance had changed. The rhythmic swoosh of cars on the road had once been comforting; now it grated. In his mind the alleyway now held some kind of menace, the shadows loomed deeper, the blackness of doorways an invitation to oblivion, and he became aware he couldn't sleep rough there tonight. But that little voice inside him kept picking away at his conscience. What if she came back? What if she came back and she needed him? And anyway, where else did he have to go? He pushed his reluctant feet forward to take those first steps down its maw. He had a job to do. He had to check it out, just in case she had returned and was there, although in his heart he knew she wouldn't be. In his mind she was somewhere, somewhere strangely like this — cold, dark, foul — and she was alone. But she was alive, he was certain of it. He had to find her.

The alleyway held a stench he hadn't noticed before. He smiled to himself at the irony of suddenly being precious about smells, when he'd reeked for so long. Her spot was empty, as he knew it would be. He looked across the way to where he used to doss down and recoiled at the sight of the darkened alcove. He moved further along the alleyway, his footfalls sounded unnaturally loud in the chasm of concrete buildings. A darkened mass to his left began to move.

'Who's there?' a cigarette-scratched voice called out from the gloom.

'It's me,' he said.

'What do you want?' The voice had changed from cautious to its usual antagonistic.

'To strike a deal.'

He heard a derisive chuckle, then as he got closer a sharp intake of breath. 'Bugger me, what have you done to yourself?' Skeet said. There was nothing wrong with his eyesight.

'The girl, Billy, she's missing.'

'So, maybe she saw sense and went home, or shacked up with some fella. What do you care?'

'I care a lot, as it happens. I need you to keep an eye out for her, in case she comes back here.'

'Why would I do that?' Skeet said, the hook in his voice indicating exactly what it would take to get him to share that kind of information.

Max slipped his hand into his pocket and pulled out a precious five-dollar note. He handed it to the wily old bugger.

Skeet held it up towards the light at the end of the alley, checking the denomination. 'Humph. It's going to take more than that. Couldn't even get myself a packet of cigs with that.'

'Call it a token of goodwill,' Max said. 'I'll be back each day to check in. If you see her, you let her know I'm looking for her. If you can prove she was here, there's a bottle of whisky in it for you.'

'A big one, not a hip flask.' It was a statement, not a request.

'Of course, the big one.'

Skeet tucked the money away and settled himself back into his digs. 'Why don't you hang around yourself, see if she turns up? Or are you too good for us now?'

Some people he could feel sorry for, with the circumstances life gave them; some people deserved what they got. Max wasn't going to miss Skeet.

'Like I said, if you see her, tell her I'm looking.'With that he turned and walked back towards the light.

Meredith

It had been over a decade since she'd last set foot in a church. She could even remember the date — as she should; you're supposed to remember your wedding day, after all. Not that she had cause to celebrate it anymore — the philandering bastard had buggered off years ago. Unfortunately it was with her sister. She didn't miss the bastard, but she did miss what she'd once had with her sister. It didn't do much for interfamily relations, of course, and after a couple of disastrous family Christmases they'd all given up the pretence of trying to make it work out, and, to her mother's great sorrow, the family had basically disintegrated. So much for love.

This church was huge — it had to be, to service its large Pacific Island community. The carpark was a sea of asphalt large enough to accommodate several basketball courts. She could hear the melodic strains of a choir practising in the main auditorium beyond the large foyer in which she stood. Through the glass double doors she caught a glimpse of colourful floral prints wrapped around big, beautiful women.

'They sound good, don't they?' A huge Polynesian man stepped towards her with a warm smile and his hand outstretched. Her hand was dwarfed in his as they greeted each other.

'Thomas Mara, minister of this church, we talked earlier. You must be Detective Peters.'

'Detective Sergeant,' she said, but didn't offer her Christian name. 'Thank you for your help with this,

185

and facilitating a meeting.'

'That's okay, I'm just glad I recognised Vilimena from the description you gave. It's a serious matter. I had no idea how serious until I received your phone call. Come this way.' He guided her towards some offices down a corridor to the left. 'It appears the Naitakus have not been honest with me about their dealings with their daughter. I had understood, after the troubles they had with her, that she had been sent back to relatives in Fiji, so I was shocked to hear she had been living rough on the streets all this time. Please believe me, if we had known the truth of the matter the Church would have stepped in and done something for the girl. I'm horrified at the thought she has been unsupported all this time.'

She could tell from his distress that he meant it. 'We appreciate the help you're giving now. Hopefully her parents will be able to give us some information that will help track her down.' She wasn't going to hold her breath on that front, given what she'd been told by the minister on the phone. Although she was supposed to go into situations like this with an open mind, she had already formed an opinion of the Naitakus and it wasn't very flattering.

'They have asked that I be present at this meeting, if you don't mind. They're just through here.' Given what she now knew of the situation, a buffer would be a good thing. He knocked twice on the door and entered. The room had several rectangular tables arranged in the middle, giving the effect of one large, boardroom-like table. The drawn curtains were an overly cheerful orange; they were complemented by inspirational pictures on the walls. Meredith tried not to scoff at a Bible quote that said 'Love is patient, love

186

is kind' — that was clearly not the case here. Billy's parents were seated side by side. Lily Naitaku looked nervous — make that guilty — a rotund woman with her coarse, greying hair pulled back from her high forehead and tied in a bun, a fake frangipani flower behind one ear. In contrast William sat with his arms crossed across a muscular chest, a sulky defiance in his eyes. Meredith knew the type straight away, and she trusted her instincts well enough to predict she would have to do a lot of tongue-biting in the course of this interview. She sat opposite them and was glad when the Reverend took a place between them along the side.

'William, Lily, this is Detective Sergeant Peters. She is here to ask some questions about Vilimena. I expect your full cooperation in this matter. Please answer as honestly as you can.' His voice was tight, the tone making it perfectly clear he was unimpressed with the two members of his flock before him.

'Did you bring a picture of your daughter with you?'

Lily Naitaku nodded and bent down, extracting a five-by-seven photograph from a large woven kete. She slid it across the table, avoiding eye contact. Meredith spun the picture around, taking in the fresh-faced schoolgirl who smiled back at her. She was a pretty little thing with sparkling eyes and an open face. And they had cast her out. Who could do that to their child?

'What is her date of birth?' Meredith jotted down the date, given in halting English by the mother: it confirmed she would be eighteen years old now. Most kids that age were still happily at school, hanging out with their friends, worrying about what to wear and how their hair looked — not trying to survive alone

on the streets. Well, she hadn't been completely alone — she had Max. Small mercies.

'When was the last time you saw her?' She tried to keep her voice carefully even, but couldn't help the hint of disapproval that snuck in.

'We haven't seen Vilimena for a year. That was when she left our home.' William spoke of his namesake as if she was some boarder, not his daughter. His English was better than his wife's, but still strongly accented. His choice of words was interesting.

'I have been told by several sources that she did not voluntarily leave your home. Can you tell me what happened?'

'She had to go. She broke the rules of our house and was being a bad example to her younger brothers and sisters. She couldn't stay under our roof.' William Naitaku spoke with the manner of a man who was unaccustomed to being questioned by anyone, and when he finished speaking he eyeballed Meredith, as if that was all that needed explaining, end of story.

'Why not? What exactly did she do wrong?'

He snorted, nostrils flared like a horse, as if it was all such a bother.

'It is a private matter.'

'Mr Naitaku, your daughter has been reported missing and we have grave fears for her safety. If you have any concern for her welfare whatsoever, you will answer my questions. What happened the last time you saw her?'

His eyes narrowed at being questioned further, and he looked to his minister for support. If he thought he was going to get moral support from that department he was mistaken.

'William, answer the questions, and truthfully this

time. Your deceptions have done enough damage already.'

Meredith felt a surge of satisfaction at the look of annoyance and embarrassment on his face, but wasn't surprised to see how quickly it was overcome by one of defiant pride.

'She got involved with a boy. She was not allowed to date until she was eighteen, that is the rules, but she went against my wishes and sees this boy behind my back. She was told not to, and was punished for it. If that was not bad enough, she then came and told us she was pregnant. How do you think that made us feel? She brought shame upon our family, and shame upon herself in the eyes of God. I am a youth pastor at this church, how do you think that would make me look? My own daughter acting like a harlot? She could not stay. I told her to leave, I threw her out.'

Meredith clenched her teeth. His actions had indeed resulted in her becoming just that, a harlot, all because he worried about what other people would think. She was sure they'd agree he was a pillar of society now. While the husband spoke like a puffed-up self-righteous git, his wife sat still, eyes downcast, hands held together so tightly, her fingers had paled.

'When you say "threw her out", was there force involved, Mr Naitaku?'

'I did what was necessary. She was no longer welcome in my home.'

'Was there force involved?' Her voice doubled in volume.

Again he looked to his minister, but this time with an edge of caution.

'Did you strike your daughter, William? Don't you lie to me. Did you hit her?' The Reverend Thomas

Mara sounded as disgusted as Meredith felt, and was most likely as bound by professional duty to be impartial as she was, but it was clear emotion had overcome the constraints of his position.

'You hit her, William, you hit her belly.'

William gave his wife a withering look as she whispered the words. He fired angry words at her in Fijian, and Meredith didn't need a translator to understand the gist — or a crystal ball to know there would be repercussions later.

'So let me get this right. Your young daughter came to you one day and confided in you she had fallen pregnant, so you physically threw her out of the house, including punching her in the belly, a pregnant woman; and you haven't seen her since? And this was a year ago?' Meredith's words were measured, cold, and it felt like she had to count a beat between each to prevent herself from screaming at the man and saying something she would regret.

'That is right.' He spat it out as if it was his God-given right to act that way, and Meredith saw that in his heart, this man believed it. The thought made her feel physically ill. 'She hasn't come back and begged our forgiveness, she hasn't repented. Until she does, she is not welcome in our home, she is not my daughter.'

'So you haven't met your grandchild?'

There was silence, punctuated by shuddery breaths from Lily Naitaku.

'Do you even know if you have one? Did she have the baby? What happened there? Do you know?' If she had hoped for a flicker of guilt or remorse in his face, she was mistaken. She decided William Naitaku was a truly ugly man.

'If she has the baby it does not matter. We would be ashamed of the child, it was the product of sin, a sin that shamed our family, before Church and God.'

Meredith had to clench everything to stop herself from exploding. Her toes ached in her shoes. She could sense the waves of tension coming off the minister to her side. She wondered who would give in to their urge to scream at him first.

'This is why you lied to me, William?' The Reverend won. He rose to his feet, towering above all those at the table. 'You told me she had been sent back to Fiji to stay with relatives. I am horrified you threw her out on the streets, all because you felt ashamed, worried about what people would think — what the Church would think?' His finger stabbed in accusation. 'Our God is a god of forgiveness. We would have supported you all, especially Vilimena, in this. I am appalled at your lack of faith in your congregation, and I am sickened by what you did to her, your own flesh and blood.'

The Reverend's face was flushed and beads of sweat framed his brow. He had a look about him of the fire-and-brimstone preachers of old. Meredith could see the situation was about to turn to custard, which, although satisfying to watch, would achieve nothing. She stepped in to deflect the attention off the men.

'And what of you, Mrs Naitaku? Do you share your husband's views? Do you know if she had the baby?' Lily looked up to her husband, mouth agape, clearly hesitant in giving any reply. Meredith caught the shiftiness about her and knew she was hiding something. 'What do you know? I can see you're not telling me something.' Silence descended on the room as all attention was focused on the woman. She shook her

head from side to side, staring at the tabletop. 'Look at me, Mrs Naitaku, this is your daughter we are talking about. What do you know?'

'She didn't have baby,' she whispered. 'She lost it.'

Max had never mentioned a baby, so Meredith had been sure it had either been dealt with, or miscarried. After hearing of her father's heavy-handedness she couldn't help but wonder if he had contributed to this. She added another potential crime to charge the bastard with, along with assault, immigration evasion, and complete failure to be a decent human being.

'Have you talked with her?'

She shook her head. 'Frankie, our oldest boy. He sometimes go see her, give her money, his money.' William fired another salvo at her in Fijian, which she returned with similar vigour. It appeared Mrs Naitaku had had enough.

'Silence.' The Reverend's bellow shut them both up.

'When was the last time Frankie saw her?'

'Two, three week ago. He find her in town.'

'How old is he?'

'He fifteen.' So a child succeeded where the adults had failed, and had showed more compassion than the girl's own parents.

'And she didn't tell him of any problems she was having with anyone, any concerns she had for her safety?'

'No, everything okay.' Apart from the fact she was a young woman abandoned by her family on the streets of Auckland. Yeah, everything was just hunky-dory.

Meredith had had enough. She'd done what she'd set out to do, found out the identity of the girl, got a photograph and eliminated the possibility her

family had stepped in to rescue her. It couldn't have been further from the truth. Listening to the father's self-righteous crap had left her mentally exhausted and sick at heart. She stood up and pushed the chair away, pulled on her jacket.

'Thank you for your time, Reverend,' she said, acknowledging him with a nod. 'Mr and Mrs Naitaku, I will keep you informed of our investigation into your daughter's disappearance. Mr Naitaku, be warned there will be charges pending, and if I hear even a whisper of any harm to your wife or children as a result of this conversation you will be in a cell faster than you can blink. I'll see myself out.' With that she turned and walked to the door. But as her hand gripped the door handle she decided she couldn't leave it at that; in her heart she couldn't let it be. She turned back to them and looked at them with contempt. 'You both should be fucking ashamed of yourselves.' And with that salvo fired she walked out and slammed the door shut behind her, blocking out the eruption of Fijian that followed in her wake.

Billy

Billy sits with her back against the solidity of the wall. Her shorn hair lies in a pile beside her, where she has gathered up every last strand she can find. She takes a deep breath and reaches up with trembling fingers to her scalp, explores what remains on her head. She lets her breath out with a groan as she feels the frizzy few centimetres that remain and the rough-cut ends that prickle her fingertips. It has always been her pride, and even with everything she has been through in the last year, she has always kept it clean, tidy, pretty. Now it is gone. The stories of her childhood fill her head and her mind casts back to Samson, betrayed, blinded and robbed of his glory, his strength. Her eyes squeeze shut and she whispers to herself, 'I will not lose my strength, I will not lose my strength.' Her hands drop back to her lap, and she lifts her eyes heavenward, looking at the water stains in the ceiling, picked out by the dim light of the lantern he has left her. But Samson came back; she recalls Samson's last act of defiance, his entreaty to God, placing his hands against the central pillars of the temple of his enemies and pushing, pushing, and destroying the temple with the last remaining ounce of his strength. And she knows she has to find that place, that well of strength within her, if she is going to survive this. Because, by God she feels her fear and her anger, and she feels her hate, but she also feels shame. She thinks of the Bible and all of those Sunday-school stories, the memory verses she'd had to rote learn, the stories

194

of those who called upon God in their hour of need. But she can't bring herself to do it. When she thinks of God she thinks of her father, and when she thinks of her father, her mind explodes with those last terrible images of his rage, of his fists, of being forcibly cast out, and her hands fly to her eyes to try and block the visions. But all she sees is his face screwed up in anger, she hears the hurtful, shameful names fall from his lips, feels the echoes of his blows, and she sees her mother cowering, impotent. She remembers the pain, the griping, the bleeding, the loss, and her heart aches at the thought of what could have been, but was stolen from her by that man. No, she can't call on God. That god is his god, a god of anger and fear and pain. She thinks back to the stories, those other stories — not the Bible ones, instead the ones her grandmother used to tell her, stories of myths and legends. She sighs as she remembers her grandmother, her Bubu. Images flood her mind, but they are different, and she feels her heart calm as she sees the grand old woman, tall, oh so tall, and big, and beautifully ugly — because she was far from pretty, her Bubu. She smiles at the scary woman the children used to run from, but to whom she was drawn. She sees her serenity, her calm and, above all, her strength, she sees her Bubu's strength. And she knows she has found that place of refuge now, that place of strength she can retreat to. She laughs quietly to herself. She has found her talisman.

Max

Max walked into the café, relieved to get out of the biting wind, and scanned its interior, taking in the retro-cool look the place had tried to cultivate, not altogether successfully. There were padded booths for the diners, and Formica tables, and 1970s-style lighting hung from the ceiling. Not even the most gifted of interior designers could manage to make walls of computer screens look cool, though, even if they were banished to the darkest recesses of the place.

He was surprised to see how many people were here at this hour of night. There was quite an array of humanity feverishly typing on keyboards. It had been difficult to find an internet café, they were few and far between now most people had smartphones. The tourists were easy to spot: some because of their silly hats and beanies. No self-respecting Kiwi would ever wear a bright, stripy beanie that covered the ears and ended in braids — especially the guys. There was one guy who looked borderline homeless — stubbly beard, holey clothes, dead eyes. Max found it hard to stop staring at him; when he finally did it was to look at himself, reflected in the window. He looked gaunt, and the hair was definitely shorter than he'd ever worn it, but he was a more recognisable self than the apparition that had stared back at him from the mirror this morning.

'Can I help you, sir?'

Max turned his head around to see a bearded young man, decked out in muso clothes. Beards looked to

have become fashionable in the time he'd been out of circulation. It was one of those changes he noticed, now that he had started looking at people's faces again. Perhaps he'd been a little hasty in getting rid of his.

'How much is it to use a computer?'

'Internet is three dollars for half an hour, or two dollars if you buy a coffee.'

The last coffee Max had drunk was a treat brought to him by Billy. That would have been, what, over a week ago? Shit, a lot had changed since then.

'Is there anywhere nearby with free internet?' he said.

'Only wireless if you've got your own laptop.'

Max shook his head.

The guy looked at him as if he was some cheap-skate. 'There's the city library, but they're closed at this hour of night.'

It couldn't wait till the morning. He put his hand in his pocket, felt the ten-dollar note, but left that, then found the last remaining coin. He pulled it out and held the two dollars in his hand, turning it over and over between his thumb and fingers, wondering what the hell he was going to do. He didn't want to break into that note.

The young man shrugged. 'That will have to do,' he said, and took the coin. 'You're at computer number twelve, over by the window there, and here's your password.' He handed back a small slip of paper.

'Thanks,' Max said, and felt touched by yet another small gesture of kindness from a stranger. It went a little way to restoring his faith in humanity. He sat down in the window seat next to a young couple who were bantering away in some foreign language, it sounded

Scandinavian. They gave him a cursory glance and went back to their banter. He logged in and stood staring at the screen, willing his mind to remember what to do. Computers had never been a passion for him. He had been proficient enough at their use, but he saw them more as a tool than a pastime. Max surreptitiously looked at what the Scandinavians were laughing over. Bloody Facebook. When he looked around at the other computers in use, they were all on social media. It had been over two years since he'd been near a computer, and then talk had been of how social media was the new way of communicating; that it would replace the need to actually talk to people. It looked to him that it had taken over the world. Last resort, he told himself.

He looked up the White Pages telephone directory website first. He felt his skin grow clammy as he typed in the name. Grimes, Helena. Nothing. Grimes, H. Still nothing. He wondered if it was still under . . . Grimes, M. No, he wasn't there either. It surprised him how that small omission made it feel his presence had been erased from the world. With an ache in his heart he typed in Goodchild, H. And there she was. She'd gone back to her maiden name. 'Fuck.' He didn't realise he'd said the thought out loud until the couple next to him turned their backs to him, more for their comfort than his privacy, no doubt. The other thing he noticed glaring from the computer screen twisted like a knife for the stab in the back. She'd moved. God, had she sold the house? But she couldn't have. She'd have needed his signature for that: despite everything that had happened, legally it was still half his — although morally? He knew the answer to that. He needed to write the information

down, but pen and paper wasn't on his personal inventory. He looked around at the people nearest him. He didn't want to bother the Scandis, they were probably wary of him anyway. The computer to his right was vacant, but the next one over was occupied by a young Indian-looking man.

'Excuse me, please? You wouldn't have a pen and some paper I could use, would you?' The guy had a refill pad and a pencil case in front of him, so Max knew it was a case of would he, rather than could he. The young guy looked surprised, as if he'd been pulled out of some alternative reality, which was probably true: Facebook.

'Yeah, sure.' His accent was one hundred percent Kiwi. Max listened to the rip as he pulled a page out and then handed it over, with a red biro.

It had been so long since he'd written anything that it felt alien and awkward as Max jotted down the new address and phone number. The letters looked stilted and large, the writing of a small kid. He looked at the phone number and pondered how to approach this. The trouble was it wasn't Helena he wanted to talk to — she was the last person in the world he wanted to confront right now — so he couldn't just pick up the phone and ring, and hope she wasn't the one to answer.

There was nothing else for it, he knew what he had to do. Given his dislike of the thing, how ironic that it was going to be the pathway for knowledge for him. He pulled up the Facebook homepage and logged in. The only reason he had a Facebook account in the first place had been to do precisely what he was about to do now. The photo of a laughing and carefree-looking Max was a lifetime removed from the man looking

at it now. He shook his head and moved on to his friends list, which was brief. He wasn't surprised to see he'd been 'unfriended' by Helena. Revenge at a keystroke. But he felt a jolt of relief when he saw the other name there. His finger poised over the mouse, but he had to take several deep breaths before he found the strength to click.

His body slumped in the chair at the sight of the face grinning out at him from the screen. Harry's face had made that subtle change from a teenager's to a man's in the two years since he'd seen him; and the torrent of guilt Max felt in having missed that transition threatened to overwhelm him. His eyes took in the new bump in the nose, the stubble, and he admitted with a groan he'd missed that vital passage into manhood: the first shave. Who had overseen that special moment? Helena? Someone else? It didn't bear dwelling on. He scrolled through some more photos, and marvelled at how tall he'd grown, how much he'd muscled out. It was undeniable. His son was no longer the gangly teenager he'd left behind, he was a carbon copy of Max at that age. The word 'abandoned' snuck into his mind, and his shoulders hunched forward with near physical pain at the accusation. Jesus, he'd walked away, he'd just walked away from all that, and missed out on so much. But at the time there had been no other way. It was either walk away or, well, do something drastic. His mind began to play like some old horror movie, that train of thought causing old doors, old, creaking, menacing doors, to creep open, the poisonous light from within edging wider and wider, spilling further and further.

Jesus, get a grip, get a fucking grip, he told himself. He had to do this, for Billy's sake he had to do it. He

clicked the 'message' box before the impetus disap-
peared. But, God, what to write, what words could
you use when you suddenly wanted back into the life
of someone you'd left like that? Keep it simple, it was
all he could do, keep it simple. When he looked at the
words, they looked cold, detached. His fingers paused
over the keys and he added one more, 'please'. He
clicked send before he could change his mind, then
sat there, spent. His eyes flicked up to the time read-
ing in the corner. He only had two minutes left. Did
he dare look any further? God no. He stood up: the
noise of the chair scraping across the linoleum floor
sounded deafening to his ears.

It felt like everyone's eyes were on him as he made
the long walk to the door and out into the night.

Bradley

For the first time in longer than he could remember he looked forward to this very moment, to walking through the doors at work and heading to his desk. His hour at the gym this morning had left him energised. He had worked out hard, probably too hard, and he tensed his thigh muscles, enjoying the slight burn that came from having pushed himself just that little bit further, beyond the pain barrier. So what if he paid for it tomorrow.

'Jesus, Bradley, where have you been the last few days? The boss is ropeable.' Jenkins had never looked more like a nervous rabbit than he did at that moment. He was the office doomsayer, everyone acknowledged it; but somehow today, in Bradley's eyes, he was a caricature, some pathetic wide-eyed creature dreamed up by a cartoonist — the ultimate loser. He had the urge to swat him away like a pesky fly.

'I've been sick, Jenkins, he knows that.' Crampton knew because Ange had taken it on herself to be the overprotective mother and to ring him. That was yet another subtle way she emasculated him. 'You are allowed to be sick, you know, even in this company. It's not illegal.'

Jenkins caught the sarcasm in his voice and looked puzzled, even hurt by it. In that moment it dawned on Bradley that Jenkins saw him as an ally, a fellow wimp among wimps. He'd have to rectify that. There was no way he was going to continue wearing that mantle. He'd had enough of being downtrodden, and

associating with that whinger and whiner just pulled him down further. The other staff were all pretty glum at the moment, courtesy of all the shit that had gone down with the restructure, but Jenkins was the worst; how the hell he'd kept his job, he didn't know. Maybe he was a relative of someone important, or maybe he knew where they buried the bodies.

Bradley walked on to his desk, ignoring whatever it was Jenkins was prattling on about. When he got there the first thing he saw was the fluorescent-yellow note strategically placed in the middle of the mess: *My office as soon as you get here.* Bastard hadn't even signed his name. Bradley screwed it up and tossed it in the bin. He looked at the piles of shit all over his desk and wondered how on earth he managed to get anything done with all that crap everywhere. He sat down and set about restoring some kind of order to it all, and after fifteen minutes of concerted effort had cleared everything away into its rightful place. It looked far more relaxing. Maybe there was something to that feng shui garbage after all.

Next he turned on his computer and waited while his email inbox filled up. Two hundred and fifty-six unread email messages. Shit. He scanned down and deleted twenty-eight without even looking at them — they were only forwarded funnies from co-workers. He was about to open the first real email when he heard a strident 'Fordyce' from across the room. The tone was unmistakably irate. 'My office, now.'

He knew this was coming, and he also knew the lines he'd been practising in the car on the way over.

Robert Crampton was a bully, pure and simple. But Bradley also recognised in him a man under immense

pressures of his own. He too had to answer to those above him, and he too had just survived the restructuring. Unfortunately for the rest of the staff, he was the kind of man who took that stress out on others; the kind who found the weakest and most vulnerable and then took it on himself to slowly pick them apart. Bradley had been the target of that campaign these last few weeks, and it galled to think Crampton saw him as an easy target.

But that was no longer the case. He wasn't going to buy into the victim mentality any longer. He felt more than capable of taking on his aggressor and standing up for his rights.

'Look, I didn't appreciate that we didn't know where you were yesterday. There's a lot going on here at the moment and the last thing we need is people taking time off at a whim.' His face, when screwed up like that, looked remarkably puggish.

'I was still sick. Ange had called in the day before, so I didn't think it necessary to call again. I would have thought it was obvious I was still home.' He'd never dared be that direct with Crampton before, and although he could feel the flutter of anxiety in his stomach, it felt good.

'Simple courtesies count. As far as I'm concerned it was an unaccounted day off, so it will come out of your annual leave.' His eyes had narrowed even further.

'I'll get a doctor's certificate if you like. I was ill, so you can't arbitrarily remove it from my leave.' Crampton looked surprised at this assertiveness, then wary; he was unaccustomed to having anyone contradict him. Bradley could see the simmering anger beneath his demeanour.

204

'You do that, then, but I expect to see it tomorrow. All the same, you're going to have to make up the time, though. We have the report for Red Co due Monday morning, so you'll have to stay as late as it takes tonight to get that finished. And the annual plan for the engineering division needs to be completed by Wednesday. You'll have to come in over the weekend to get up to speed on that.' He sat there and rattled off more demands and expectations of overtime. Bradley stood there, calm, taking it in and smiling on the inside, waiting for his moment to play his trump card. The boss paused; Bradley played.

'No, I'm sorry, I can't do that.'

Crampton shook his head as if he hadn't heard properly. 'What do you mean, no?'

'I won't be coming in on the weekend, and I won't be working overtime tonight. I will work my utmost for you in the hours I have here, but I will no longer allow work to spill into my family time.'

A shade of deep red began to creep up Crampton's neck and blotch into his face.

'That's impossible,' he said, his voice in combat mode. 'Everyone else here is doing extra hours, it's part of the job, and I don't need to remind you there are plenty of other people who would be happy to step in and take over your job if you aren't up to it.' The volume of his voice had risen, and Bradley let his rise to meet it. He was very aware of the fact the door was open behind him and an appreciative audience beyond.

'Perhaps the fact everyone else is having to do overtime is because the amount of work you are foisting on us is impossible. Since the restructure everyone left has been doing the work of two people, but with

205

the same time restraints, resources and the same pay. It's inhumane and it's unworkable. Look at them all — everyone is stressed out and up to their eyeballs in it. If you want all this work to get done you need more staff, it's as simple as that.' There he was, champion of the cause, and it felt great, he felt he was on a roll.

Crampton rose to his feet. 'If you think there is going to ever be more staff, you are mistaken. Get real, Fordyce, you know the current economic environment. And don't you dare go stirring up this kind of sentiment among the others. They choose to stay and work overtime, they aren't lazy shirkers like you.' The conversation had changed tone: Crampton's voice was rising in pitch, but Bradley's remained rock steady, even.

'They don't choose to: every single one of them would rather be at home with their families, or out having a life. You and this profit-driven, shareholder-pandering company give them no choice. They know damn well if they don't do it, you'll turf them out on their ears and they'll be stuck in the dole queue, struggling to pay their mortgages and scrape up enough money to feed their families. They are blackmailed into staying late, pure and simple. The work doesn't get done because there is far too much of it for the number of staff we have, so they are here doing overtime because you force them to.'

'Well, that's your opinion, and I can see clearly you aren't coping with your job.' Crampton started straightening papers out on his desk, indicating this conversation was about to come to an end. 'I'm sure I won't have any difficulty finding a replacement for you; and after this conversation, where you have taken

time off without notice and are causing unease among the staff, inciting them, you'll be receiving a written warning.' And there he played right into Bradley's hands.

'And if you so much as think about going down that track I'll be filing suit against you for constructive dismissal. I know the union would be very interested in all of this, in the way the workers are being treated in this company. So don't you dare threaten me with losing my job, and don't you dare threaten the others either, because by God, I'll get the unions and the lawyers involved and you and this company will not know what has hit you.'

Before Crampton had a chance to retort, Bradley turned his back and stormed out of the room. He emerged from the door in time to see a scurry of bodies heading back to their desks, and as he walked, slowly and with back straight, to his cubicle, his chest rose at the smiles and thumbs-ups he got along the way.

Max

Sleep had not come easily last night. His dreams had again been infiltrated by dread, the same distorted images of Billy's face and that other one, but this time joined by the Red Cross girl, Jess's, and Harry's, all billowing in an ethereal mist, wraith-like and being hounded by something hooded and reaperish, something that felt incredibly old and cold, something dredged from the collective fears of humanity. This time he'd awoken disorientated and afraid, and it had taken him several panicked moments to figure out he was back in the dark of the boxing gym. Matt had reluctantly let him in last night. No doubt Max had the young woman's potential wrath to thank for the roof over his head and the comfort of the pile of gym mats he'd dossed down on. In thanks he'd found a broom and swept the floor before the first people arrived in the morning. But despite a warm and dry night and even the luxury of a hot shower first thing, nothing could remove the taint of the nightmares, and he felt a blanket of gloom smother his mood.

He trudged back up the familiar route to the Central Police Station and put in his usual request to the officer at the front counter. There was someone new on today, but either word had got around about his business there, or he looked semi-respectable in the young woman's eyes; she paged Meredith without question. Although he no longer experienced that near-crippling panic when he entered the building, it still wasn't what he'd call a comfortable experience,

and his radar was on full alert, waiting for something bad to happen. It took an age for Meredith to come down, and he couldn't help but wonder if she did it on purpose. When she finally appeared at the side door and indicated for him to come through, they followed the uncomfortable dance of silence and polite distance — at least up until the second landing in the stairwell, where she opened her mouth.

'You look like shit. Do you want a coffee?' She always was concise. But he wasn't going to turn down an invitation for coffee, even if soured by insult. Besides, she was probably right. She led the way up to the staffroom. He was relieved to see they were the only occupants; it was too early in the day for the first round of morning tea breaks. His eyes drifted to the cabinet of cakes and sandwiches, and his stomach audibly informed him of how hungry he was. Billy's disappearance had provided a large distraction in his life but he knew if he was going to have the fortitude to see this through, he was going to have to remember to eat.

'Oh, for God's sake, choose yourself one, I'll get it.' He didn't turn down her grumpy charity. She might have been a bitch, but she was a generous one. They took their supplies to a table over by the window. She had her standard black coffee, no food. You didn't get a figure like that by snacking. His own methods of weight loss had been a little extreme.

'I take it you want to know where we're at?' she said, getting straight to the point.

He just about said, 'Well, I'm not here for the charming company,' but thought better of it, so instead nodded and bit into the sandwich. God, he'd forgotten how good bacon and egg could be.

She reached into her satchel and pulled out a

photograph, slipped it onto the table in front of him. He almost spat out the mouthful.

'Is that your girl?'

The image blurred as his eyes welled up, an instant reaction to seeing that face. God, for a man who never used to cry he'd been doing a hell of a lot of it lately. He guessed that was what happened when you were a wreck, in every sense of the word; but he couldn't accept it. To him this tendency to tears taunted him, reminded him of the pathetic creature he'd become. He needed to be stronger than that. He reached out and picked up the picture, careful to hold it by its edges. The photo must have been at least two years old, but despite the rounded cheeks and schoolgirl plaits, it could only have been Billy. Billy without the street-weary look, Billy with an innocent smile. He looked at Meredith and nodded. She frowned at his emotion and looked away.

'How did you get this?' he asked. That was quick work — but, he reminded himself, that was the exact reason why he'd called on her help. She was the best.

'We found her parents. Played a hunch on the churches. You were right about her father being a youth worker; we picked the biggest Pasifika church we could find, and, bingo, there he was. I figured if you were of dodgy immigration status you'd try to lose yourself in the biggest organisation you could, among all the other people with dodgy immigration status. The minister picked her and her parents from the description straight away, and called them in for a meeting at the church last night. He must hold a bit of clout — they came in immediately.' Never underestimate the power of the Church.

'Were you there? What were they like?' he asked, his

210

eyes still transfixed by the picture. What he wanted to say was, *What were they like, the bastards who could throw their young daughter out onto the street?* But he was afraid, with the prickle of anger simmering under his skin, that if he went down that track he might lose what little vestige of control he had.

'They looked very nice for a pair of self-righteous, hypocritical, arsehole pricks . . . Well, the mother had the grace to look embarrassed, but the father was definitely a self-righteous, hypocritical, arsehole prick.'

Max was startled by the vehemence of her words. She was never shy at speaking her mind, but this was something more. He grasped, with gratitude, that she was taking this personally too.

'Why, what did they say?'

'It wasn't what they said, it was what they didn't say. I had to sit there and listen to them justifying their actions and grit my teeth because they never once made any apology for throwing their daughter out, and to my mind they didn't look that concerned. It was all this "it's in the Lord's hands" righteous crap; "she shamed our family in front of God and the Church" rubbish. And do you know why they threw her out? Did she tell you what happened?' She had a real head of steam going.

'She wouldn't tell me exactly what, although I think it was to do with a boy. All she said was her father got pretty rough, and her mother just stood there and let it happen, except where her little brother tried to step in and protect her, but her mother pulled him away.'

'The gold standard of parenting. It was a boy, alright. She got pregnant. He scarpered, naturally.' Max had suspected something of that magnitude. No parent would abandon a child without an immense

211

cause — he of all people knew that — but he had never outright asked. She wouldn't be the last teenager to find herself in that position, but he'd have thought most parents would do their best to support their child, not vilify them.

'What galls me, though, is that they sat there explaining why they had done the right thing in throwing her out, because she had disobeyed them and God, and tarnished their good name, and all this crap about being a bad example for her younger brothers and sisters. Not once was there concern for her welfare. And worse, they had no idea that I was sitting there shocked that they could have thrown a vulnerable young woman out onto the streets; they honestly thought they had done the right thing. They threw her out the day she told them, and they haven't seen her since. When I asked if they'd gone looking for her, the father did his best to make out how badly he had been wronged, and what a strange thing for me to ask. Fucking bastard. Never once asked if she'd had the baby, and if so where it was.'

'What is her name?' Max asked. He touched the face on the photo. 'What's her proper name?' Jesus, she'd been pregnant. But she'd never looked that way, and there was certainly no baby on the scene. She must have aborted it or lost it. He felt a visceral ache in his chest as he calculated this must have all happened around the time when he'd first met her, those first nights. No wonder she looked so sad, so scared. She'd coped with all that by herself. The thought of the physical toll it must have taken, let alone the emotional, made the spark of anger he felt leap into a flame. No one should ever have to go through that alone.

'Her name was Vilimena Naitaku.'

'And her father?'

'I'm not giving you that.'

He looked up at her, and was met by those tough green eyes. 'Why, what do you think I'm going to do, go over there and deal to him? Look at me. I'm hardly a threat.'

'Yeah, well I'm not going to have you running around town like some avenging angel. I will keep you up to date with progress, but I'm not about to give you any details that you can rush off and follow. You'll just get in the way.'

'She's not dead, you know.'

'I never said she was.'

'I owe it to her to find her.'

'Don't turn this into a crusade, Max. I realise how hugely important this is for you, how personal it has become, but I'm not going to let you fuck it all up this time.'

Her words were a slap to his face. Finally it came out — after all of the tiptoeing around and avoiding, it finally surfaced. This was how she truly felt.

'It wasn't my fault,' he said; defensiveness crawled into his voice.

Accusation had leapt into hers. 'Well, whose fault was it then, Max? I trusted you. I gave you his name, and what did you do? You jumped in there like some bloody hero, instead of trusting me, trusting us to do our job, and it all turned to fucking shit, the worst kind of fucking shit.' She stood up, the chair nearly falling over with the sudden movement, and she paced back and forth, her hands on her hips, before she stopped and pointed at him to deliver another salvo. 'And do you have any idea of the hell I had to go through, the trouble I got into for trusting you? It was alright for

you, resigning and buggering off to avoid the heat, but I got dragged through it all, the investigations, the accusations, I was on trial for what you did, I copped the blame, it was my career that nearly went down the toilet. All because I stupidly trusted you. You fucked it up for everyone.'

Max leaned over the table clutching at his chest, praying the pain shooting through it was a heart attack and it would all be over fast. But then anger flared over mortification, anger hot and bitter, and it was as if some dam had broken and every hurt, every soul-shattering ounce of grief and guilt that had lain on him these past two years burst through.

'You selfish, fucking bitch.' And he too was on his feet, finger pointing. 'You think this is all about you? You weren't there. You weren't the one that got to watch her die, you weren't the one that got to see that mongrel bastard psychopath slit her throat.' As the words escaped his lips, he was thrown back into the memory with such force his back hammered into the wall, his eyes clamped shut, and the vision that detonated in his head took him there, back to that one moment in hell, and he could smell the mustiness of the house, see the cigarette smoke-stained walls, the light diffused through the drawn purple curtains, the grinning teeth of the man, his face obscured by the shadow of his hoodie, always those grinning, disembodied white teeth, as he held her in front of him, defenceless, her hands tied behind her back, he saw him grab her head, one hand under her chin, the glint of the blade, the terror in her eyes, the thin red line across her neck that opened like a mouth when he pulled her head back further, the hot, metallic smell of blood, the sound of his own screaming.

Bradley

He loved this. He couldn't recall the last time he'd experienced such clarity and focus. It was as if his processors were in overdrive and running at one-hundred-percent efficiency. He'd machined his way through the Red Co report in two hours, and it wasn't some cobbled-together rubbish, it was good, really good. He was taking one last double-check through the numbers to make sure he hadn't missed anything obvious when a *whump* beside him on the desk made him jolt with shock. He whipped his head around to see what had made the noise, and was surprised to see a large cardboard box. He looked up above the box and saw the puggish face of Crampton, dangerously impassive.

'Clear your desk, you're fired. You've got five minutes before the security guard arrives to escort you off the premises.'

It took Bradley a few moments to register what he was saying. 'What do you mean, I'm fired?'

'Are you deaf as well as stupid? No one talks to me that way and gets away scot-free. You might think you're shit-hot with your threats of unions and lawyers. Well, bring it on, because I can tell you now, you will be the first to give in, it will be you who runs out of money way before this company does, and it will be you who doesn't know what's hit him.'

Bradley sat stunned for a moment; he hadn't anticipated this. In his mind there had only been one path for the bastard to take, and that was to capitulate.

Like all bullies, he'd cave in at the first sign of true opposition. He looked at the now-smirking face and knew he'd made the wrong judgement. But he wasn't about to run off with his tail between his legs, no; the old Bradley might have done that, but he was through with being pushed around, by anyone. He clenched his jaw and took several large breaths before he stood to his feet and eyeballed his assailant.

'You can't fire me, Crampton. You can't fire me for telling the truth. What's the matter? Can't you handle it? Is that what this is, you can't handle anyone telling it like it is? Standing up to you? Well you wait, you're not the be-all and end-all, there are other people who will be bloody interested to hear about this.'

Crampton smirked. 'Oh, yes? And if you think you can go crawling to the head above me, think again. Who do you think I've been on the phone to all morning? I've fully briefed them all on your performance back there, and the way you encourage dissent against the company. And I've filled them in on your less than stellar employment record. They are one hundred percent behind me: your arse is gone. Pack your things and get the fuck out of my sight.'

Bradley's jaw clenched hard and his hands balled into fists. He could imagine how it would feel to smash them into that smug, self-serving face; the heat of rage that built in his chest was urging him to take the bastard, and show him exactly what would hit him. Just as he was about to lose the battle between anger and good judgement, out of the corner of his eye he saw the security guard making his way across the room. He looked around and saw the ashen, staring faces of his colleagues, and he had the sense to recognise this was one battle that would have to be fought another

day. He would stay the hero.

Quietly, so no one else but Crampton could hear, he uttered under his breath, 'You wait, you fat, smug shit. This isn't over, this is far from over. You wait, you bastard, you just wait, and you watch your back.' With that he whacked the box with the back of his hand, and it knocked the penholder over with a clatter as it sailed through the air and hit Crampton in the guts. Then he grabbed his wallet and his car keys and stormed for the door. He was metres from the exit when he stopped and turned. Bugger this, he wasn't going to go down quietly, he had to make a stand.

'Crampton,' he yelled, loud enough so every head in the office whipped up. He waited until he had all of their attention. 'You can't fire me because I now refuse to work the outrageous amount of overtime you demand of your staff, time that is outside of my contracted hours. This is utterly illegal, and bullshit. You will hear from the union, and you will hear from my lawyers. This is not over.' And with that exclamation mark on his performance, he stood tall, his shoulders back, and slowly walked out of the room.

Max

'Jesus, Max, you pull yourself together or I'll call the mental-health team, you know I will.'

He became conscious of the fact he was curled up in the foetal position under the table. Meredith was crouched down at his side, one hand resting on his hip. Shit, how the hell did he end up on the floor? His head was pounding and it felt as if someone was stabbing an icepick behind his left eye.

'Speak to me, Max.' Her voice was full of concern. The sound of it brought everything back in a flood, but although he physically wavered under its onslaught and it made the stabbing sensation worse, he found he could face it. He pulled himself up into a sitting position and held his head in his hands.

'I'm okay.'

'Jesus, I thought for a minute there you'd had a stroke or something.' She sat on the floor opposite him, and they rested in uncomfortable silence for several moments. 'Have you ever had counselling since Jess died?'

That name, it reverberated around in his head, each echo amplifying the previous one so it became louder instead of fading. He tried to blink it away.

'They made me. It didn't do any good.'

Again the pause.

'Look, I'm sorry if I—'

'You were right. You were absolutely right, about all of it.' The self-flagellation hurt like hell, but in an odd way it dulled the pain at the same time, a numbing

218

that was welcome relief in his new state of heightened awareness. The tsunami of facing the past had passed, and he felt like a survivor who had been caught in the deluge, but who was alive, if battered, exhausted.

'You can't go on this way. You need proper help. Look at you, it's killing you.'

Her face was earnest, her concern real. He knew from years of working with her that she was damn good at maintaining the stern facade she had built, and that she rarely gave a glimpse of any vulnerability, so he was touched by the sentiment.

'I know, and I will, after this is over, I promise. But I can't right now, not yet. I have to find Billy, she means everything to me, and until I do, it's pointless even thinking about help.'

'I'll hold you to that promise.'

'I know you will.' They weren't idle words, they had a pact. It made him think of that other pact he'd made.

'So what are you going to do now?' she asked.

'That depends a bit on you and the hunt for Billy. I need to do something to help — anything. You know why I have to.' He looked up at her again. The weight of his exhaustion made it a monumental effort to lift his eyes.

He could see the conflict of emotions on her face, knew damn well the position he was putting her in.

'Max, I can't, you know I can't. You've done the right thing by this girl by coming in, and I know how big that was for you. But you have to trust us now — trust me. We have her name and her family, and we're working our way through all of the car owners. Which reminds me, the pimp who gave you that photo, what's his name? We'll need to interview him.'

It hadn't exactly been a gift, and Max couldn't

imagine the guy being too pleased about a visit from the fuzz.

'Can't we play quid pro quo? I give you something, you give me something?'

'I can give you a night in the cells for obstructing justice. That's not how it works, and you know it. Do you want to help her or not?'

He sighed. 'He's the huge Polynesian guy on K Road with the designer beard and the orange jandals. They call him Tiny, I think. He had a special interest in Billy, wanted to control her, so he probably took quite a bit of notice of her movements. He didn't mention anything to me about the car or man involved, just gave me the picture. Mind you, he may be more forthcoming for a woman.'

'I doubt that,' she said, 'considering he basically keeps them as slaves.'

'Can you—?'

'Max, don't even ask. Unless you're suddenly going to become sworn staff again, I can't give you anything.'

They both knew that wasn't about to happen.

In his heart he knew he couldn't expect her to hand-feed him information; and the fact she was so bloody black and white and perfectly untrusting made what he planned next all the more guilt-inducing. He admired her for her dedication to the cause of justice, but sometimes you had to circumvent justice, and this was one of those moments — because the rawness of his self-revelation had made him aware now, more than ever, that he had to find Billy, for her sake and for his.

'Look, I appreciate all the work you've done, looking into this, I really do. It's just, well, I'm worried sick about this girl — and you can see the parallels for

yourself.'

'I'm doing everything I can.'

'I know.' He slowly got to his feet, holding on to the corner of the table to stave off the head-rush after being down low for so long. 'I'd better go.'

'Will you be okay?' The concerned look on her face stirred feelings he hadn't felt for a long time, but they were all too soon swallowed up by guilt.

'I'll be fine.'

'Where are you staying? How can I get hold of you if there are any developments?'

That was a damn good question. He knew he'd outstayed his welcome at the boxing gym. He didn't possess a cellphone, and didn't have the means to change that.

'I'll keep checking in with you here.' He turned and headed to the door.

'You didn't answer the first part of the question.'

He paused and turned back towards her. 'That's because I don't know.'

He could see the tussle going on inside her, the freckles and features certainly no camouflage for a poker face. Was she going to make an offer?

'I'd better show you out.'

He realised he'd been holding his breath. 'No need,' he said. 'I know full well how to get out of here.'

Bradley

The car ride to the factory had been a white-knuckle journey of reckless distraction. The squeal of brakes and honks of horns drew his attention to the fact he'd run a red light. He'd driven far too fast, narrowly missed a lady pushing a pram at a pedestrian crossing, and as he pulled up outside the building it was only a split-second reconsideration that stopped him from purposefully driving the car into the concrete wall.

Fuck, fuck, fuck, fuck.

The main door into the workshop slammed behind him, the noise echoing around the cavernous building like cannon fire. He strode across the floor, pausing in front of the pile of old tyres only to kick at them, once, twice, God, seven times before the pain in his foot overrode his will and he stopped. God, he just wanted to throw something, anything. He picked a tyre up and hurled it with a roar, but it did nothing to release the anger that burned magnesium white-hot in his guts. And as his eyes roved the building, looking for something, anything with which to quench the fire, that other door beckoned. He looked at it, nostrils flaring, knowing he shouldn't go in there, not when he was this agitated; but oh, he raged so much, he raged so deep, and before he could stop himself he jammed the key in the lock, turned it viciously and threw the door open with so much force it banged against the wall and ricocheted back so hard that pain fired through the arm he thrust out to block it.

She was cowered there in the corner. The sight of her, hiding, timorous like some mouse, like that pathetic Jenkins, riled him further and he needed to hit something, he wanted to hurt something so badly, and he looked at her, then over at the table, at the whip, and he looked at her, and he had to, he just had to, and then it was in his hand, and he raised it up, and brought it down hard on her back, and he heard her scream and the sound of it, white and pure as it cut through the red haze of his rage was cool bliss, it was climactic, and finally he began to feel that release, the release of all that anger and frustration and hatred, and his soul craved more, and he raised his arm and brought it down again, and again, and again, and he found his voice, each explosive word contrapuntal to the heavenly rhythm of his arm descending again and again,

'Bitch.

'Whore.

'Slut.'

Billy

Her body is a temple to pain, she feels the sear of the stripes across her skin, the scream of her back muscles in their futile attempt to immobilise and protect her from the incessant hurt. She is stunned by disbelief at the ferocity of the attack and in mortal fear of what might happen next. He will kill me. She knows this with absolute certainty; he is gone for now, but he will be back. She has seen the fire in his eyes, burning incandescent with anger and something else; and what terrifies her is the realisation it was the look of lust: he had enjoyed it. Overwhelmed with fear she thinks of her grandmother, her Bubu yalewa, she clings to her solidity and strength and, taking deep breaths, feels her pulse start to slow, her panic ebb. She is not ready to die, even the thought of the word spikes her heart up again, but what can she possibly do from here? She is trapped, bound, powerless. All hope of his mercy flayed with the lash of his whip. But who will save her? When she thinks of her family all she feels is more pain, her abandonment complete. There is only one other, one other hope. She calls on Max. In her mind she paints him as an avenging angel, black-clothed and caped, stealthy, hardened and relentless in his search for her. His X-ray eyes seeing through the concrete of her prison, his arms casting aside doors, smashing through walls, throwing all aside in his mission to reach her. 'I need you, Max.'

Max

He walked out of the police cafeteria and over towards the exit, his mind still reeling with the force of everything laid bare, but somehow relieved. As he descended the stairwell he could hear the click of her heels as she followed him. He hoped she wouldn't follow him all the way, and when the click stopped at the next landing and he heard the heavy smoke-stop door pull open, he allowed himself a sigh of relief. With his moment of self-revelation had come conviction. He had to help Billy and he was prepared to do anything, even if it meant deception. He continued down another flight of stairs and then waited a few more moments before entering the next floor. This was where he prayed for luck. It was amazing how you suddenly developed the urge to invoke a higher power when the stakes were truly high. He walked past the door of the first office, his peripheral vision noting the two people in there. It felt like his heart was lodged in his throat, and he made himself keep walking on with the same cadence, like he was meant to be there and not the interloper he was. At the second door he used the same approach and again noted it was occupied. The third was the charm, though, and he slipped in and pulled the door slightly closed after him so he wouldn't be obvious to anyone else walking past. There were three computers in the office. He moved to the one furthest from the door and clicked the mouse to wake it from its sleep. He hoped the system hadn't changed at all in the last two years. He doubted

225

it, because that would have involved expenditure and budgets were tight enough, so any changes would be minor. Sure enough, everything was pretty much as he'd remembered it. Alas, the previous user hadn't been sloppy enough to leave it logged on, which was a bugger; security training must have sunk in. He didn't sit down, instead he stood, and leaned over the desk and chair, poised to escape, which was a bit ridiculous considering there was only one entrance and if someone came through it he'd be screwed. He typed in his old ID and password, on the off chance it was still valid. The big error message on the screen soon clarified that. He'd known it was never going to work, but he'd felt compelled to try as a delaying tactic from the little piece of deception he was about to pull. He went back to the log-in page and typed in a different ID and password. He paused before hitting enter; his face suddenly felt hot. If it worked, he prayed she would forgive him. His finger hit the key. Oh Jesus, he wasn't sure if he felt elated or mortified when Meredith's password failed. It was a little something he'd acquired without her knowledge in those devastating times when Jess had first been kidnapped and he'd been excluded from certain information. He hadn't needed to use it then because he'd persuaded her to keep him in the loop, but she wasn't about to make that mistake again. Now he had no choice but to try it. Jesus, think. They'd both been at the security meeting when the hierarchy had had the little password chat, about what was a high-security version, with enough letters and digits, punctuation, upper and lower case to stymie the best guesses of a hacker, and about changing them regularly. They'd also shared a coffee afterwards and unanimously agreed, stuff that, who

the hell would remember. He'd told her he worked on a rotation of three passwords involving his kids' names and the current year with a hash. She'd laughed and called him a lazy swine, and then confessed to using her pets' names and her street number with a full stop. How many times would the system let him try to log on before it sent an alert somewhere or froze him out altogether? And what the hell were the names of her other cats? He knew the pattern of upper and lower case from the password he'd carefully observed and memorised that time. In a way it was a huge victory that he could still recall it. It was funny what trivia your brain would cling on to while carefully forgetting other, more obvious things. Scotch had been the old cat, the weary battler who had been getting near the end of his days. He was probably dead by now. What were the kittens' names? The replacements? He smiled when they leapt into his head: Jack and Danielle. Anything was worth a crack, and he was fast running out of time and options. With every second that passed he expected someone to come walking through that door.

Jac23K94
ERROR
Fuck.
Dan23Ielle94.
It worked, it bloody well worked. With the jubilation came a flicker of remorse, but it was soon swamped by urgency. He logged into the motor-vehicle registration network and typed in the scant information he had — those magical two digits. He looked at the screeds of matches and knew he had to narrow it down, so he filtered it through colour and region like Meredith had; but he also added an age range.

Although he wasn't a complete car fanatic, he knew enough to be able to narrow the shape and design features of a vehicle down to a five-year manufacturing range. That still left thirty possibilities, but it was still too many numbers. He clicked one more filter. He was ninety-nine percent sure the car in the picture had been a Nissan Primera. They were a dime a dozen. He was having to rely on memory here, as the photo was now, no doubt, part of a file on Meredith's desk, and he wasn't about to try and sneak into her office. But that extra information narrowed it down to five numbers; five names and addresses. That was manageable.

He looked around the room and was relieved to see a printer in there. Some rooms had shared printers, so it was a stroke of luck. He was going to need a lot more of that if he had a hope of making this work. He hit the print icon but had to wait for a few agonising heartbeats until he heard the whir of the printer as it came to life. The sound of footsteps approaching down the corridor made him freeze; the cramp of panic gripped his bowels and he held his breath as they paused outside, and released it through tight pursed lips as they walked on. Shit, he wasn't cut out for this clandestine crap. He logged out of the computer and made sure it was on the right screen before putting it to sleep — anything to help this interlude go unnoticed. The sheet of paper he grabbed from the printer seemed so insubstantial compared to the amount of stress needed to acquire it, but it held the vital piece of information, he knew it did. He folded it as small as he could before sliding it into his back pocket, and then slipped over to the door, leaning his head against it and listening before he poked his head

around the corner to check the way was clear. There were two women down the far end of the corridor, talking. Fuck. He pulled his head back into the room, trying to decide what to do. They weren't between him and the exit — at least that was something — but what if they saw him? The longer he stayed here the greater the risk of being discovered, but if he stepped out now he could be challenged. Damn it, he had to go, he had to get out of the building before he was discovered, before his bowels exploded or he had a nervous breakdown, whichever came first. He took three steadying breaths and then, with as much confidence as he could muster, walked out of the room and straight towards the stairs. He didn't look back, he didn't look to the sides, he tried to exude a nonchalant air of *I belong here.* The stairs were only a few strides away, and when he reached them the door felt insurmountably heavy and it took all his strength to open it. He stepped through into the cooler air of the stairwell and let out a sigh of relief.

'Max, what are you still doing here?' He froze, felt the acid tang of bile rush into the back of his throat. Fuck, it was Meredith. He turned around to see her four steps up from the landing, making her way down. Going by the dark look and the drawn eyebrows she wasn't pleased to see him.

Jesus, how was he going to bluff his way out of this one? His innards felt hot and liquid and he thought if he didn't get to a toilet soon the consequences would be dire. That spark of an idea was his saviour.

'Sorry, I had to stop in at the toilets. After everything that happened up there, I, well, you know.' He was pretty sure he looked pale enough to sell it.

Her face softened and he knew, with both relief and

Bradley

He stood in front of the mirror. The face reflected at him looked like the same old Bradley — same coarse skin, same sprinkling of wrinkles around the eyes, same mousey blond but greying hair, slightly receding hairline. But the Bradley on the inside felt inhabited by some strange alien creature. If he had to put words to it, it was as if the mild-mannered Bradley facade was a host, a host to a new and improved being, a creature of power, a superman, a god. He laughed to himself at the childishness of the image, and then laughed all the more when he saw his teeth were still the same old Bradley teeth. In a weird kind of a way it reminded him of that first time, when he'd lost his virginity, that moment where clumsily and nervously he'd crossed some magical border between boyhood and manhood. But there had been nothing clumsy or nervous about this crossing. His hand clenched and unclenched at the memory of that feeling, the intense satisfaction of emptying his anger, of emptying out his frustration, of emptying out his impotence. He had crossed a border, a crossing that made him something despicable in the eyes of most; but the odd thing was, that didn't worry him. Because he had felt power, true unbridled power, power and control. And he could carry it hidden in his heart, his own special secret. Was this what it felt like to be a woman, to be pregnant, to carry such a mystical and magic secret so deep within? He thought of Ange, how easily he'd swept aside her fears of his infidelity, how easily she'd

231

surrendered herself into his arms, how good it felt to satisfy her, to be in charge, to dominate her. He felt his prick stiffening, and he looked at that face in the mirror again, looked at the proud and self-assured look in its eye. Who gave a fuck that he'd been fired? He'd fix them. He'd fix them all.

Max

This was an agony of waiting. Uniformed students had started pouring out of the school ten minutes ago, and his eyes had searched the face of every boy who walked past him. He had enough sense not to wait right outside the entrance, he knew Harry — well, any teenager — well enough to know you didn't want to meet your parents out front. Instead he'd asked to meet him at the park a couple of hundred metres up the road, far enough away to be private, but public enough to be non-threatening. The bench he sat on was set ten metres back from the footpath, under the shade of a huge, old pōhutukawa tree, and the whole thing shook with the vibration of him jiggling his legs. It was a bit late to be having second thoughts about this; the invitation was out, and it couldn't be rescinded. And he'd had to catch a bus across to the Shore. That had chewed up a huge chunk of his precious money — prices had hiked in the time he'd been in his self-imposed exile. He didn't have enough for a return fare; but then there were more immediate things to worry about than how to get back to the city.

Jesus, what if he didn't show? What if Helena had intercepted the message and banned him from coming, or, worse, showed up herself? His head swivelled around, and his eyes leapt from woman to woman. The blonde? No. The grey? Too old. Shit she was brunette, was that her? No, a long-haired boy. What about that other brunette? His eyes flicked back to her face with a jolt of apprehension before discounting her

and moving on to the next. He also took in every car, registering colour and shape, number of passengers. Did she still have the white Subaru? Or had she got rid of that like she'd got rid of the house? It irked him that he was so bloody paranoid, but he'd been through enough emotions today without adding her to the load. He didn't know if he had the emotional strength to get through meeting his son, let alone the wherewithal to face her and handle the fireworks she'd set off. The knot of tension that had cramped in his stomach began to loosen when he noticed there weren't any more women around. The noise of a large group of boys announced their approach. He cringed at the language, the f-word dropped in as an adjective as casually as the basketball being dribbled along the pavement. The boys in this group wore their uniform in every imaginable way except the proper one, and Max recognised them as the kind of boys who often found themselves in trouble with the police. They were harmless enough, but stupid. He'd come across enough of them in his police career to pick the type instantly. Unfortunately most of them were equipped with equally stupid parents, who did everything they could to protect little Johnnie instead of letting the little shit see the consequences of his actions. The herd was parallel with him now, and as they walked past a tall boy peeled off the back and walked stiffly over to him.

'Max?'

Max climbed to his feet, his eyes locked on that face, his jaw slack. To see it in the photo had been one thing, but to see the boy, the younger version of himself standing before him, flesh and blood, shook him more than he imagined. The reminders of the years

he missed were there, accusing him. The light stubble where he'd shaved, the soft fuzz of the areas that weren't quite there yet. A smattering of acne across his cheeks and a few blackheads on his now manly nose. The boy who never used to care about his appearance now sported a hairstyle that must have taken considerable time to achieve.

Tears sprang into Max's eyes, he tried to blink them back, and a shiver traversed his entire body. He had no idea what to do next. What did you do when you finally met up with the son you hadn't seen in two years? Shake his hand? Hug him? Did Max deserve that right? After all, he'd essentially abandoned him. Harry stood before him, hands jammed into his pockets, shifting his weight awkwardly from foot to foot. Max could see his Adam's apple bobbing up and down as he tried to fight his own feelings. Harry gave a half-smile and the sight of his teeth, straight and true, braces gone, pushed Max beyond the edge of control, and the tears escaped his eyes; he felt their wetness crawl down the skin of his face to his jaw.

Still he stood there, frozen, incapable of anything. He willed himself to say something, anything. The boy looked embarrassed and turned aside to look at the backs of his retreating friends.

'What do you want?' The words were quietly spoken. They contained no anger, no disrespect, no warmth, no nothing. They sounded empty. The knife twisted in his heart. This was not how he'd imagined this moment. In his heart he'd thought the father-son bond would break down all barriers, and they'd fall into an embrace and tears and mutual backslapping. The awkwardness of this was excruciating. What did he want? So much, probably too much — too much to

articulate in words in this place and at this moment.

'I need your help.'

'Why would you want my help?' Again, the tone was quiet, sober.

'I have no one else to turn to.'

The boy met his eyes then. Max saw a reflection of his emaciated self.

'Why should I help you?' The challenge was clear.

Max felt his resolve crumple as the heat rose in his face. Why indeed? What right did he have to even ask? Why had he even harboured the hope his son would want anything to do with him? This was stupid, he shouldn't be here, this was all wrong. The urge to bolt rushed over him, the need to escape those eyes, to escape that question. He stood gawping like a stranded fish for a few moments before abruptly turning and obeying his heart's command to escape. He had to get away, and fast. What had he been thinking? There was no way in hell he was ready to face this, face him. His feet led him away from the guilt, from the pain: it took every ounce of his self-control not to break into a run. There were thirty paces between them before he began to slow, before the cogs of his conscience pulled him to a halt, and it dawned on him that he was doing it again. He was walking away from his son, his only son, because he couldn't face him, couldn't face the truth, couldn't face himself. He stood stock-still, looking up to the heavens, taking in the seagulls soaring overhead, so carefree. He dropped his head. *Jesus, just turn around, you only have to turn around.* With what felt like a monumental effort, he turned his shoulders and then his body, his eyes searched to find the boy, find his son. But he was gone. For a panicked few moments Max looked up the road,

before he saw Harry had sat down, was on the park bench, leaning forward, elbows on his knees, head in his hands. Max took the long walk back, and carefully lowered himself onto the seat next to the boy. No, not boy, he thought, young man. He leaned back, looked up into the cloudless sky and pushed the air out from between his lips in a big sigh.

'You left us.' The voice rippled with suppressed emotion.

'I know. I'm sorry.' Powerful words, softly spoken.

'After everything that happened, how could you do that?'

God, how? He'd asked himself that very question constantly in the last few days. How could he describe the desolation, the darkness? 'I was fucked in the head. I was in a really bad space and made some awful decisions. But I was shattered, utterly shattered. I had to get away before I did something rash, did more harm.'

'It never occurred to you running away was rash?' It was said without humour.

'I wasn't thinking. I...' He couldn't find the words to express how the aching sorrow and guilt in his heart had painted his entire landscape black, how he'd blanked out the world. How he'd had to — there had been no other choice, other than ending it all, and it had come so very close to that.

'What happened?' Harry spoke with a whisper. 'What happened to Jess?'

Max froze. 'Did Mum never tell you about that?'

'She wouldn't tell me anything — she couldn't talk about it, refused to talk about it. You might have run away, but she may as well have, because everything changed, it was like living with a ghost. She just said Jess had been killed and it was your fault.' Max closed

237

his eyes against the impact of those words. 'I found most of it out from my friends. But I need to hear it from you. Was it your fault?'

He swallowed, and then told the simple truth. 'Yes.'

'How?'

He looked at him then, their eyes locked. 'Do you honestly want to know?' Did he want to tell? But for Max, that dam had already burst, and the aftermath of ruin and destruction was inevitable after the initial deluge. He was ready.

'Yes.'

God, where to start? 'He was supposed to be her boyfriend, but he was bad news. Jess,' he still winced when he said her name, 'was going through a difficult time, a bit rebellious, and he was part of that. Except he was a P smoker, in a gang and right on the edge, you know. He was every parent's worst nightmare, and we tried to tell Jess that, to make her see, but the more we tried to warn her off him, the harder she clung, and the worse he treated her. We had to back off and let her find out for herself, which was heartbreaking for us both, because it felt like we were abandoning her to him; but eventually, she finally saw through him, saw him for what he really was and tried to break it off. She came back to us for help, but that was when things got truly ugly. He was an evil, evil young man. He took her. He kidnapped her and took her away. We hunted them for days, but he was always one step ahead.'

This was where it got hard, and Max took several deep breaths before he carried on. When he did speak, his voice sounded hollow and dead.

'I was a detective then, of course, but because I was too close to it all I'd been kept off the case, which was

the most frustrating time of my life; I felt hamstrung by them, stonewalled. But they finally got a handle on where this guy was, where he had her, and I, well, persuaded a colleague to tell me.' He rubbed his hands together, trying to figure out how to justify himself, how to spin it, but in the end, Max knew Harry would draw his own conclusion.

'You have to understand how worried, how terrified I was for Jess, we all were. I was mad with worry. I went there, went after them by myself, I thought I could talk him into releasing her, make him see sense, give her back to me.'

'But he didn't, did he?'

'He was high, high as a kite, and manic. He . . . he . . .' The visions assaulted Max's mind, and he had to clasp his hands together to stop them shaking. 'He killed her, right there in front of me.'

'How?'

The thin red line, gaping, the awful sucking sound.

'He slit her throat.'

Max could feel the shaking of the seat, hear the quiet sobs beside him. He reached out to put his arm around his son, but Harry shook it off. Max pulled it back like he'd been burned. The sound of the man's mocking laughter filled his ears, overshadowing the question from his son.

'Sorry, what did you say?'

'They didn't get him, did they? The papers I looked at later said he'd died, that he killed himself, but I don't know what to believe. Mum wouldn't let me see anything at the time, television or newspapers, so I had to ask my friends and they told me a bit about it. But they didn't say much — I guess they wanted to protect me too.' He paused before asking the next

239

question. 'Did you kill him?'

He'd fantasised about that so many times — that he'd snatched the knife the bastard had used to butcher his daughter, that he'd taken that knife and stabbed it into his heart, and that he'd twisted and twisted that knife as he listened to the screams for mercy. But that wasn't what had happened.

'No. No I didn't. As they said, he killed himself.' Again Max heard the echoes of manic laughter, the laughter as the crazed young man had brought the knife up to his own throat and with theatrical decisiveness had ripped it across. 'He killed Jess, then he killed himself.'

'How?' God, why would he want to know that? Why would he possibly need to know that? 'Please?'

'He slit his own throat. He slit his throat too.' And it all came back then, the iron stink of hot blood, the wetness of it as it seeped through his clothes, across his skin as he cradled his girl, her long blonde hair stained red as it fell across his arm, as he cradled her body and rocked and cried out to God to take it all back, to bring her back to him, as he cried out to anyone, anyone who could hear, as he screamed for help. Max slumped forward in the seat as grief and pain wracked his body, and he cried, he cried the hard, hot tears that had locked themselves away for so long. Through the torrent of his own outpouring he heard one more question, one more devastating question.

'If you hadn't have gone there, would she still be alive?'

He answered in the only way he could. 'Yes.'

Billy

Billy wipes the tears from her face and the snot from beneath her nose. She aches in ways she never imagined she could ache. The ferocity and anger of his attack flashes her back to that other attack, when *He* had slapped her and punched her and called her whore and slut and castigated with his fists and his tongue, and *She* had stood there, cowering and had done nothing, nothing. But whereas then she had been cast out to find her own way in the harsh world, now she was imprisoned. Then she had been among family, those who should have loved her and cared for her; now she was at the mercy of a stranger. But that was where the differences stopped. The strands of the two intertwined on so many other levels. Both men had beaten, belittled, accused and humbled. *Whore, bitch, slut* — both had showered the words over her, and they had stung as much as the cuts of the whip or the throb of the fists, and threatened to erode her strength. But she can't allow that to happen, she won't allow that to happen, and she scrunches her eyes closed and casts out in her mind to her strength, her talisman, her Bubu. She invokes the memories of her, happy memories of hearing mythical stories and of wonderful hours spent creating, crafting, plaiting and weaving. Of her sitting cross-legged on the exquisite flaxen mats, a flower tucked behind an ear lending its scent and beauty to the moment. Of the gap-toothed smile and warmth of her Bubu telling her what great work she was doing; that she was pretty, and clever

and good, that she was a good girl; and how much that made her heart soar and her soul sing.

'I am good,' she whispers to herself, 'I am a good girl.' And with her fingers she reaches out for the pile of hair, of her beautiful, beautiful hair, feels it spring beneath her touch, and she thinks of her Bubu and those tranquil, happy moments together, and her fingers pull out three small bunches of strands, and she starts to plait them, twisting them together, left over right, right over left, falling into that comfortable rhythm, with one hand then the other hand, over and hold, over and hold, rocking gently with each movement, over and hold, over and hold, because she is a good girl, over and hold, over and hold.

Max

How long had they been sitting there? It could have been seconds, minutes, hours, he didn't know; all he was aware of was pulling himself out of his reverie and being aware Harry was still in his. He looked back up at the sky; it hadn't fallen. He had squared off against that which he had been hiding from, and the world hadn't ended. But he hadn't come through unscathed. He ached, his body responded like some hollowed-out creature, not quite human, some automaton acting out a prescribed series of movements, but not capable of anything further.

'What did you want with me?'

It was back to the questions. Harry had sat up and blown his nose, and now looked at him. The burden of knowledge made him look old beyond his years.

'I need your help with something.'

'What kind of help?'

How a barely seventeen-year-old could help he wasn't sure, but in a world where the only person he trusted and relied on had been stolen from him, it was his only hope.

'I have a friend and she's in trouble.'

'Is she your girlfriend?' He could hear the wariness and hurt in his son's voice.

'No, no way, she's my friend, that is all. I know my word probably doesn't count for much, but there's never been anyone for me but your mother.'

He heard his son inhale and let his breath out slowly. 'She's got a boyfriend.'

Max thought he'd grown immune to pain, but that news cut like a claw raking across his back, exposing nerve and bone. Of course he had no right to expect her to hang around for however long and wait for him to have his crisis — after all, he'd left them, left her; his brain told him that — but his heart was another matter altogether. His mind flooded with questions. Who was he? What was he like? Was he good to her? Was he good to him? Silence hung on his lips.

'She said she didn't owe you anything, that she couldn't wait forever for you to make your mind up, sort yourself out.'

Was he doing this on purpose? Were these knives, thrust with such deadly accuracy, Harry's revenge? He looked at his son, but the boy's face was guileless, and he recognised someone just telling it like it was.

'Fair enough,' he said.

'You don't hate her for it?'

'No, of course not.' And it was the truth. He couldn't hate her; and with that knowledge Max knew he was coming right, that he would be alright. There was more he could offer to the boy, a sliver of comfort so Harry could justify what he perceived to be his mother's disloyalty. 'I didn't give her much choice, did I?'

They sat in silence again, although this time it was as if a critical test had been passed for both of them, and it was a lot more comfortable. It was time to steer the conversation back towards its main purpose. The clock was ticking, and Max felt the weight of exhaustion after so many self-revelations.

'This girl, we look out for each other, on the streets. She is young, doesn't have anyone, any family who care for her. I was, well, pretty troubled, and her presence gave me purpose, gave me a reason to get

through each day. She kept me alive. But she's gone missing, and I'm worried sick about her. Something bad has happened, I know it.'

'You mean Billy?'

Max's head spun around, and he searched his son's face. Had he heard right? He saw the concern there, and though he tried he couldn't mask his astonishment.

'You know her?'

'The Fijian girl?' Harry's face flushed, making the pimples flare out even more.

'But how do you know her?' There was no way their lives would intersect, not a street girl in central Auckland with a schoolboy from the North Shore. All sorts of scenarios went through Max's mind, none of which was very comforting. He looked closer at his son.

'I, ah . . . ' Harry looked away, his Adam's apple bobbing up and down as he tried to swallow. 'I saw you with her.'

'When?' His interrogation voice had crept in, and in response Harry's became defensive.

'A few times, when I've been in town. I . . . ' He hesitated, as if he was embarrassed. 'I came looking for you, okay? I had to know if you were alright. Mum didn't seem to care, or didn't want to know, so she wouldn't check up on you; but I had to know how you were. I never told her what I'd done, she'd have been pissed off, she wouldn't have understood, so I kept it a secret.' He blurted out the words, and Max felt a fresh wave of guilt at the worry and stress he'd caused wash over him. In his self-survival state he'd never considered the impact it would have all had on his son. He hated having to admit to himself that, after Jess had been murdered, it was as if he'd forgotten he

had a son. What despicable creature could do that? Forget about his own son?

'How often did you come?' The detective voice had been replaced by one of infinite tiredness. 'Why didn't you talk to me?'

'I didn't know what to say. I just wanted to make sure you were alright. Someone had to. I saw you with Billy a few times, so I went up to her one day, and we talked about you. She was nice. She told me you were having a hard time, but you were getting by.'

'You talked to her?' He was aghast. It had never occurred to him his son might seek him out. His astonishment was mixed with something — what was it? Admiration, pride? And Billy had never said. She'd probably promised Harry not to breathe a word, and one thing about Billy was she always kept her promises. Another suspicion jumped into his mind when he thought of Billy and the numerous occasions she had brought him food, drinks, even medicine when he was sick. 'Did you give her money?'

'Sometimes. I had to do something. I've got a weekend job, so I didn't take it from Mum.' Jesus, the child carrying the burden while the parents went to hell. A barrage of guilt hit him again. 'Did she give it to you, the money? God, I hope she did. I thought I could trust her.' The poor boy looked so worried.

Max laughed then, the noise a crackle in his swollen throat. 'She knew me too well. Knew if I had cash I'd just buy booze and cigarettes. So she bought me food, bought me things when I needed them. You put your faith in the right person.' He turned then, rested a hand on his son's shoulder. 'Thank you.' Harry just nodded, a grim expression on his face, but this time he didn't shrug off the hand. 'Billy's missing, and as

246

you know she is always trustworthy, always reliable. She would have told me if she was going off somewhere for a few days, but she didn't. She's vanished, and I know she's in trouble.'

'Have you been to the police?' The obvious question.

'Yeah, and they are doing what they can. I gave them as much information as I could.' The vision of Meredith slipped into his head, and his deceit. 'They won't include me in the investigation, for obvious reasons. But I have to do something, I have to do something before it's too late.'

'So how do you think I can help?'

He laughed. 'I don't know, I really don't know.' He looked at him then, this boy-turned-young-man. Jess had always been the spirited and playful one, the one who brought equal measures of colour and joy and trouble into their lives. Harry had been the quiet and resourceful one, the observer, the problem-solver, the serious one. Had he changed that much? 'You tell me: how can you help? Will you help?'

'I've got a car.' He said it with the first hint of a smile. The sense of relief was overwhelming.

'That's a damn good start. I've got some people I need to call on.'

Bradley

The sound of a sharp knock at the front door pulled his head up.

'Are you expecting anyone?' he asked Ange as she hurriedly pulled on her jeans and then threw a jumper over her head. She didn't bother with a bra, and Bradley enjoyed the way her nipples pulled at the knit, it made him want to grab her and drag her back to bed, to hell with the front door. It was probably just the Jehovah's Witnesses or Mormons, or someone peddling home-ventilation systems.

'It's the pool boy, come for his turn.' She leaned over and gave him a kiss and a wink as she left the room.

'Hurry on back now, you hear?'

He leaned against the pillows and smiled to himself. Fuck this was good. It was as if every electron in his body was supercharged, every hair standing to attention. Ange had always been a very generous and enthusiastic lover, and a little giving on his part had resulted in the kind of gymnastic and playful romp they'd enjoyed as twenty-year-olds. Who would have thought it could ever go back to this? He felt so alive. No longer the downtrodden underling, he was in control, control of Ange, out of that fucking hellhole of a workplace, and most of all, in control of *her*. He was master of his universe, and the world was a bottomless well of opportunity for him.

Ange had opened the door, and he heard her voice change from one of greeting to wariness. That

difference in inflection caused the afterglow of afternoon lovemaking to be washed away by the cold shower of caution. He jumped out of bed and started to pull on his trousers.

'Bradley?' he heard her call, and noted the alarm in her voice. He pulled the merino top over his head and came out to the hall. A glimpse of a blue hat, and his heartrate skyrocketed. What did they know? Had they found something; had they found her? No, don't jump to conclusions; it could just be that fuckwit from work. He hadn't done anything there to bring about a police complaint, had he? No, he hadn't nicked off with the office stapler on his way out — apart from keys and wallet, he'd left empty-handed. Why were they here then? He made himself breathe regularly, approached the door and gave a hopefully convincing smile at the young woman officer.

'Hi, what can we do for you?'

'Hi, sorry to disturb you. We're doing an investigation into a missing person, and I just needed to ask some routine questions.' Just breathe, he thought, just breathe. 'We are visiting all the owners of cars in Auckland with numberplates with a range of digits that may include those of the last person this particular young woman was seen with. That covers a lot of vehicles, but we do have to talk to everyone.' She sounded apologetic for disturbing him. A lump of fear cramped in his belly. She looked oblivious to his discomfort — as did Ange, who stood by his side. Surely she could feel the heat that was emanating from his body in waves. 'I understand you drive a Nissan Primera, numberplate—'

'Daddy, Daddy, why is the police lady here?' Ellie had pulled herself away from *Paw Patrol* on the

TV — the electronic babysitter they had put on to keep the kids occupied while they fucked each other senseless. Her arrival had broken the tension. He swooped her up onto his hip and, after brushing away the fringe of her strawberry-blonde hair, planted a kiss on her forehead.

'The nice police lady has to ask some questions about cars, sweetheart, it's nothing you need worry about. Off you go, back to Katie.' He placed her down, and she gave a shy little wave at the policewoman before heading back towards the lounge. 'Sorry about that.' There was a look that could be taken for longing on the policewoman's face, and Bradley promised himself he'd buy Ellie that Sylvanian Families set she had been asking for. 'What were you wanting to know?'

The young woman looked back down to her clipboard, smiling. 'Your car numberplate has some digits in common with a vehicle we are trying to trace.' How the hell did they get part of a numberplate? Did K Road have surveillance cameras now? Surely not. It had never occurred to him there could be some record of him picking up the girl. Where had it come from? He had to know, but there was no way he could ask, not without arousing suspicion.

'Did you want to see our car?' Bradley asked. He made sure his words made it sound like the family car, safe in the knowledge the constable had been charmed and was now on their side. He felt the tension begin to leak out of his body, control resume its rightful place. He could play along with this game, be helpful, like he had nothing to hide.

'Yes, please.'

'I'll just go and grab the keys.' Before he picked them out of the drawer, hidden from sight, he held

250

his hands out and smiled when he saw all traces of tremor had disappeared. He clutched the keys in his fist and made his way back to the constable, who was chatting amiably with Ange. All good.

'The car is down in the garage. It's easier to go through the house, along this way.' Nothing to hide, nothing to give away. 'Did you say someone was missing? I haven't seen anything on the news about it. Who are you looking for?' His voice sounded calm and even, just interested enough, but not too keen. He congratulated himself on his deception.

'A young eighteen-year-old woman. I imagine it will be on the news tonight.'

Ange followed them down the hallway too, with Ellie and Katie tagging along behind. It was a family trip to the garage.

'I also need to ask you what you were doing on the night of Monday the eighth?'

It was obvious he'd be asked that question, he should have expected it, but still it threw him. God, Monday night. How could he possibly forget, it was only the most fucked-up night of his life. What was he going to say? He'd come home a little later than usual, because he'd picked up a prostitute, bashed her on the head and kidnapped her, taking her off to a vacant industrial property he owned? Hardly. He wasn't about to confess to anything.

Ange came to his rescue, and for once he didn't resent it. 'That would be the night you were sick, wouldn't it? He was vomiting his head off that night.'

'I think you're right,' he said. He wasn't about to correct her or offer a detailed timeline. It appeared to satisfy the officer. He opened the internal access door to the garage and flicked on the light switch.

251

His run-of-the-mill Primera was closest to the door; Ange's hybrid Toyota Rav4 on the far side. The officer did a lap around the vehicle. He'd always been very careful with cars, had them serviced regularly, washed them once a week without fail, made sure they were well maintained, tyres inflated properly and with sufficient tread to be in good safe order. His father had impressed upon him that a car was an asset and had to be maintained. God, he hadn't thought of his old man in years. He'd died a decade ago, after a short battle with cancer, and Bradley felt a flicker of shame at what his father would think of all this, before he shook his head of it and continued on with his careful web of lies. He had to remember exactly what he said here. It was the little things that tripped you up. He'd learned that from all of those TV programmes — *Criminal Intent, CSI, Bones*. The killer always gave themselves away with some little thing, an inconsequential detail. He wasn't about to make that mistake.

'I'll need to take a photograph of your car, for our investigation.' She'd moved to the front but was hindered by the workbench. The tool drawer with its illicit lock of hair seemed to scream out, *Look in here!* and he had to divert her attention away from it.

'Of course. Is there enough room for you there to take the picture? Do you want me to move the car back a bit?'

'That would be great, thanks.'

Ange pressed the button on the wall for the automatic garage door opener, while Bradley unlocked the car and climbed into the driver's seat. His eyes did a quick scan of the interior, making sure he hadn't left anything there by accident. They fell on a small receipt caught under the mat in the passenger footwell; shit,

it was for the emporium. He glanced up to see if he was being watched, but the officer was leaning over, talking to Ellie, holding her hand to keep her out of the way of the backing car. He bent over, pulled the receipt out with his fingertips and slipped it into his pocket. Its presence burned in a thrilling kind of way. The buzz was tempered with a cold prickle of panic when he remembered the small bag of rubbish he'd left in the boot. *Jesus, don't ask to look there, don't ask to look*, he chanted in his mind. He started up the car, feeling the vibration of the engine as it rumbled to life, slipped the car into reverse and slowly rolled it out the door and onto the paved driveway to make the most of the late-afternoon light. He flicked the switch to lower his window.

'Is here okay?'

'That's fine, thanks.'

The officer went about her work while he sat in the car, and the penny dropped — his face would probably appear in the photographs. If they had a picture of a partial plate, did they also have one of the driver? The officer walked around to his window.

'That's all I need for now. Sorry for disturbing you, and thank you for your time.'

The relief was giddying. If they had a photograph of the driver, surely she would have asked to take a portrait of him. Someone had seen the car, but not the man behind the wheel. As she walked down the driveway and hopped into a patrol car parked on the street, he prayed for her to drive off, to drive off now, but she appeared to be writing notes. He turned the engine off, leaving the car in the driveway. Although he'd coped with the whole episode well, kept it under control, it had brought home just how careful he was

Max

The house in Glenfield screamed blue-collar. Tidy enough, but the paint peeling on the eaves and around the window frames told him the owners lacked the extra cash or time to keep up with the maintenance.

'Park up there, up past the corner.' He pointed to a spot beyond the bus stop.

'What are you going to do?'

That was a damn good question. Now he was here, he became aware he didn't have a plan. The lack of a warrant card or a blue uniform meant he couldn't legitimately knock on the door with some polite queries. Some stranger turning up on the front step asking questions would only arouse suspicion. And he had to make the assumption that if this house was on his list, it was also on the police list, so they may have already paid a visit. Being timid wasn't going to get him anywhere, though.

'I'm going to get out and have a look around.'

'But, Dad?' Max stopped dead at the realisation that was the first time his son had called him Dad. He turned around to look into worried eyes. 'What if something goes wrong?'

He gave what he hoped was a reassuring smile.

'I'm just having a look, nothing will go wrong,' he said and pushed the car door closed. There was a small amount of traffic going past, but no one would take any notice of the likes of him here; at least he blended in with the neighbourhood. A few lumps of ill-placed dogshit meant a sidestep or two as he headed towards

the house. He had no idea what he was looking for. There weren't any cars in the driveway, of that he was glad — chances were no one was at home. He took the bold approach, rather than the furtive, which was far more likely to attract attention than someone acting like they were meant to be there. He walked up to the front door and gave a resounding knock. His heart banged under his chin while he waited a reasonable spell, after which he stepped off the porch, grateful there had been no reply, and walked around to the back of the house. In that time he picked up that the house was occupied by a couple, and they had at least two children, from the accumulation of shoes and gumboots on the porch. The front left room was a children's room; the front right the parents. Around the side there was an empty garage, and a kids' swing set and a trampoline with safety-netting sides sat in the tidy, fenced backyard. He was just about to open the gate when there was a wooden thud of something big getting to its feet and then the fast-approaching bark of a dog. That he hadn't expected, and he staggered back with shock as what looked to be a pitbull-ridgeback cross leapt up at the fence, making enough noise to alert the whole neighbourhood. Shit. He couldn't believe people kept those mongrels as pets; who the hell would let something that vicious near his children? The thing looked like it would rip his leg off, given the chance, but he wasn't about to offer it the opportunity. He needed to see the people, he needed to see the guy to be sure. He'd have to come back later when someone was home. It would be a hell of a lot riskier to snoop around then, but at least now he knew the lay of the land and, more importantly, knew about the bloody dog. He walked swiftly back to the

car, but not too swiftly — that would look suspicious, given the barking. He pulled the printout from his pocket and looked at the list. They were spread out all over the city, but there was one other on this side of the harbour bridge, so that was the next logical stop.

'When's your mother expecting you home?' he asked as he sidled back into the car. The last thing he wanted to do was get the boy into trouble.

There was silence.

'What time do you have to get back?' The seatbelt clicked in loudly.

Harry hesitated. 'She's away.'

'So she won't be in until late?'

'No, I mean she's out of town. She and Greg have gone away for a few days.'

'So they've left you at home alone?'

'Jeez, Dad, I'm seventeen years old, I'm old enough to be home alone, it's no big deal.' But to Max it was a very big deal. He thought back to all of those out-of-control parties and kids he'd seen come through the juvenile court system because their parents hadn't been there or didn't care, and he thought back to the fact he and Helena had always vowed they wouldn't be those kind of parents, the kind who would bugger off and leave the kids to fend for themselves. Some-one would always be home. Then his own hypocrisy struck him in the chest like a missile, and he bit back the comment he'd been about to let loose.

'Of course you are, I'm sorry. I forget things have changed.' Everything had changed, beyond recognition. 'Do you mind going to one more house today?'

'How many are on your list?'

'Five.'

'That's not many, I can do them all.'

Max felt a surge of gratitude and marvelled his son was being so cooperative — he'd never thought it would be this easy. As if in answer to his thoughts the boy added, 'I'm doing this for the girl. I liked her.'

Put in his place.

The fourth house on the list was in a newish, swanky subdivision in Albany, the sort of place where middle-income families mortgaged themselves up to the eyeballs so they could be seen to live in an over-sized new home in a good neighbourhood and near a desirable school. Max knew this because that was precisely what he and Helena had done. They had pushed their finances to the limit so they could look the part, send Jess and Harry to the right college, one with lots of doctors' and lawyers' kids and where the majority of the faces were white. Diversity was for the poor. But soon enough their lives had disintegrated in every way possible, including financially. Once upon a time this place would have been utopia. Now it just presented a sad veneer for hopeless aspirations and unrealistic dreams. They drove through the curved streets towards yet another cul-de-sac.

'That's the street there,' he said, 'Joy Street.' As Harry turned right, Max saw a navy-blue Nissan Primera approaching the roundabout from the other way. His eyes dropped down to the number plate and the last two digits: 59 — shit, it was the very car from the list. His eyes slid up to the driver just as he pulled past, and he had about two seconds to take in a light-haired guy, late thirties, early forties he guessed, probably the latter, with the slightly receding hairline, reasonable build, from what he could see . . .

'Shit,' he said, 'carry on around, Harry, that's our guy, that car that just went past.' He craned his neck

258

around to see the car disappear around the bend. 'Quick, you need to follow him.' It felt like an eternity while Harry slowly circumnavigated the roundabout. He fought against the urge to yell at him that he was driving like a granny and to get on with it. He'd never imagined he'd complain that his teenage son drove too carefully. He felt a surge of relief when the Primera came back into view a hundred metres ahead, waiting at the intersection to turn onto Gills Road.

'I want you to follow this car. Keep well back — we don't want him to suspect he's being tailed — but close enough so we don't lose him. Do you want me to drive?'

'Dad.' The disparaging tone said it all.

By the time they got to the back of the Mairangi Bay shops, Max was impressed with his son's driving. He'd kept exactly to the brief, as well as negotiating the increasing amount of traffic. It was almost five o'clock, so the streets were filling up, heading towards the inevitable Auckland traffic jam. The Primera pulled right off the main street and then took a quick left into the street behind. It meant that Harry's Honda was directly behind it as the car went down the narrow street. Shit. He didn't want to be that close. Then it indicated to pull over to the left.

'Fuck,' he said, as Harry slowed behind it. 'Go on past and to that intersection up there, turn left and pull over. I'm going to hop out.' Harry pulled past the car and drove steadily on, no hesitation, indicated and turned left. There was a driveway entrance that he pulled into. 'Good job,' Max said. 'You did that like an old pro.'

'I've been watching telly,' Harry said.

'Wait here.'

259

Max ran back to the street and looked down. He saw the boot being closed and the man look up the street. He pulled his head back, hoping he hadn't been seen, counted to five and then slowly looked around again. In that first glimpse he'd seen the man had been holding a half-full grocery bag, tied at the handles. Now, as the guy got back into his car, the bag was gone. He waited a few seconds to make sure he was getting into the car and then turned and headed back to Harry. The car had disappeared. Fuck, he looked up and down the street, before he heard a toot, and his eyes found the Honda slipped into a parking spot. He climbed back in.

'Get ready to go, he's coming this way.' They had a fifty-fifty chance of facing the right direction. It was a T-junction: the Primera had to go right or left.

'Shit, he's turning the other way,' Harry said as he waited to pull out. 'There's too many cars, I'm never going to be able to do a U-ey here.'

Max craned over his shoulder to see, and could see he was right; there was too much traffic at this time of day, and the Primera had already disappeared into it.

But they knew where the guy lived. 'Don't worry about it. I want you to go around the block and back down that side street.' Most people didn't drive five kilometres across town to dispose of the rubbish — that was what wheelie bins were for. He needed to know what was in that bag.

Bradley

The mad pounding in his chest finally dropped below that of imminent heart attack. Although he'd been the picture of cool, calm and collected while the police officer was at the house, he'd had to hide the shaking in his hands that had restarted once she had gone. Ange appeared not to have noticed. He marvelled at how completely guileless she had been, and how little she questioned him afterwards. In fact it annoyed him. The police come knocking at your door, and all she said about it afterwards was, 'We'd better watch the news tonight.' He should have been happy about her complete lack of suspicion, but something about it galled. Was he such a patsy in her eyes? He'd made the excuse he was off to the supermarket and to run some errands, and then took off in the car. Simple things, he reminded himself, simple things. Jesus, what stupid, stupid mistakes to make. Imagine being dumb enough to leave a receipt in the car, let alone what was hidden in the boot. He should have got rid of that before he got home, but no, he'd been so distracted by the moment, by the sheer rapture of the experience, it had dulled his cunning. Never again. From now on he had to stay sharp. The police were looking for the girl. Thanks to the efforts of his darlings, the officer didn't suspect a thing, but they would follow up again, and again, and he had to be squeaky clean. It also meant he had to revise his plan. He snorted out loud at the thought. What plan? It wasn't as if he'd planned any of this; so far he'd been flying by

the seat of his pants. He turned left into the alleyway behind the shops. The first step was offloading.

Sure enough, there were rows of dumpsters servicing the cafés and retailers. He pulled over and, after a surreptitious look around, threw the bag into a skip, making sure it was a designated rubbish bin, not a recycling one. No simple mistakes, Bradley. He climbed back into the car and sat, hands on the steering wheel. Next he had to go to the car cleaners and vacuum out the car. He wasn't going to wash it, that would be too obvious, Ange might notice. No, he'd wait until the weekend for that, same as usual. But the girl had been in the boot, he'd chucked her in there after he'd knocked her out, and as he'd seen on all those crime shows on TV, there was the potential for the police to go over the entire interior with a fine-tooth comb. So he'd vacuum — vacuum like his life depended on it, and then mess it up a little, so it didn't look too clean. He'd already wiped down the passenger side where she'd been, and the window — he remembered the sound of her head hitting it and winced — he'd done that immediately after, but he'd go and sit on that side for a while, make sure he touched things so there were prints, lots of prints, but only his. He could stay one step ahead, even two. He felt the smile crinkle up to the corners of his eyes. This was a game of cat and mouse now. The yo-yoing of his emotions from fear to excitement had been confusing and exhausting, but one thing was for certain: he'd never felt more alive in his life.

Meredith

Used-car salesmen were up there with her most hated individuals. As a profession they had taken their usual hammering in the recent nationwide most-trusted poll, filling in the last places along with politicians, real-estate agents and celebrities. She had more cause than most not to trust them, which was why it had taken her all day to work herself up to this visit. Even the walk across the forecourt with its gimmicky helium balloons only served to remind her how crap her own car was, and how she was in no position to do anything about it.

'Is Aaron in?' she asked the young blonde woman behind the counter.

'Sure, I'll just get him for you.' As the pert butt in the clingy short skirt tottered off on too-high heels she couldn't help but wonder if he was shagging her, too.

When he appeared from the end office she had to admit to herself her ex-husband was still a looker. She couldn't bring herself to call him hot, because that kind of arsehole didn't deserve to be glorified. As soon as his eyes found her, his rapid steps slowed to a more cautious pace and his face took on that ever so familiar defiant, defensive look.

'What do you want?' He could at least have made an effort to be civil. It was very tempting to flip him the bird and walk out, but unfortunately he had something she needed.

'I want you to identify a car for me.'

His eyebrows rose, causing a ripple of furrows up his forehead. 'You're asking me for help?' He said it like it was a major victory, which was precisely why this course of action had been an absolute last resort. But love him or hate him, the bastard had an encyclopaedic knowledge of cars, and he was the one person she knew would be able to tell her with absolute certainty the make and model of the vehicle Billy had got into. If it narrowed down the field of suspects, it would be worth the antagonism.

'Don't be a prat,' she said, and she pulled the photograph of the vehicle from her bag.

'You could be a little more pleasant if you want my help,' he said. It was a bit ripe, considering he'd set the tone of the conversation. The man hadn't forgotten how to push her buttons.

'Look, Aaron, I wouldn't be here unless I absolutely had to. If it will help massage your ego, then yes, I do need your help, and you know damn well how hard it is for me to be here asking for it. So let's just get on with it. Will you look at this or not?'

The smile he gave her bordered on smarmy, but he pulled a slimline pair of reading glasses out of his pocket, slid them on and leaned over the picture. She knew he would never turn down a challenge.

'This is all you've got?' Even though the image had been enhanced, it was a grainy, low-light shot with only part of the car visible, including those three precious digits. A lamppost and the vehicle parked in front obscured the car's badge and most of the grille. The most distinguishable were the headlight and the trim. Unfortunately any glimpse of the driver had been blocked out by the obstacles too. Life was never kind enough to throw you such gifts.

'That's it,' she said.

'All I need. The car's a Nissan, a Nissan Primera. It's pretty old. From the shape I'd say the year is 1998 or 1999.'

'You're certain?' She didn't have to ask this question, because she knew he'd be right, but she felt an overwhelming need to undermine him.

'Of course. You know I am, otherwise you wouldn't have come here.' It was moments like this, when he was full of this ego macho crap, that she wondered what she'd ever seen in the man in the first place.

'Are they very common?' Short sentences helped quell her burning desire to scream at him.

'Common as dirt and reliable as hell. That's why, even though they're old, there's still plenty of them around. You see them everywhere.'

'Thanks.' Another hard word to force out. 'Thanks for the help.' She picked up the picture, placed it back in the bag and turned around to leave.

'That's it then? No how are you, how's your sister, nothing like that?'

Dropping her sister into the conversation like that was a point-scoring step too far, even for that sod. She decided that her beloved sister was welcome to him.

'No,' she replied, and walked out the door.

Max

The dumpster was close to full, which made his job easier; he only had to lift up the lid and lean in to grab the bag. Its pale-grey plastic was in stark contrast with the large, black polythene bags from the shops. His eyes fell on a cardboard tray of discarded sandwiches and cakes. He grabbed a couple of triangular plastic containers of what resembled ham and chicken salad and three clingwrapped slices. Old habits died hard, and besides, he was ravenous. Waste not, want not. Harry looked agitated when he got back into the car — even more so when his eyes set on the food.

'Oh, Jesus, tell me you didn't just pull that out of the bin?'

'There's nothing wrong with it. Do you want one?' He offered a box of sandwiches. Harry shrunk away from it like it carried the plague.

'No, thanks, lost my appetite.'

Max set the food aside on the floor of the seat well and set his attention to the disposed-of plastic bag. Other old habits died hard, too. He opened the glovebox and poked around until he found a first aid kit. He knew it would be there, it was one of Helena's things: she was a good Girl Guide and took the 'be prepared' motto to heart. He was certain she'd have insisted on Harry carrying the right safety gear. There were probably jump leads in the boot, too. He pulled out a pair of rubber gloves and put them on.

'Shouldn't you be taking that to the police?'

'Yes,' was the simple answer, but life was seldom

266

that simple.

The handles were knotted loosely and it only took a few moments to release them. The contents of the bag were hardly the stuff of conspiracy: muesli bar wrappers, empty takeaway drink containers. He gave them a sniff: hot chocolate. This was the sort of rubbish that went into the wheelie bin at home, not the kind of thing you drove kilometres away from home to dump around the back of the shops — unless you had something to hide. This was his man, he knew it, he knew it as certainly as he knew his own heart. He rummaged deeper into the bag. Tags — there were several clothing tags, and he pulled them out to examine them in the light. The sizes were all SW — small women's.

For the first time Max felt a true glimmer of hope. Meredith had challenged him with the likelihood Billy was already dead, and although his heart had refused to believe it, his pragmatic head had told him it was a possibility. But dead people didn't need new clothes. He rummaged again, and his fingers crinkled against a cellophane wrapper. He brought it to the top and his face curved into a smile as he recognised the small rectangular shape. Tampons, this had held tampons.

'She's alive.' He looked at his son then, and repeated the words to validate them, make them real. 'She's alive. This is our guy.'

'You have to take that to the police then, you have to let them know.'

He should, he knew he should, but even as he envisaged Meredith's face, he knew he wouldn't. This was too personal. He had to do this himself. If he delivered this piece of information he'd be thanked and then excluded yet again, probably after being

reprimanded for meddling. He couldn't allow that to happen. Besides which, Meredith was damn good at her job, so she'd come to the same conclusion about this guy and probably sooner rather than later; but for the moment he felt it was up to him. It had been a long time since he'd felt the excitement of the hunt. It was game on.

'Harry, this is our man. We need to find out everything we can about him so we can find Billy.' He felt a twinge of guilt at putting the next question to the boy. 'I know your mother would have a fit, but I really need you to take me to your house so we can get on the internet and do some hunting. I know this puts you in an awkward position, and if she finds out you'll be in the deepest shit imaginable, but we have to do this, for Billy's sake.'

'This isn't just about Billy is it?'

An astute boy, but then he'd always been the observer, the one who stood back and waited until he was entirely sure and comfortable with something before he'd participate. It was in stark contrast to his sister who, if it looked like a good time was to be had, was in, with no questions asked. To her, parents were just the fun police — and in the end he'd failed to be even that.

'No, it's not.' There was no point in lying.

'Oh well,' Harry said, and pulled the car back out onto the street. 'It's not like I'm not used to being in trouble.'

Billy

The fine twine of hair feels soothing as she rolls it through her fingers. Beads of sweat pepper her forehead, and when she closes her eyes she can smell the damp sweetness of tropical forest, her skin feels the waves of heat that beat down with the sun and her ears buzz with the murmuring of the sea. She knows she is getting sick, that her back burns like fire and she is hot with fever, but it is comforting to let herself relax into the visions that merge with her reality, and she doesn't fight them. Her Bubu sits cross-legged on the mat before her, hands moving with hypnotic rhythm and grace over the flax *kato* she is weaving, while Billy plaits her own strands. Her warm brown eyes hold Billy's, a smile crinkling the edges with wisdom and knowing. A hibiscus flower flares a bloom of red behind her ear. Bubu is talking to her, but her words sound filtered through water, indistinct and muted. Billy leans closer, closes her eyes to concentrate on each syllable, and like a photographic image the words come into focus. *He's coming back, sweetheart. He's coming back. Be strong. I love you.* He's coming back? Her senses are wrenched back into the present. He can't be coming back already? She strains to listen, trying to hear over the whoosh, whoosh of her racing heart. And with a sense of dread she hears something, something that chills her. She hears the turn of the key in the lock.

269

Bradley

Coming back here was dumb, every ounce of his being told him it was; he should have just driven straight back home to his wife and kids, and sorted his shit out. Yet somehow, here he was, standing again outside the nondescript grey door, arms spread, hands leaning against the door jamb, rocking side to side. That this one door and what lay behind it should hold such a power over his future beggared belief. He was in some warped horror movie: go on, choose a door, they're all bad. Jesus, the police were looking for her now; he couldn't take the chance of them finding her here. He had to get rid of her. Fuck, if only she'd taken the money when she had the chance, they would both be free of all this. But she had made her choice, and now, one way or another, they would both pay the price. He leaned his forehead against the door, but its cool surface didn't do anything to quell the turmoil of his thoughts. How the fuck was he going to get rid of her without her turning around and dobbing him in? Sell her into slavery? If only it was as easy as Googling a solution. What would you type in for that? 'I accidently kidnapped a girl. How do I fix it?' Could he still buy her off after all this? Not now he was fucking unemployed; he was going to need every cent he had — but it might be a sacrifice he had to make. With each thought he could feel the pressure building in his chest, the pulse of blood aching its way across his temples, a tic in the corner of his eye. This was all her fault. If she hadn't smirked at him when he couldn't

get it up, if she hadn't rejected his offer of cash and freedom, if she hadn't turned into such a huge fucking millstone around his neck, he could be getting on with his life, he could be plain old Bradley Fordyce, living a simple life, a life that didn't involve having to lie to his wife. The thought of Ange brought corporeal memories so intense his skin shivered. If there had been one golden lining to all of this it was the reawakening of his lust, and the fulfilment of those feelings of dominance and command over her. It had been divine. But even that could slip away because he was losing his grip on the wheel — and it was all the girl's fault, the fact his life had turned to such total shit was her fault, it had been fine until she came along, and as the throb in his forehead intensified, and the pressure of his rage built so high he could taste it and he felt overwhelmed by that need, the need to take it all out on something, someone, and the need was so intense and so unbearable, he could imagine the leather of the whip cool in his hand, and his heart began to race in anticipation, anticipation and excitement of what he knew he shouldn't do, mustn't do, but knew he would, he had to.

He turned the key and stepped through the portal to his other world, the world where he was God and his heart sang as his subject genuflected before him. He would allow himself five minutes, five minutes to soothe his frustrations before he went home and faced the potential fallout of being out of a job, if he even had the guts to tell Ange. Five minutes was just reward for his shit of a day, he deserved it. He felt his breath quicken as his fingers curled back around the smooth leather of the whip.

Max

Helena's new home was more humble than he had imagined. It pained him to admit his retreat from life had cost them both, on many levels. His need to run had been so powerful, so consuming, he hadn't even considered what it would mean to her, and to Harry. His instinct to protect himself ignored everyone but him, so he had lost all capacity to hold the needs of others in his heart, even those most dear. The blackness had descended with such finality it was irresistible. Now, emerging from the dark, it shamed him to see what he'd done — to them all. Looking at the 1970s carpet, the faded curtains, smelling the faint mustiness, it all weighed his heart down further. They had been living the dream in their new home in the poshest subdivision. It hit him like a punch to the chest that they — well, she — had probably lost the house in a mortgagee sale. It would have been yet another insult after so much trauma.

'My room is this way.'

Max followed Harry down to the end of the hallway and then paused in the doorway, felt the floor shift beneath him. Gone was the bedroom adorned with All Blacks posters and his cycling heroes; the sports trophies were nowhere to be seen. It was clear the last remnants of Harry's fourteen-year-old self had been overlain by what appeared to be some slave to Satan. The curtains were black; the posters on the wall were all of death-metal bands with images of skulls and demons and creatures that brought a shiver to his

272

spine. The room had a television and a games console on a dresser over by the window. They'd always been adamant they would never let the kids have a television in their room. It appeared many standards had slipped. Harry had slid into a chair in front of a large computer screen perched on a cheap and tiny wood-veneer desk. He hit the space bar, and Max noted the boy had password-protected it; from his mother's prying eyes, no doubt. He pulled up Google.

'What's the guy's name?'

'Bradley Fordyce.'

The letters appeared across the screen and within seconds lines of hits scrolled down the page. 'It's not a common name, so most of these hits must be for him. You can find out all sorts of shit about someone on Google. It's always a good place to start.'

Max's urge was to correct the boy's use of language, but judging from the room, it was probably just symptomatic of the newfound attitude. Harry's fingers flew across the keyboard and guided the wireless mouse in a minute ballet. 'Here we go, he works at Prime Insurance Company. Looks pretty geeky in the photo.' Now he was in his own territory, it was as if Harry was coming out of his shell.

Max leaned over to look at the photo. Bradley Fordyce had blondish hair, slightly receding, but well cut to hide it. His face looked open and friendly, and boyishly handsome, with just a sprinkle of wrinkles around the smiling eyes. Was this the face of a kidnapper? A felon? A murderer? Looked like a typical middle-aged male. Actually, not all that typical. His face was lean, he had the look of someone who looked after himself well, someone who hadn't succumbed to the extra kilograms many men of that age packed on

when they decided they were too old to bother working at it.

He was still examining the picture when Harry flicked it onto another screen. This one was familiar. Facebook. 'We can look at his profile.' Wife, Ange; two kids, Katie and Ellie. Cute. Max had barely taken it in when Harry had flicked onto another page — his rate of absorbing information and moving on was phenomenal. Each time he changed pages there was a gentle whirr from a printer on the floor by his feet. 'Ha, he's particular about his privacy settings, but his wife's not. There's all sorts here on her page.'

'Have you done something like this before?' Max asked.

Harry looked a little uncomfortable. 'We had to search a few things for school projects.' Max knew a lie when he heard one, but he wasn't about to pursue it. He'd come to the conclusion everyone was entitled to their secrets; the world worked better that way. Mind you, if what they were doing right now was anything to go by, it didn't stop people trying to pry into them. It would seem his son wasn't the squeaky-clean kid he'd left behind. Part of him felt bad about that, but another part . . .

'Do you smoke?'

The boy's head snapped around, a look of mild panic in his eyes. Max fixed him with what he hoped was an indifferent look. Harry pushed his chin out and looked him in the eye.

'Yes.' He didn't add the 'and what are you going to do about it?' Well, not in words, anyway.

'Good, I need a cigarette. You got one?' The boy's face changed from one of shock to a shy smile. He leaned over to the bottom drawer of the desk, pulled

out a pencil case, unzipped it and removed a packet of cigarettes and a lighter.

'Mind if I join you?'

After a short break on the back porch and then another fifteen minutes of searching, they had a reasonable background for the guy — it was scary how easily they had amassed information. They knew that Bradley Fordyce attended a gym in the city centre and had come eighteenth in its 2011 annual stationary rowing challenge, which was fifteen spots better than the previous year. They knew his paternal ancestry back for one hundred and eighty-seven years, courtesy of a relative who was into genealogy and had posted it all online. Fordyce's family had emigrated from Britain and been in New Zealand for five generations — which didn't help them much for the purposes of today — but dear second-cousin James had been kind enough to post everyone's birth date. That was handy. They also discovered that his wife, Angela, or Ange as she was known, sold Tupperware and belonged to a book group called Readers Anonymous. Not so Anonymous after all. So far, so ordinary. It was good background stuff, but Max wanted specifics.

'Go onto the Auckland City Council website.'

'Sure.' The fingers danced over the keyboard. 'What are you wanting?'

'Rating information, I want to find out about their home.'

Harry typed in the address and the information flashed up in moments. 'Rateable value of 1.6 million dollars. Newish. Sweet. Bet that's flash.'

'Probably just pretty average. This is Auckland after all. In some suburbs that would barely get you

a shack, especially if it was a shack with a sea view or was in the right school zone.'

'True,' Harry said as he scrolled further down the page. 'Bet they have a decent mortgage, though.'

'Not necessarily. Look, the house is owned by a company, Robinson Group.'

'That's the wife's maiden name, isn't it?'

'Can you look up the company? Go to the Companies Office. I want to see if they have any other properties.' This guy had Billy, he was sure of it. But where? If you were holding someone against their will, you had to be pretty confident she wouldn't be found, and that she wouldn't escape — which meant having somewhere secure to keep them — secure and isolated. Otherwise the neighbours might notice the screaming. He couldn't picture Fordyce secreting her away in a hallway cupboard at the house. The wife would be sure to notice. Auckland was a sprawling city, there were plenty of places to lose someone.

'Okay, here we go, they have eight properties. Not a bad portfolio for a mum-and-dad company. Odd they've done it as a company instead of a trust. Probably some creative form of tax evasion. I thought the government was tidying up those kinds of loopholes.'

Max looked at his son again. Things had changed a lot in a few years. Here was his boy talking about portfolios and company structures. He had a lot to catch up on. 'We can Google Street View them all if you want?'

'Knock yourself out.'

The first four properties were clearly residential rentals, all modest-looking homes in modest suburbs. She's not there, his head told him. Too many nosy neighbours, too close. You'd hear any kind of

commotion — hell, one of the houses looked close enough to the neighbours' boundary you could probably hear them fart. The retail and industrial properties were more likely prospects, but the Street View photographs showed all of the premises were occupied and there were plenty of vehicles around. It was a good idea, but looked to be a dead end. Max went to push the hair back from his forehead, but was met by stubble — there were plenty of new things to get used to. His eyes flicked to the time, shit, it was after eight o'clock, he'd completely forgotten to check in with Meredith. The intensity of the day weighed down on him, and he slumped forward, eyes closed, resting his forehead on his hands.

'You alright?' Harry asked.

He pulled himself back up and blinked several times to remove the film that had formed across his vision. 'Yeah, just tired, that's all.'

'You can stay here tonight.' He'd been debating with himself whether he should even ask, but Harry saved him the awkwardness, for which he was grateful.

'You sure? Your mum would go ballistic if she found out.'

'Yeah, I know,' he said and looked terribly pleased about that idea. Max knew he shouldn't laugh, that it wasn't good that the boy was going out of his way to piss off his mother, but he couldn't help it. A large part of him was delighted with the apparent male sorority thing going on; it was unexpected. Harry shrugged and Max caught the blush in his son's face before he turned aside to get the printouts from under the desk.

'Thanks Harry,' he said, 'brilliant. But do you feel like getting some takeaways and doing some old-fash-

Bradley

Ange was in the girls' room, finishing their bedtime story. Bradley paced the lounge, the anticipation building. His skin was itching with need, he had felt the pressure of it pushing below his ribcage all evening, ever since he'd left her. He hadn't meant to push it that far, he'd just wanted to test it a little, to see if he could hurt someone, on purpose, not when he was angry or when he had lost control, like the other times. He wanted to see if he could go against all the conditioning, if he could override his mother's echo in his ears, *You don't hit girls*. He'd been surprised to find the answer was an emphatic yes. And the elation, oh the sweet sense of power at doing it. He had chosen to do it, and he didn't wimp out. He had assumed his conscience would kick in, pull on the brakes, make him step away. But his conscience had let him down. No, that wasn't right, he told himself; his conscience had finally allowed him to explore a different morality, a morality that he was beginning to thrive on. He felt like he was the movie character when he first puts on the superhero outfit. He longed to know how far he could take it, what he could do. Could he fly with it? The feeling of utter liberation that revelation had brought with it had altered another adage he'd spent his life abiding by: *Do unto others as you would have them do unto you*. He fingered the belt around his waist. The touch of the leather made his prick engorge with blood. He groaned. Hurry up, Ange. He wanted to feel that leather, feel it sting his flesh, hear

279

it sing. And she would do it, too, he knew she would.

A sharp rap at the door made him curse out loud. God, who would be out at this hour of night? Jesus, he hoped it was just collectors or door-knockers and not some friend who wanted to stay for a drink, because all he could think about right now was a hot bitch swinging leather. He flicked on the porch light and swung open the door. Lucky after all. Jehovah's Witnesses, going by the clothes — a man and a woman. And the woman was damn sexy in that alien kind of way. She was tall and redheaded with freckles smattered across her nose and cheeks. She wasn't what you'd call beautiful, but there was something feline about her features, especially with her long hair pulled back into a ponytail. Bradley envisaged her dressed in a studded bustier and panties, and thigh-high boots, punishing him for his sins.

'Bradley Fordyce?' Her voice was slightly husky, just as he'd imagined it would be, and he wondered if God would strike him down for fantasising about one of his flock.

'Yes?'

'Detectives Peters and McCarten.' A bucket of icy water washed over his fantasy. 'We'd like to have a word. Can we come in?'

'Is this about the visit we had earlier from the constable looking at the car?' His voice sounded remarkably calm. It was in stark contrast to how he was feeling. But among the turmoil in his head he heard a cool, clear voice telling him to keep calm, to play the game; if he held it together it was a game he could win.

'Yes. We'd like to ask you a few more questions, if you don't mind.'

280

Those feline eyes suddenly felt very penetrating, and what before promised exoticism now felt intimidating, and that was appealing too. Ange walked into the room. Her eyes flicked between the two guests and back to Bradley.

'These are detectives,' he said, answering her unspoken question. 'They want to ask us some more things about this afternoon's visit.'

'Oh.' She sounded taken aback. 'Was there a problem? The officer was pretty thorough.' She walked across the room to stand next to Bradley, hooking her arm through his. It was as if her response to having a stunning woman in her living room, even if official, was to go on the offensive and show exactly who belonged to whom. The show of possessiveness was flattering. The detective appeared to recognise this as she directed her comments to his wife.

'As the officer would have told you, we have been looking for a missing young woman, as we're very concerned about her safety. The last sighting was of her entering a vehicle that shared licence-plate numbers with your own. We have since had further information that has narrowed the vehicle down to a make and model, which again reduced the possible vehicles it could have been. One of those is yours. So as you can see, we will need to ask some more questions about your activities on the night in question, and also we would like to make a closer examination of your car.'

The woman's manner was clinical and even, but Bradley could detect a steel in her voice that told him that she was not someone to be trifled with. Ange must have sensed this too, as she sat down on the sofa, indicating for him to do likewise.

'Of course,' he said as he sat next to his wife. 'Please,

sit down. How can we help?' He noted the length of her legs as she sat, and her heels. Those weren't standard police-issue footwear. They were sexy, high and black.

'Were you on Karangahape Road at all on the night of Monday the eighth?' The directness of the question startled him. He'd expected a more gentle line of questioning.

'No, no,' he said, stuttering. 'I was at home that night.'

'That was the night you were sick, wasn't it?' Ange chipped in. 'He was vomiting.' Said like a mother discussing her baby's bowel motions at a coffee group. There had once been a time that he would have been pissed off at the way she always answered questions for him, but he certainly didn't mind now, especially as her memory of the night was helpfully wrong, and he wasn't about to correct her. 'We told all that to the constable this afternoon.'

'Yes, that's okay, but we need to go over everything again, if you don't mind. We are in the process of eliminating people from the investigation, so every bit of information you can give us helps.' She directed her question back to Bradley. 'Were you home for the entire evening? Had you been into the city centre at all on that date?'

'Well he'd been to work, and I think you went to the gym after work, didn't you honey?' She looked at him, but continued on before he could reply. Now he fervently wished she'd shut the fuck up. 'But it was at the gym when he first started feeling sick, wasn't it? So he came home. That would have been early evening, definitely by six.' Silence hung in the air and Bradley felt a buzz of gratification at the look the detective

282

gave Ange.

'If you don't mind, Mrs Fordyce, I'd like your husband to answer the questions.'

Ange's face reddened and she made some put-out noises. Bradley would have laughed had the situation not been so precarious.

'Yes, I went to work that day. I work at Prime Insurance.'

'That's in the city, isn't it?'

'Yes, Hobson Street. Then I went straight to the gym after work.' His mind ran over the gym's check-in procedure. It was just a tag system — you handed in your gym card when you arrived and picked it up when you left. He was pretty sure they didn't record attendance on a computer or anything, and he didn't think they had video cameras, so unless someone specifically remembered him not being there no one would be able to corroborate that he was lying his arse off.

'Which gym do you belong to?'

'Freedom Gym, that's in Swanson Street.'

'So you came directly home from the gym?'

'Yeah. I started feeling really queasy, so I wanted to make sure I got home before I threw up.'

'And your route home: did you travel along Karangahape Road?'

'No, I park the car off Albert Street — I lease a space — so I always go up Victoria Street to get onto the Northern Motorway. I don't go anywhere near Karangahape Road, it's way off my route.' She looked at him directly, and her eyes seemed to penetrate his mind. Shit, you wouldn't want to be on the receiving end of a full interrogation with her, he thought. His skin tingled, and he decided that the idea of being interrogated by her was turning him on. Again, he

had to suppress the urge to laugh. He thought about card nights with the boys and the little tricks he used to keep a straight face.

'And there is no way you might have taken a different route on that evening?'

'No, as I said, I was feeling awful, and I just wanted to get home as fast as possible before I started vomiting.' She must have accepted that, as she moved on to a new question.

'Have you ever seen this young woman before?'

She held up a photograph of a very young-looking woman. His eyes focused on the hair, glossy and dark, pulled tight in two braids down the sides of her face so the curls were less noticeable. She then held up another picture, this one grainy, and going by the shelving and stock in the background looked like it had come from a security camera in a petrol station.

'That's the girl who's gone missing. I saw both these pictures on the news tonight. After the visit from the constable this afternoon we thought we'd better watch and find out what was going on. But other than that, no, I've never seen her before.' Even he was amazed by how calm his voice sounded, with just the right tinge of concern. His pulse was elevated, but not hugely so. In a bizarre kind of way, it was exciting.

'We would like to take a closer examination of your car.'

'Of course, I'll take you down to the garage. Do you want to look at it in the garage, or do you want me to park it in the driveway?' He congratulated himself on having the foresight to clean it out. As well as a vacuum he'd wiped down any of the exposed metal or smooth surfaces she might have touched in the boot. One step ahead, that was all he had to stay.

'Thank you, but we will need to take the vehicle away, so our people can do a full forensic examination of the car.' That he hadn't anticipated, and for a few wild heartbeats he panicked, then he told himself not to be so stupid. He'd done the job well, it would be alright.

'But he told you he hadn't been on K Road. Why do you need to take the car? And don't you need a warrant to do that?' Ange's voice was strained with annoyance.

'As I said, we are in the process of eliminating people from the investigation. This will enable us to eliminate your husband faster. We are examining all of the vehicles on our shortlist, not just his.' The manner reminded him of a school principal, when you'd just been caught throwing paper balls at the teacher. This detective was the first person he'd met who could put Ange in her place. He was unaccustomed to seeing his wife back down from anyone, let alone a woman. 'Unless you have any objections we will have a truck arriving to remove the vehicle soon. We should have it back to you in a couple of days.'

Ange began to open her mouth to protest, but Bradley held up his hand to stop her. 'It's okay, I don't mind. If it gets things sorted out faster so we get left alone then that's good. It will be fun car-sharing for a few days. Just as well it's the weekend tomorrow, huh?' He gave her a reassuring smile and thought he'd done a superb job acting as if it was no bother to him whatsoever. This was pure front, though, because a niggle was worming its way into his head: he was beginning to worry about blood. She'd been bleeding when he'd bundled her limp form into the car that day. At the time he'd wrapped her head in a sports towel, and

when he'd cleaned the boot of the car he hadn't seen any traces of blood anywhere. But that didn't mean it wasn't there.

He felt like an automaton while he watched his car winched up onto the flat-deck truck, and as they saw the detectives to the door. Although he'd been a picture of calm on the outside, inside his mind was whirring through all the possibilities, trying to find a way to salvage this. If they found blood he was fucked. He only had a day — if that — if worst came to worst. If they found blood they'd start looking into his background, and when they found the investment properties, they'd find the girl. The game had changed and now one thing was for certain. The girl had to go.

Max

They both slid down low in their seats as the car head-lights came around the corner. Despite the windows being wound down slightly to stop them from steaming up, Harry's car still had the unmistakable fug of stale fish and chips and end-of-day male.

'Who'd be dropping by at this hour of the night?' Harry asked as they watched the Holden Equinox pull into the Fordyces' driveway. Max had a suspicion as soon as he saw the vehicle — he knew an unmarked police car when he saw one.

'Oh, shit.' The tall redhead who climbed out of the driver's seat was unmistakable. He smiled to himself. He should have known she'd be on the ball and would have narrowed the numbers down fast. 'That's the police, come around for a little chat — although I pity anyone who finds themself on the receiving end of one of her chats.'

'Is she hard?'

'That's one way of putting it.'

Max heard the note of admiration in his own voice.

'You like her, don't you?' Apparently it had betrayed him. He was surprised at the question. It was rather personal, considering they had been carefully avoiding anything that could be vaguely challenging or confrontational.

'I respect her. There's a difference.'

There was silence for a while, before he heard Harry suck in a deep breath. Max wondered what was coming next.

'Don't you want to know what Greg is like?'

'Who?' He played dumb.

'Mum's boyfriend.'

Truth be told he was dying to know what Greg was like, but had restrained himself from asking. But it was an odd question, and one that set vague alarm bells ringing in his head.

'Why? Has there been a problem with him? Do you want to tell me something?' The thought of some strange man giving his son or his ex-wife grief riled him. If there was trouble going down he would be quite prepared to deal with it.

'No, there's no problem, he's nice, and he's good to Mum, and me. It's just . . . '

'Just what?'

'Well, I kind of feel bad that Mum didn't wait for you, you know. I was a bit mad that she went and found someone else. I might have been a bit, well, difficult.'

Not a conversation he thought he'd be having any-time soon, but he felt gratified Harry had stayed so loyal to him, after everything he'd done.

'You know, I don't have any hard feelings towards your mum because she found someone else.' A lie felt appropriate at this time. 'What I did, walking away from you all, was pretty despicable, and I only did it because I was utterly desperate and didn't know what else to do. It wasn't because I didn't love you, or love your mother. I still love you both. But things had started to fall apart between us after Jess died. The strain on us both was huge, and then, well, I ran. Plain and simple. I ran. It was the wrong thing to do, I know that, but believe me I was at my wits' end, I was a mess, a head case. So I don't blame her at all that

she wanted to find someone else. So don't you blame her either.'

Harry's hands rested on the bottom arc of the steering wheel, his index finger tapping away against the leather.

'Did you miss me?'

Cold nausea hit his stomach. How the hell did he answer that question? Because the sad truth of it was, he hadn't.

Honesty seemed to have worked so far, or degrees of it.

'Look, Harry, I know you're a bright kid, and you can sniff out bullshit a mile away, so I won't insult you by saying, yeah, of course I missed you, because it wasn't that simple. I think the best way to describe it is I shut down, I shut everything out. I had to or else I would have gone insane. I shut out Jess, and I shut out your mum, and I am ashamed to say I shut out you.'

He dared to look at his son, and the boy was staring straight ahead, tears streaming down his face. The sight made him feel as if someone had wrenched his ribcage apart and was ripping away at his heart with a cheese grater.

'It was like a blackness had descended over me and on the occasions I emerged from it, the pain of it all seared so much I willed the darkness to return. I existed but I wasn't really alive. The only thing that kept me from tipping right over the edge was Billy. These last few days have been an awakening, and I've had to face up to a lot of things. One of those things is the horror and shame I feel at the thought of missing so much of your life.'

'You're a fucking nutcase.'

'Yeah, I know.'

Harry turned and looked at him then. The hurt in his eyes cut to the bone. 'I hate you for leaving us.'

'I know that too.'

They sat for several minutes in a silence that was uncomfortable, but not excruciating. They'd both said their piece, and Max didn't feel the need to add anything to the conversation. After a time, he noticed neither did Harry; and with a wry smile he realised his son was an awful lot like himself.

'What do we do now?' It was Harry who broke the ice.

The question could have meant many things, but Max took the pragmatic approach.

'We go home.' They had watched as a tow truck had arrived and started to haul Fordyce's Nissan aboard. 'The game has changed. He's our man, I know it, and this is going to force his hand. So we go home, we get some sleep, then we come back in the morning, early, really early, and we wait for him to make his move.'

'Why don't we just stay? Won't he do something straight away?'

'No, he'll think and he'll wait. If he went out now he'd be signalling to his wife that he's guilty of something. He won't act till morning, and when he does, we'll be waiting.'

290

Meredith

There was a chill wind, and she shuddered as she stood on the footpath with crossed arms and watched as the navy-blue Nissan Primera was winched onto the tow truck. The spasm wasn't only due to the cold. She watched the Fordyces, standing arm in arm on the driveway, a picture of unity; but most of all she watched him. He had been helpful, he had been polite and, apart from the bits where his domineering wife had taken it on herself to speak on his behalf, he had been communicative. He hadn't whined when they asked to take his vehicle, he'd been most obliging. Even when his wife had mentioned the warrant word, he'd not taken up her objections. He was hiding something. From the moment he'd opened the door she didn't trust him. She didn't like the way he'd looked at her, she didn't like the way it made her feel when he'd looked at her — defensive and even a bit grubby — and most of all she didn't like the fact he'd answered the door with an erection. Detective McCarten hadn't noticed, but she had. It wasn't her usual practice to greet a man by looking at his crotch, but she'd seen what she'd seen.

McCarten wandered over towards her as the truck drove out of the driveway and headed up the road.

'We're all done,' he said. 'I've told them we'll be in touch as soon as we can release the vehicle.'

They walked across the street to where she'd shifted the unmarked patrol car out of the way. Again she shivered and, unable to shake off an uneasy feeling,

glanced further down the street, but there was nothing out of place, just a few parked cars. She must have been tired — but then it had been one hell of a strange few days. Max's reappearance in her life had rattled her more than she cared to admit, and she couldn't get the sight of him, emaciated and derelict, out of her head. He was the ghost who walked. They climbed into their vehicle and she waited until McCarten had clicked his seatbelt before she started the engine.

'Well, that was a waste of time,' he said.

'You're kidding me, right?' She looked at him in amazement.

He looked puzzled at her response. 'What do you mean?'

'Bradley Fordyce is our man, I guarantee it.'

'What on earth makes you think that?'

She'd thought it was perfectly obvious, but she wasn't about to dignify him with a full explanation. 'Because I know. He's the one. He's the one we're looking for.'

'And this is based on what? A feeling? Woman's intuition?' She noted the sarcasm in his voice. He was new to the station, and relatively new to the job. No one else would have dared doubt her so-called woman's intuition — well, not to her face.

'How long have you been a detective, McCarten?'

'This is my first year qualified.' Jesus. Bloody newbies thought they knew everything.

'Right, tell you what, then. When you've been qualified for more than five minutes, then you can sit there and give me your opinion on whether I'm right or not. Until then, you can shut the fuck up.'

292

Billy

Her muscles scream out in protest with the slightest movement, lines of fire scorch across her back, buttocks and arms. Her body burns, her heart weighs heavy in her chest, and her mind still reels from his latest attack. He has transformed and been reborn as some terrible creature from myth and legend, a chimera; he has become a god, a god of war, a god of hatred, a god of pain. Gone is the frightened man with the desperate eyes who kidnapped her. He has been possessed, possessed by something evil. Her hands finger the long rope of hair she has plaited, finger it like the rosary, her lips whispering prayers and entreaties to a kinder god, prayers for help, prayers for strength. The air becomes warm and the scent of frangipani makes her smile. Her Bubu begins to talk to her again, the soothing rhythm of her voice tells her tales and stories of bravery and valour; of demons and gods and the heroes who vanquish them; of heroes who cast aside their fear and weaknesses and draw on all of their courage and strength to banish the evil back to the hell it emerged from. Her face relaxes and despite the flare of pain as the T-shirt that has stuck to her bloodied back rips away from her torn skin, she leans back against the wall, settling in to listen to her Bubu and the stories that lull her to sleep.

Bradley

Sirens surrounded him, enticing him, luring him into a sea of tarry blackness. They called to him, husky, sultry voices, their long, lustrous hair flowing, caressing, swaying just enough to reveal the curve of breasts, the hint of nipple. A tall red-headed woman moved to the front, and as her face came into focus, the freckles across her skin glowed with vitality, her feline eyes burned with desire, and her arm reached out, her hand slid in behind his neck, pulling him forward to her, he could smell the scent of frangipani infused in her hair, the warmth of her breath as she pulled his unresisting lips onto hers, he felt their softness meld with his, then press, press harder, and harder, and he pulled his head back, trying to escape their pull, but she was unyielding, and he felt his breath being sucked away, and as he tried to draw another, the wave of panic flashed cold through his body and he tried to run, but she had dragged him into the tarry water, was dragging him deeper and deeper and his leaden legs couldn't find purchase and he tried to scream, but all that came was a muffled groan, and another, and then a shaking, and a shaking and a voice, a voice calling his name, 'Bradley, Bradley,' and he flew back into consciousness, heart pounding, breath rasping, Ange's hand on his shoulder, shaking him.

'Wake up, you're having a nightmare, wake up.'

'Jesus, what the . . . ?'

'You were moaning and kicking like an animal.'

'Ugh, sorry.' He tried to shake his head, shake away

the bitter taste left in his mouth, but it wouldn't budge. His heart still banged in his chest, and he took a deep breath and held it, to try and force it to slow down.

'Is it getting to you?' Ange asked, her voice soft with concern.

'What?' he said, although he had heard her.

'This business with the police coming back. Is it upsetting you?' She rubbed her hands over his back, trying to ease his fear away.

'It must be,' he said. 'But it is kind of strange, isn't it? It's not every day you get your car hauled away on the back of a truck. I hate to think what the neighbours made of it all.'

'Well, we might not get invited over for dinner for a while,' she said, and he appreciated her attempt to make light of it all. 'At least the police will be able to eliminate you, and then we'll be left alone.'

'Yeah, you're right.' He was wide awake now, his legs twitched and he had an overwhelming urge to run. 'You go back to sleep, I'm going to get up for a bit.' He pulled on a sweatshirt and slippers and padded out to the lounge. His eyes flicked up to the clock, it was only 2.00 am. Too early to go without arousing suspicion. He felt the need for something to drown out the turmoil in his head, so he turned on the TV. There was nothing that screamed out to be watched and he flicked channels, through the BBC, endless infomercials, home shows, music, sport, kids cartoons and documentaries before flicking back to the crime channel. The programme followed the investigation into a man who had murdered his wife in the United States. They were always in the US, and there was apparently an endless procession of men dissatisfied with their lives and their wives for

whatever reason, who saw murdering them as the only way out. And as the images scrolled by, of the woman's body, the plastic bag over her head, the staged break-in, the police forensics, the news footage of the distraught husband appealing to the public for information on who might have done this dreadful thing to his beloved wife, so convincing, so grief-stricken, his own scattered thoughts began to take shape and form as he came to the realisation that for him there was no alternative. That the police would keep coming back until they found the girl, whether it be days, weeks, years or decades. Because it had come down to that. Unless, by the grace of God, they found absolutely no trace of her in the car, he was a suspect. And even if crossed off the list, his name would still be sitting in a file somewhere, ready to be probed again when they came to a dead end. The simple fact was he had everything to lose. So he had no choice, he had to clean up this god-awful mess he'd got himself into, he had to finish this properly, because the only way he could escape the net that was drawing ever tighter around him was for her to disappear, forever. Every last trace of her had to go. He'd have to scrub out and bleach that room and make it as pristine as an operating theatre. That would be the easy part. But was he capable of dealing with her? Was he capable of doing something that drastic when his mind couldn't even bring itself to use the word 'kill'? *Can I kill her?* He forced himself to think those exact harsh words. And his heart began to race, and his breath quickened at the thought. There were many things he'd proven to himself in the last week: he'd done things he'd never dreamed he was capable of, guilty pleasures that thrilled and excited him, sinful acts that made him

feel masterful, in control, more alive than he'd felt in his life, and he knew he didn't want that feeling to end, ever. And he thought of the girl, that stupid, greedy girl, waiting in the dark, because it was her fault it had come to this. She'd had her chance, but she'd fucked it up, she'd brought it on herself. His eyes took in the scene on the television — the body. How would it feel? How would it feel to have the power of life and death in his hands? His stomach tingled with the stirring of nervous excitement and anticipation, and he noticed it wasn't just his gut that was eager, his cock stirred too. He could do this.

Max

He sat in the dark in the armchair. The tick of the lounge clock split the air with its repetitive click. His body felt like every nerve ending was simultaneously firing, and his mind was sharp, so sharp the clarity hurt. He had his man, he knew it, and he would lead them to Billy. And it would be over. In the morning he would track his prey; he would find her and she would finally be safe, safe in his arms, safe under his protection. It would be different this time. 'Jess, it will be different,' he whispered.

Billy

She feels a frisson in the air, that feeling of pressure intensifying before a storm and the dull headache it brings. She imagines the bulbous steel-grey clouds gathering on the horizon, leaves scattering and flags whipping with the first fluttering of wind, the scent of ozone on the air. The tempest is building, and in her heart she knows everything is coming to a head. He is coming. He is coming back, and this time he will finish it. She thinks of her brothers and sisters, and her heart saddens, and although she tries not to, the thought of her mother intrudes, and with it the sour taste of disenchantment. Such weakness. How could she not have advocated for her own daughter, protected her? But no, she had cowered before that man, that murderer. She was not strong. The image of Max drifts into focus, and she smiles. He is steel under that wasted exterior, she feels it; and so is his son. She recalls the young man's smile, his shy approach but understated strength, a quiet guardian. Hope, they bring her hope, and hope brings strength. The soothing voice of her Bubu whispers in her ear. *He is coming, but you are strong.* Because the storm is breaking — but she is ready, she is ready for him, and her fingers run across the bobbles of her plaited hair, of left over right, and the love and strength of her Bubu's stories are woven into each strand of her rope, her Bubu's stories of gods and demons, of warriors — and heroes.

Max

It was dark; it felt darker than dark. Not even the amber glow of the streetlights could penetrate deep into the night. No moon, no stars, instead a brooding blanket of black and the heady promise of rain. Harry had already been awake when he'd entered his room to rouse him, and had moved with quiet solemnity as they dressed and took the drive over to Albany. In the city that never slept there were scant cars on the roads at 4.00 am; the trucks ruled the motorways. As they traversed the arteries, and then the arterioles of Auckland, the car's engine sounded outrageously loud in the curtained and locked world of suburbia. They entered the cul-de-sac, each oversized house shoulder to shoulder with its neighbour, looking much like queens and kings on a chessboard, their wheelie bin and recycling bin pawns guarding the footpaths.

'Drive past, turn around and park over there, so we're facing out.'

Harry did as he was told without comment, turned off the headlights, killed the engine. Their vantage point gave a clear view of the garage door. There were no lights on in the house: all seemed deathly still, eerily silent.

'Now we wait.'

Bradley

He nuzzled into his wife's neck and murmured, 'I'm off to the gym.' She mumbled a dreamy 'Goodbye,' and he slipped out of the bed. He found his clothes in the dark, trying to be as quiet as possible. His toe caught the corner of something and he swore with the jolt of pain. When he bent down to move the culprit he felt the soft nylon shell of his gym bag. Jesus, what an idiot. He would have forgotten it. That could have spoiled everything. No simple mistakes. Only when he was in the garage did he dare turn on a light: her car looked lost, alone in that vast space. He unlocked it and slung the bag in the boot. Then he went over to the laundry and utility cupboards that lined the back wall. He searched through until he found the grocery bags, each one carefully tied in a half knot to prevent one of the kids accidentally suffocating. The irony of it made him snort. He sorted through them and selected four that didn't appear to have any holes in them. A bundle of black polythene bags caught his eye and he decided to take them for good measure, as well as a small box of disposable gloves. Lastly, he went to the tall end cupboard and pulled out a spade, a blue plastic tarpaulin and a bundle of nylon rope. His hand hovered over his tackle box, and then Bradley opened it and retrieved the sheathed fishing knife. Just in case.

Max

A flood of light bathed the driveway as the garage door of the house slowly rose. It was 5.13 am. Harry sat up in his seat, but Max pulled him back down, out of sight. A red Toyota Rav4 reversed out of the garage, its headlights cutting an arc across the front of the house as it swung into the street. As if an omen of the pending storm, the first drops of rain began to spit onto their windscreen, distorting the red of the tail lights as the car pulled away into the distance.

'Keep well back, and don't turn your lights on yet.'

Harry started the engine and drove off with deliberate calm. The beacon of red had disappeared left around the roundabout, and when they caught sight of it again it was indicating to turn right into Gills Road. It was ironic to Max that a man on his way to continue the perpetration of a heinous crime was being so law-abiding as to indicate in the wee hours of the morning when there was no one to see. He would have laughed if the situation hadn't been so serious. Harry instinctively hung back, keeping as close to the kerb as possible. If Fordyce looked in his rear-vision mirror, he'd just think it was a parked car. They drove this cat-and-mouse course down through to the turnoff joining up with the main road. Fordyce turned left onto the highway. As they rolled up to the intersection Max was surprised at how many cars were on the road at this hour of the morning.

'Lights on,' he said. 'We don't want to get pulled over now.' The rain was falling hard enough now to

require the windscreen wipers; the buzz of the tyres on the tarmac, the orange glow of the sodium lamps and the hypnotic swish of the wipers made it feel surreal. There were now two cars between them and Fordyce, which suited them fine.

'I'll bet he's heading to the Northern Motorway, towards town.'

'Good. He'll be easy to keep track of then. We'll be able to slot in behind like any other commuter with an early start.' Harry was the essence of calm and concentration, and Max felt a surge of admiration for how the boy was handling all of this. He was certain he'd never been that mature at his age. But then Max, by his very actions, was the reason the boy had to grow up ahead of his time. 'You're doing a great job,' he said. Harry just nodded and kept his eyes on the road.

The pitch of the wheel buzz changed as they crossed the harbour bridge. The lights of the city were blurred by the haze of rain that had descended upon it. The Sky Tower pierced the sky like some science-fiction light sabre thrust up from the cityscape. The Rav4 passed the off-ramps that led into the city and continued south. It finally veered from the motorway at the Mount Wellington off-ramp, slowing to a halt and then turning north. The traffic lights in front of Fordyce changed to orange, and the Rav4 sailed through, but the car occupying the place between them decided to be a good citizen and stop. The lights, for what felt an interminable length of time, stayed red.

'Shit, we're going to lose him in traffic if he gets too far ahead,' Harry said, fingers drumming on the steering wheel and frustration edging into his voice.

Gotcha, Max thought, a smile creeping onto his face

Meredith

'Got you, you bastard,' she uttered to herself as the automatic door crawled up and a red Rav4 backed out of the garage. The door started its slide back down and Meredith's eyes followed the vehicle as it drove up the street.

'Next,' she said, and on cue an old white Honda pulled out from the kerb, headlights off. She'd staked out the house since 4.00 am; the phosphorescent face on her watch now glared 5.14 am. The other car had sidled in around half an hour ago; the intrusive glare of its headlights had woken her from a doze. Although she had been mortified she'd fallen asleep on the job, it had done her good and she now felt semi-human. When it had first driven past she'd sunk down low in the seat so she couldn't be seen, but unfortunately it meant she didn't get to see them either. It didn't prevent her from guessing who one of the occupants was, though. It had taken a huge effort of self-control on her part not to walk up there, pull the door open and give him an earful. She stretched out as far as she could in the cramped confines of her car, twisting her ankles around and around to try and get some circulation going, then turned the key in the ignition and with her headlights off, joined the tail of the convoy.

'What the hell does he think he is doing?' she muttered to herself, although part of her felt a grudging admiration that he'd managed to narrow the field down to this one man, this one house. It was also a confirmation that she was right, this was the man

they were looking for. Max Grimes had always been a hell of a good detective; given the choice she would always want him on her team. She got down to the main highway and the opportunity to blend in with the early-morning traffic. The rain was becoming more insistent, further dampening her mood. The old Honda had turned its headlights on now, and she did the same, settling into the traffic flow one car back from it, just another commuter on the road.

Something bugged her. Actually many things bugged her about this case, but this conundrum bugged her more than most. How the hell had Max tracked down Bradley Fordyce? Sure, he'd provided the three digits, and would have kept a copy, no doubt. But to get registration details he would have had to access and search the database, so he must have had someone on the inside to help him. But who? She couldn't think of anyone who would risk censure for providing information to a civilian. And considering the state he was in, she couldn't picture him charming it out of anyone.

A horrid sinking feeling dropped its way into her belly. Yesterday, on the stairs, when she'd stumbled across him coming out of the second floor. He'd certainly looked sick enough to sell her the story. *You bastard.* He hadn't spent the time shitting his ring out like he'd hinted; no, somehow he'd snuck in and hacked into the computer system. *You deceiving, lying bastard.* It was the only way he could have done it, surely. But she didn't recall him being a computer geek, and his registration was well and truly out of the system. *How did you do it?* Despite feeling pissed off at the ease of his deception, she felt a grudging admiration and also a touch of reassurance that he

was along for this ride because, to be honest, she had no idea what she was going to do when they reached their destination, wherever that was. On the passenger seat beside her sat her baton and pepper spray. She wished she had a side arm, but considering this was not exactly official time on the clock, trying to procure one would have raised too many questions, and she hadn't felt inclined to explain, because she had been teetering on the edge of wanting to rip people's throats out. McCarten's had a few good teeth marks on it. After the removal of Fordyce's vehicle the rest of the evening had been an exercise in frustration.

Which was why, in the end, she had resorted to sitting alone in her car at some ungodly hour of the morning outside the house of a man only she suspected. It hadn't taken much digging to find Bradley Fordyce had a few rental properties — but could she get leave to apply for a warrant to search them? No. It was all, 'You must have probable cause', or 'What evidence do you have? You'll have to wait until morning, or until the forensic examination results come in from the vehicle.' It was all bullshit. She could have screamed in frustration — she had screamed, once in the soundproof confines of her car. Fordyce was evil, and that girl, if she was even still alive, was running out of time. In her mind she saw the fresh-faced, innocent girl, and she recalled the face of that other young girl they had hunted for, all those years ago, and she felt the steely determination, tempered by the cold wash of uncertainty. There were so many things that could go wrong.

'Oh Jesus, Max, don't fuck it up this time.'

Max

Google Street View had lied, or was at least hopelessly out of date. The building was nothing like in its picture — the whole block had changed. It was no longer the bustling hive of industry depicted in the photo. Now, with the moody weather, it resembled a deserted filmset from some gothic horror. The engineering sign had been taken down, leaving a cleaner rectangle in the sea of grey and making the building a vast concrete-panelled bunker. The Rav4 wasn't anywhere to be seen.

'Drive past, go up a few hundred metres, then turn around and come back.'

Sure enough, from this different perspective they caught a glimpse of the Rav4 in their headlights. It was parked around the back of the building.

'Right, drive past, a couple of buildings further up and then pull over.' Harry followed instruction without comment, and then turned off the engine.

'Now what?' He had to yell to be heard over the sound of the rain pounding on the roof of the car. It was a bloody good question. Max had been thinking about this moment all night, about what he'd do. Or at least what he wouldn't do. Now it was here the moment verged on the unreal.

'You are going to stay here in the car.'

'But . . . ' the boy's face was a gripe of hurt.

'No argument. I don't know what's going to happen here, and I've put you at enough risk already.'

Harry wasn't going to give up that easily. 'But two

are stronger than one, we could overpower him.'

Max felt a surge of love for this young man, this son who was a virtual stranger but who, after everything, everything he had done, was still prepared to lay it on the line for him. He reached out and grabbed his forearm.

'Absolutely not. Promise me you will stay in the car. I'm not going to risk you, like I did . . . ' The words died on his lips, and a look of understanding passed between the two of them. He took a deep breath, thoughts of Jess tore through his head. 'Harry,' he said, his voice charged with emotion. 'I lost Jess, I'm not going to risk losing you. End of story.'

Harry looked back at him, lips pursed, and nodded. 'Okay,' he said, though his face said it was anything but okay.

Max reached into his hip pocket and pulled out the slip of paper he'd written during those long hours of wakefulness. He handed it to his son. 'When I go in, I want you to ring this. This is Detective Meredith Peters' number. I want you to tell her where we are, who we've followed and that we need immediate back-up. If she doesn't answer the phone, dial 111 and tell them it's a life-and-death situation. Say anything to get them here. Then you wait. You lock the doors, and you wait here.'

'But what if he's armed?'

Jesus, if Fordyce was armed, he was fucked. 'I'll face that when I come to it. If you hear gunshots, you get the hell out of here, you understand, you just drive.' He glanced back towards the building, the view blurred by the rain. Billy was here; it was the perfect hiding place, an abandoned industrial area, isolated, dead. He turned his attention back to his boy, gave

him a wry smile. 'No matter what happens, do not follow me, you understand?'

The boy nodded, his eyes grim. 'Be careful, Dad.'

Max leaned over and gave him a fierce hug, whispered 'I love you' into his ear, and then opened the door and disappeared out into the rain.

Meredith

'Jesus, where the fuck have they gone?' The teeming rain had made visibility a nightmare. She'd only noticed at the last possible second that they'd turned off the glistening motorway at Mount Wellington, and she had nearly skidded the car into the side rails when she'd wrenched it onto the off-ramp. Several vehicles had snuck in between them, and now, as she waited, stuck second in line at a set of lights, fingers drumming on the steering wheel, there was no sign of the white Honda. She reached over into her bag and grabbed the printout of properties owned by Fordyce, or at least by the company sporting his wife's family name. She had to wonder about that relationship, and who wore the pants. She certainly hadn't warmed to the wife, and she'd straight out detested the man. One of their industrial sites was somewhere around here, she was sure of it. Out of the corner of her eye she saw the traffic light turn green. She dropped the piece of paper back onto the seat. As she sat back up she noted the green Hyundai directly in front pull into the intersection. And then just as Meredith was about to ease her foot down on the accelerator she caught the flash and blur of something hurtling through from the right on the red light. Her foot shot to the brake, shoulders automatically hunched, and she cringed in anticipation as the squeal of brakes and rubber sliding across wet road climaxed in the inevitable crunch of metal on metal and the dampened tinkle of falling glass.

'Holy shit,' she said. She watched in horror as the two cars slid across the intersection in front of her, joined in some terrible dance-like embrace. She leaned forward to the dash and flicked on her hazard lights, grabbed her cellphone and jabbed 111 while she climbed out of the door and ran over to the wrecks. What a fucking mess. She pulled open the passenger door on the T-boned car; she had to yank hard and lift to get the warped door open.

'Are you okay?' she yelled to the driver. It was clear she was far from okay, slumped forward in her seatbelt, blood streaming down her face, the spent airbag drooping down from the steering wheel like some burst bubblegum bubble. 'Hang in there, I'm getting help.' She relayed the information through to the emergency services as she dashed around to the other car. She pulled the door open to find a dazed but intact-looking young man.

'What happened?' he said, like it wasn't bloody obvious what had happened.

The urge to scream at him, 'You ran a red light, you fucker,' to hit him, beat some sense into him was so strong, so intense that she slammed the door shut again, hit her fist into the side of the car and instead yelled out into the dark. 'Why now? Why fucking now?'

★ ★ ★

The pulsing red flash of the ambulance lights reflecting off the slick streets and mangled cars gave an eerily strobe-like effect to the scene, and standing there in the rhythmic drumming rain it was hypnotic. The shrill ring of her cellphone broke the spell. It

resisted being pulled out as the damp fabric in her pocket gripped the plastic cover, and when she finally looked at the screen it was an unknown number. Who the hell would be rude enough to ring someone at six o'clock on a Saturday morning? She pushed aside a tendril of sodden hair and raised it to her ear.

'Hello?' she shouted over the background noise.

'Is that Meredith Peters?' The voice was young, and carried the kind of tremulous tone that sent her already jumpy nervous system into hyperdrive.

'Yes, who's this?' A chill passed through her body.

'It's Harry Grimes, you know my dad.'

Bradley

The anticipation had built so much in his chest that by the time he got to the workshop he felt he would explode. His heart pounded, and his breathing was so fast and so shallow that his head spun with nauseous, giddy excitement. Calm down, he told himself, just calm down. The raindrops that had soaked into his hair and shoulders steamed from the immense heat that came off his supercharged body. Once more he stood before the door; he laughed at that symbol of choice and change. How far he had come. As he stood there clutching the bags that would help him carry out his goal, it was absurd to think it had been mere days since he had made those dents in a frenzy of frustration and disbelief at what he had done. He'd achieved such heights in the last few days, he couldn't stop now, not when he was so close to that ultimate act of power, of taking control of his life. He wasn't going to be beaten, he was going to save himself.

Billy

The click of the key in the lock pulls her back to the present, the echoes of her Bubu's voice whispering in her ear. The door swings open, and he is silhouetted there, a black shadow against the glow of the lamp on the ground behind him. With the image comes the sound of a million nails hitting the tin roof. His hands are full, and she watches, the sharp edge of fear cutting in her chest as he comes in, places the goods on the table and then turns around to face her, his back to the door.

'This is where it ends, I'm afraid,' he says, his voice raised loud above the sound of rain. 'You know, I tried, I offered you a chance, you could have taken the money and gone and made a life for yourself. But no, you didn't take it, you didn't take the path that could have led to redemption for both of us. So if anyone is to blame for what happens, it is you. You could have put a stop to it, you could have prevented things from escalating any further.' As he speaks she can hear his voice rising, can feel him building himself up, the air tight with anticipation as he works himself up to that point of explosion. She feels her heart racing, tastes the salty tang of her fear, but she tells herself to stay calm, and wills her breathing to slow. The voice of her Bubu whispers in her mind, the words reassuring her, *Be strong, have faith, wait your time.* Her fingers slide into her pocket, find the comfort of her rope, the strength of her hair.

'This is your fault,' he says as his hands work with

something, untying it. 'It is all your fault that it has to end this way.' Her heart gives a jolt as she sees it is a plastic bag he has in his hands, a plastic bag he shakes out to open up, and her mind foresees that immediate, terrible future, and he steps towards her then, towards and around, trying to get behind her, and she swings up onto her knees and cringes into the wall, turning to face him as he steps closer and closer; her eyes are mesmerised by the bag, and her innards feel like molten metal as the wave of terror threatens to engulf her. *Wait,* her Bubu says, her voice firmer, commanding, *Wait Billy, the bag is thin, be ready.* Her legs tense, her muscles poise to act and all sound is sucked from the room as her entire being microscopes in on anticipating the slightest action of that man, but as he looms above her and is about to try to reach over her with the bag she senses a streak of movement from outside, and her eyes flick to the blur of someone hurtling across the room, slamming into him, the momentum throwing them both to the ground.

'Billy.'

She hears him scream her name, and her heart soars as she recognises the voice. He has come for her, Max has come. But it isn't Max, it can't be — the clipped head, the clean-shaven face — but then their eyes meet, the sunken, razor-sharp eyes, and she knows it is him, he has not forsaken her, he has come. The man roars in fury and shock, and Billy watches in dismay the speed with which he rolls over, throws Max off, and her eyes take in the inequality of the combatants. Max lashes out, his fist connecting with the man's chin, but there is little force behind it, and the man wriggles and wrestles his way on top of Max, and then too easily he is straddling him, his muscled arms

huge in comparison to the sparrow-like proportions of Max. She sees the power in his back as he draws his arm back, and the force unleashed as he punches Max in the side of the head. Her lips mouth his name, as the arm draws back and hits Max again and again and again.

Meredith

She spotted the white Honda the second she careened around the bend, and without hesitation she screamed up alongside, driver's windows aligned, barely missing clipping the wing mirrors. She wound her window down, the rain driving into her face. The other window came down, and she saw a young and very scared-looking version of Max. The sight of him tore at her heart.

'Where is he?' she yelled over the drumming on the roof.

The boy thumbed behind him. 'Three buildings down, the big concrete one, there's an entrance around the back on the far side.'

'You stay here,' she yelled, and then drove on and turned down the side of the building. A movement out of the corner of her eye caught her attention. Shit, the boy had jumped out of the car and was following on foot. But she didn't have time to think about that right now. Right now Max needed her.

Billy

Her breathing synchronises with the punches, and over the sound of the rain on the roof and the rush of blood in her ears, she hears the long, dry whisper of her Bubu's voice — *Now* — and her hand reaches into her pocket, and her fingers find the cord of hair, her glorious hair, Sampson's hair, and she stretches it out between her hands, and she prays they are close enough, that the length of chain he gave her for freedom is enough to reach, and in one swift and decisive movement she lunges forward and slips her rope over his head and under his chin and then she leans back and pulls with all of her might. She prays that it will hold, that she has woven it strong and true, and she wraps it around again as he falls backwards into her, his hands flying up in surprise. She pulls harder, begging for strength, digging, delving for every last bit of energy inside of her, and she can feel him scrambling, scrambling for a foothold, to regain his balance, but to do it he has to move backwards closer towards her, towards the wall, and in that moment of slackness, she grabs the rope ends into her left hand, and she swings, she swings the chain that imprisons her, swings its cold, heartless metal around his neck and then she is on her feet, pulling up, pulling up with all her might, and she sees his arms flail, they tear at the air, furiously, but she can see he is gaining purchase, he is regaining balance, the element of surprise has been lost, and she feels the pulse of horror, because she has nothing left, nothing left to give, she is drained, it

319

is her one and only chance and it is failing. Then she sees Max move, slowly, slowly, Max pulls himself to his feet, and his eyes search her scalp, the lacerations on her face, the swelling of her lips, before they meet hers, and they understand. She watches as he staggers around behind her, past the monster, the writhing and struggling monster, and Max puts his arms around her and she sinks into him as his arms link hers, his hands grasp the chain, and he takes part of that load, he takes part of that burden and they pull, together they pull.

Meredith

There was one source of light from down the far end of the cavernous building, and like a moth to the flame she ran towards it. She slid to a halt before the door and edged along the wall of the room, straining to hear anything over the deafening hail of the rain. If she couldn't hear them, they couldn't hear her. Her heart raced, and she gripped her hand tighter on the baton she'd brought in with her. On three, she told herself.

One. Two. Three.

She dropped low and threw herself around the corner.

Her senses reeled as they took in the scene before her. The pile of people caught her attention first, followed by a fetid stench. At the bottom of the pile was what was barely recognisable as Max. His lip was swollen tight and split right up to his bloodied nose, the unnatural angle of which made her stomach lurch. One eye was completely swollen closed, but the other fixed her with a look that was both exhausted and triumphant. For nestled in his arms lay the girl. Her face bore the ravages of abuse, and it took a second for Meredith's brain to register the irregular brownish stripes that cut into her clothes. Were they whip marks? God, was she even alive? The question was answered when the eyes opened and wearily found hers. Meredith felt a quiver as they met, and then she followed the girl's gaze to the man. As she took in the sight she rose from her crouch and walked

cautiously around to stand before him. Bradley Ford-
yce lay spread-eagled on his back, his head rested on
the legs of the girl. His face was still, a bloated gri-
mace of agony. But what was remarkable was the chain
wrapped around his throat, a chain and — what was
that? a rope — a very fine rope? Her eyes followed the
chain from its source attached to the wall, around the
throat of the man, and to its terminus, clamped to the
girl's wrist, no, not just the girl, Max's hand gripped
it so tightly his knuckles were white, and she realised
they were still pulling.

Jesus, was he still alive?

She crouched down and reached forward, fingers
pushing into Fordyce's neck, probing for a pulse, but
there was nothing. Then she moved them a fraction
to one side and there it was, the barest flicker beneath
her fingertips, the bastard was still alive. Jesus, that
meant she had to do something to save him; it was her
sworn duty. But then she looked up, beyond the gro-
tesque face of Bradley Fordyce, and into the broken,
emaciated face of Max, and the battered, exhausted
face of the young girl. She looked around at the room,
saw the bucket in the corner, the water, the food; she
took in the table with what looked like a horse whip,
and the bags with bin liners, gloves and a knife, and
the plastic bags, and then she looked back at the wall
at that chain, that chain that had tethered the girl,
making her his slave in this prison, his toy, and some-
thing in her heart knotted, it knotted with such anger
and such hatred that she could taste its bitter bile in
her mouth, and her hand clenched, it clenched on the
solid handle of her baton and she knew what she had
to do, what she wanted to do to make it right. And she
began to raise her arm.

'No, Meredith.' The words froze her actions. 'Meredith, don't.' Her eyes found Max, saw the steel and determination in his face, heard the command in his voice. 'This isn't your battle.'

She dropped her arm, took a steadying breath. 'He's still alive,' she said, and as she spoke the words the face of Harry appeared at the door. She stepped forward quickly, blocking the boy before he could enter, turning him away. 'No, Harry, they are fine, you can't go in there, you don't need to see that,' but she could tell from the ashen colour of his face he'd caught a glimpse.

She turned back to Max then, again acknowledged the girl and marvelled at the extraordinary serenity that emanated from her, as if she was some saintly figure, some angel. In the midst of this scene of torment and death, she was somehow radiant, victorious. 'The emergency services are ten minutes away.' This was their moment, theirs alone. 'Call me when you're done.'

323

Max

The afternoon sun slanted into his eyes, and it seemed a sacrilege to reach his hand up to shield them. Sitting here on the bench, looking out over the viaduct harbour at the rich-boy-toy yachts, his body soaking in the warmth, he felt at peace for the first time in as long as he could remember. The Sky Tower stood sentinel over the city, a guardian piercing the sky. Kids on scooters squealed their way over the drawbridge, weaving between the pedestrians and cyclists relishing the autumn day and fresh air.

'Why won't anyone come and sit near us?' Billy said and followed the question with a small giggle. His face burst into a smile. Small wonder, they did look a sight, both artfully adorned with butterfly closures and bruises fading to purplish yellow. He hated to think what people would make of the pair of them, one resembling an accident victim and the other a tiny scrap of a beat-up Island girl. His head was covered with the sheep-dip beanie, an article of clothing he felt curiously attached to. Billy's head was bare, her ragtag shorn hair defiantly on display to the world. This time the ache he felt in his chest was not despair, but love — something he was rediscovering his capacity for.

There were still hard days ahead. There were the legal ramifications of taking a life, even if in self-defence. The man's wife was pushing for a manslaughter charge against them; Angela Fordyce was in denial that her husband could possibly have been

responsible for what was done to Billy. It would go nowhere, though; and what happened in that room at the end would never be disclosed — it was a private matter between the four of them. But he'd shield Billy from the fallout and from the media as much as he could.

'Have your folks been in touch?' He sensed her stiffening at the question.

'Yes, they turned up at the hospital, wanting to fawn all over me, probably because the cameras were out front.'

'What did you do?'

'Told them to fuck off.'

Max smiled again. He was doing that a lot lately.

'And did they?'

She laughed properly then, a gift to his ears. 'Only after that detective friend of yours told them to fuck off too. I like her, she's a good lady, she scares everyone.'

'She's a good ally. Wouldn't want her as an enemy, though.'

'Hell no.' She paused, hesitant. 'Would she have . . . you know?'

Max thought back to that morning, his body responding with a deep involuntary shudder, his aches intensifying. He recalled the anger, the raw and seething anger in Meredith's face, the way her freckles stood out flaming orange against her pallid skin, the eagle-like look in her eyes, the feeling of something incendiary entering the room.

'Yes.'

They sat in silence a while, the shrill cry of the seagulls filtering through his conflicted thoughts.

'I'm glad you stopped her.'

He turned his gaze from the soaring movements of the birds to his companion; saw the resolute look in her eyes.

'I needed to kill that motherfucker.'

'We both did.'

The honk of a ferry horn cut through the air, making them both look in its direction.

'What are you going to do now, Max?'

That wasn't an easy question to answer. Life had changed irreparably; it wasn't like he could just step back in and resume from where he'd left off. There would be no winding back the clock. But one thing was certain, he now had the strength and determination to start again. This whole affair had gifted him that much.

'I don't know yet. I have a lot to sort out.'

His eyes caught the slightly gangly figure of Harry walking down the waterfront towards them. He gave him a wave and noted the form move in their direction in reply. He saw her face brighten at the sight of his son. 'And I've got a few major bridges to mend. What about you? What are you going to do now? Who's helping you?' he asked.

'Your friend has been great. She's trying to sort things with immigration, and she's got the minister from Church trying to find me a place to stay and a job. No one dares stand in her way, so I'm hopeful it's all going to be okay.' The humour and spunk with which she spoke made him marvel at the resilience of the girl. Her spirit reminded him of his Jess, and although his heart ached with the thought of his daughter, it didn't shatter.

'Good. Because you mean a lot to me, Billy, you know that, don't you? I'll always have your back. And

you can't go back on the streets again, ever. I won't let you.' He thought of the unsavoury deal he'd struck with a certain pimp on K Road. That was one promise he was happy to break . . . But still, she'd have to be careful. Guys like that had fingers in many pies and friends everywhere. He would have to make sure that never came back to bite her. He'd confess to the price he offered for information to find her — one day, but not yet.

'I know you won't,' she said, 'and believe me, I don't want to.' She reached over then and grabbed him by the hand. The expression in her eyes so intense it hurt him. 'Thank you,' she whispered. Those eyes began to well with tears, and he felt his start to blur. 'Thank you so much for coming for me. I knew you'd come.'

He reached his arms out for her, encircling her tiny form in his embrace, placing a kiss on her bruised forehead. 'Thank you,' he said, 'thank you for saving me.'

'You did that all by yourself.'

'Not entirely, I needed a bit of a push.'

'Yeah, but ultimately, it came down to you, you decided to act. I'm glad you did.' She had the slightest of dimples when she smiled.

Harry had almost reached them, and Max hauled himself to his feet, his muscles reminding him just how much he'd put them through in the last week. It still made him frown to see how uncomfortable it was for Billy to do the same thing. She tried to hide it, but her face couldn't disguise the pain she was in. He found it hard to fathom what she had been through, physically and mentally.

'You know,' she said, a shyness replacing the bravado with which she'd been talking. 'I was thinking,

this is kind of like a new beginning, a new chance at life. Would you think I was stupid if I told you I wanted to go to art school?'

'Are you kidding? I think that's a brilliant idea. You could show the lecturers a thing or two when it comes to art.'

'You mean that?'

'Billy, your work is amazing. I've never seen anything as beautiful, anywhere. They would be fools not to want you.'

She broke into a grin that wavered into a grimace at the twinges of pain, and then determinedly back into a grin. 'Good, because I've got something to show you, a new piece I was working on. It was going to be a surprise, and it's not quite finished yet.' She paused and looked Max in the eye, her face becoming serious. 'I don't usually show people unfinished work, but as you know, stuff happened and I got a bit sidetracked, discovered life can be short.' They both chuckled at the understatement. 'Come with me,' she said as she grabbed Max's hand and pulled him towards the city.

Acknowledgements

I am eternally grateful to Karen Sullivan and her wonderful team at Orenda Books for taking a punt on this gal from the other side of the world, and to Craig Sisterson for placing that first book in Karen's hand and telling her she needed to read it. Look where that lead to!

Faceless has been in the world for a while, and it has been a delight to revisit the characters in this book. Thanks to Jane Gregory and Stephanie Glencross at Gregory and Company and the team at Penguin New Zealand, who originally published the book as *The Faceless*, especially Katie Haworth, Emily Boyd and the wonderful Gillian Tewsley.

Thanks to Laura Cope for being my porridge and tea buddy, sounding board and for not flinching and fleeing at my warped mind. Eternal thanks to my long-suffering family, who put up with my absent-mindedness and total neglect of them in the process of bringing this work to life.

And a special thank-you to you, the reader.

We do hope that you have enjoyed reading this large print book.

Did you know that all of our titles are available for purchase?

We publish a wide range of high quality large print books including:
Romances, Mysteries, Classics
General Fiction
Non Fiction and Westerns

Special interest titles available in large print are:
The Little Oxford Dictionary
Music Book, Song Book
Hymn Book, Service Book

Also available from us courtesy of Oxford University Press:
Young Readers' Dictionary
(large print edition)
Young Readers' Thesaurus
(large print edition)

For further information or a free brochure, please contact us at:
Ulverscroft Large Print Books Ltd.,
The Green, Bradgate Road, Anstey,
Leicester, LE7 7FU, England.
Tel: (00 44) **0116 236 4325**
Fax: (00 44) **0116 234 0205**